PULL

Dedicated to my nephew, Craig Houston, Jr.
The world lost a wonderful young man far too early.

PULL
B.A. Binns

WestSide Books
Lodi, New Jersey

Published by WestSide Books
60 Industrial Road
Lodi, NJ 07644
973-458-0485
Fax: 973-458-5289

This is a work of fiction. All characters, places, and events
described are imaginary. Any resemblance to real people,
places, and events is entirely coincidental.

Library of Congress Cataloging-in-Publication Data

Binns, B. A.
Pull / B.A. Binns. -- 1st ed.
p. cm.
Summary: After his father kills his mother, seventeen-year-old David strug-
gles to take care of his two sisters--and himself--while dealing with his grief,
guilt, and trying to fit in at a tough new school while hiding his past.
ISBN 978-1-934813-43-0
[1. Coming of age--Fiction. 2. Brothers and sisters--Fiction. 3. Orphans--
Fiction. 4. Guilt--Fiction. 5. High schools--Fiction. 6. Schools--Fiction. 7.
African Americans--Fiction. 8. Chicago (Ill.)--Fiction.] I. Title.
PZ7.B511853Pu 2010
[Fic]--dc22

2010031473

International Standard Book Number: 978-1-934813-43-0
School ISBN: 978-1-934813-45-4
Cover design by David Lemanowicz
Interior design by David Lemanowicz

Printed in the United States of America
10 9 8 7 6 5 4 3 2 1

First Edition

PULL

CHAPTER 1

It's fourth period, and so far not one teacher has questioned who I am. Like everyone else, the gym teacher accepted the transfer papers for David Albacore and waved me over to join the rest of the rejects in this class. We're supposed to be practicing basketball passing drills. Not one of these guys, especially the nit wearing a dirty Chicago Bulls jersey, could even beat my sister. They're laughing and joking, and they barely know what to do with a basketball. I never wanted to go back to any school, but at least Farrington's a place where I can be invisible.

Then it happens—again.

The pain that's made its home inside me for so long that I've learned to ignore it suddenly roars to life, flexes its claws and tears at me from the inside. The voices around me fade, and sweaty bodies vanish as memory catches me in a strangle-hold and I'm back. Back in that house, caught up in that horrible night.

Only this time things are different. This time I see him raise the gun. Hear the shot. See the bullet racing toward her chest.

This time I *will* save her.

Sweat pours from my forehead and salt stings my lips as I step into the path of death. I have no delusions—I know what's about to happen. I'm just David, not some superman. I brace for the impact, my hands clench and my muscles tense, grateful for this chance to set things right.

My life for hers. This time I will not fail her.

The bullet slams into my chest, sending me hurtling through the air. Falling, I slide on the polished hardwood floor—*Hardwood?*

From the corners of my eyes I see the basketball rolling across that floor. I turn my head slowly but I already know. My mother's not here. She's gone. I didn't save her.

A voice calls out, "Hey, Albacore, eyes open!" This provokes a round of laughter from the rest of the losers in the gym.

The gym teacher's whistle shrieks as he runs over from the sidelines where he's been talking with another man. His wide, worried gray eyes stand out from his pale face. You'd think he'd never seen a guy downed by a basketball before. Probably hasn't been teaching in the inner city very long. Probably still has ideals and intends to do some good or something.

Probably needs to get the hell out of my space.

"You okay, David?"

I'm tempted to answer *no* to his stupid question, but I'm not ready for the paperwork that'd be involved in a trip to the school nurse on my first day. Besides, I don't want to call too much attention to myself or strain the high-tension wire of fraud I've strung here at Farrington. I nod and sit up. The world spins as the cracks in the paint dance.

Over the teacher's shoulder I see a larger man approach. He's wearing an orange polo shirt with a wide black band around the left sleeve. I recognize the dark eyes and square chin from the picture in the trophy case outside the school's main office: Hakeem Kasili, the new varsity basketball coach.

The gym teacher reaches out to help me up. But I'm a senior—I don't need help—and I jerk free of his grip. The effort is too much—my legs tangle and I fall to one knee as laughter rings through the tiny gym once again.

"Fish-face can't even stand," someone taunts.

Only three hours in this school, and already I've picked up a nickname. But it's better than hundreds of voices in the stands yelling, "Don't hassle Murhaselt." I'm free of that despicable name. Anyone around here says that, they're dead.

The shuffling and muttering grow louder. Another joker says, "Get Fish-face a pair of glasses."

Kasili steps into the circle around me. He turns to look at them. Slowly. No more laughter now. No further shuffling of feet. More than thirty guys in the class, but every one of them has gone silent.

Total control. First teacher I've seen around here with that kind of power.

He reminds me of Coach Anderson back at Grogan Hills. Except this guy can't be much more than forty. Skin almost as dark as mine, with deep lines in the corners of his eyes. If I were ever to play ball again, it'd be for a man like him.

If.

The gym teacher points to the bench. "Sit and rest," he commands.

Coach Kasili just stares—as if he's sending me a silent message. As if he knows.

When class starts up again, I sit with elbows on my knees and my head in my hands, pretending to look at the floor while I watch the court. The teacher and coach are talking again.

The students don't matter. It's easy to ignore their grunts and sighs as they practice ball handling. But that coach—he keeps throwing glances my way. If he's here recruiting for this school's team, he's shit out of luck. My clumsy display of ball-handling should remind him it takes more than height to make a player. If he forgets, I'll play the fool until the school year ends.

I relax once class lets out and I'm in the showers. Didn't expect water so hot in this rundown excuse for a school. The backs of my legs still burn from the fall, but the near scalding water relieves the pain and loosens my tight muscles. I take extra time under the stinging spray.

When I go back to the locker room, all conversations cease. The guys sneak glances at me as I dress. *That's right, guys. I earned these muscles. Go ahead and look. You want a set, come to work with me tonight. Let's see how long you rejects last carrying around forty-seven pound sacks of Portland cement.*

Why shouldn't I be vain? At six-foot seven, I can do a hundred yards in twelve seconds, a five-minute mile, and last year I played almost an entire double overtime game for Grogan Hills. Can't wait to see their faces when we get to the weight room.

Next period's lunch so I take my time. No worrying about introductions to another new teacher until sixth period. Just three more classes and I'm done with my first day.

As I'm buttoning my shirt, the gym teacher steps into the locker room and looks at me. "Got a minute?"

Why do so-called intelligent adults insist on giving orders by asking a question? We both know what he means, and "no" isn't an option. But what the hell, no point pissing off a man I'll have to see five days a week until June. After slamming my locker shut, I follow him down the hall to the athletics office.

Kasili's sitting behind one of the desks. Behind him on the wall hangs a diploma that says he's got a psychology degree. Helps with motivating the team and all that crap, I guess. Won't help him in his dealings with me.

There's a picture on his desk of him with his wife and two little kids. From what I read in the papers, he uprooted that family and moved into the neighborhood when he got this rinky-dink job. Wonder if the kids'll thank him, once they're old enough to attend this sorry excuse for a school? He's a new coach who's been handed a team with no chance of ever achieving a thing.

His unsmiling face gives me the once-over. "Haven't seen you around school before, kid."

Kid. Why do these old guys always have to say *kid*? Or *son*?

The sound of the gun I never heard echoes in my ears, but I hold onto reality and force myself to stay in the here and now. "Today's my first day at Farrington."

He's got no business interrogating me. If he expects

fear, he's dealing with the wrong guy. Nor will I make a mistake and volunteer information.

Kasili shuffles some papers on his desk and glances at the gym teacher before turning back to me. "Your name's David...Albacore. Right?"

My heart beats as loud as a crowd counting down a game's final seconds as I nod and wait for his next move. There's no way he can *know*.

"You transferred up from...Oroville, is it? In California?"

"Yes."

"Small town to Chicago. Must be a bit of culture shock."

I shrug.

His fingers drum on the desk. "You play football?

I could say yes. It's October, football season's well underway. No one would think of having me try out for that team this late. But I'm in no mood to waste a lie so I say no.

I turn to leave. The bell ending the period should ring any second.

"What about basketball?"

"No."

"You're what, six-four, six-five?"

"Six-seven." Damn. How'd I fall for that trick? He knows how tall I am. Coaches size up players in seconds, just like I sized him up at six-three.

"You've got size and strength," he says. "Don't pretend you haven't played before."

The inside of my mouth feels like someone shoveled a load of hot tar in it and down my throat. "I don't play now."

Where the hell's that bell?

"Come down after school and I'll give you a tryout."
He smiles like he expects me to jump for the bait. "Being
on the team gets you out of gym class."

Part of me admires the man's determination, and part
of me wants to hate him. And a tiny part tries to whisper, *Go
for it.* After stamping down hard on that thought, I say, "I'm
fine with class. You saw me out there. Take a miracle to turn
me into a player."

The bell rings, ending the period and freeing me.

As I close my hand over the doorknob, he says, "Miracles can happen."

My heart burns with the memory of hours spent praying. If Kasili could turn back time and send her back to me,
I'd do anything for him. But I'm too old for fairy tales and
fantasy will get me nowhere.

CHAPTER 2

Grogan Hills had signs everywhere reminding us we were the best, and the ones in the cafeteria claimed they were feeding America's future leaders. Farrington apparently doesn't expect much from its students. There are no signs in this cafeteria—just grim-faced old ladies in hairnets and dark brown aprons I bet they picked to hide the stains. It doesn't work.

I'm left staring at stale, shriveled fried chicken, thick greasy fries and a gooey pudding that I pick up only because it looks less disgusting than anything else in the dessert section. I won't touch those rocks masquerading as cookies. People on *Survivor* eat better than this.

A bunch of girls are hanging out in the dessert area. Only one of them even looks like she ever touches a sweet. I've seen her before, in my second-period English class. Unlike her stick-figure friends, she's got curves I'm itching to grab. Luscious brown thighs descend from a skirt that's just the right length to torture me. Muscular arms show she's a Mighty Mite; barely five feet tall, even in the high heels that don't belong in high school, except she carries them off.

I'd let her carry me off, too. Mighty Mite could easily stop a few buses. Or an airplane or submarine. She's scowling at the so-called cookies as if she agrees with my assessment. Suddenly she whips her head around, sending the beads at the ends of her micro braids rattling against her back. "What do you suggest?" she asks me.

Her voice is softer than I expect. She's got big brown eyes and dark chocolate skin.

I could just toss my tray and eat the girl. She'd be spicy hot and sugar sweet.

I place my pudding on her tray.

She laughs. "I don't want you to starve."

"Don't worry." *I've never felt less hungry. Not for food, anyway.*

One of the other girls nudges her. "We don't have time."

Mighty Mite frowns. "Right." She throws me a glance over her shoulder as she joins her group.

If not for my sister, I'd go after this girl. But the only reason I even dropped back into school is so I could take care of Barney. She should be easy to spot. A lost-looking six-foot freshman with a big braid hanging down her back ought to stand out like a giraffe parading on the Magnificent Mile.

I leave the food line and enter the lunchroom, where I look around at the tables. Farrington's school colors are black and orange, laughable if you're a Halloween person, but depressing otherwise. Probably why I've seen so few

Goths around. They'd blend into the scenery and be lost, and isn't the point of dressing like a zombie wannabe to stand out?

I don't bother to scan the two tables of white kids by the door or the back corner where the football types hang. I don't even look at the dead-heads, thugs and wannabe's. What I'm looking for is neutral territory, a place where Barney and I can find peace for the next seven months until I collect my diploma. That may not be all I want, but it's the most I can expect. Mom believed in reaching for the moon. But Antwon—my father—said be a realist. I hate being forced to agree with him.

When I do catch sight of Barney, she looks anything but lost. She's in a seat at a table by the windows and I smile in relief. She's already found friends. Maybe this won't be so hard.

One big dark-skinned dude next to her has gleaming ear studs and sits with his ass on the table. Black gangster pants leave his blue and white striped underwear visible. He leans over and says something that makes Barney laugh. Why any girl would find a guy dressing like somebody's prison-wife a turn-on beats me. But there's Barney, looking at him like he's Denzel or something.

I'd better get over there and check out my sister's first guy.

But before I can move, a female voice behind me says, "Oh, no. Hell, no!"

Thinking the angry voice is directed at me, I step aside, saying, "Sorry."

The Mighty Mite and her friends push past me and advance on the table. She and the other girls form a semi-circle around Barney.

"We've been invaded," the Mite says.

The guy beside Barney jumps away from the table. He's tall, almost as tall as me. "Relax. She's cute."

"This isn't about you, Malik." The beads at the ends of the Mite's braids clack together like a snake's rattles. "That girl doesn't belong here."

Barney's trying to look like she isn't scared of the angry female horde surrounding her, but her fingers clutching the edge of the table give her away.

I drop my tray on a nearby table and push through the crowd just as one girl says, "Don't know who you are, but you're a fool to be where you're not wanted."

When I touch my sister's shoulder, I feel her trembling. It's not like she understands the maze of unwritten rules and set out to provoke a war. The treatment center they put her in after Mom got killed sheltered and protected her, and this is only her first day in a real high school. She's so young, she still believes the world wants to be her friend.

Pushing back rage, I say, "Let's go, kid. You don't belong in the land of the bitches."

One girl with a wide red stripe running through her black hair turns to me. "Ohhh, lord, they finally found us some cute guys." She moves close and presses herself against my side. "I'll be your bitch if you want, big guy."

"The day I'm that desperate, I'll cut it off."

The guys behind her fall out laughing.

Red Stripe screams, "Kiss the shit off my crack, faggot."

The Mite's lips tighten. She remains silent, but her eyes move from me to the still shaky Barney as I lift my sister's tray. Turning my back to the haters, I escort my sister to the table where I left my lunch.

"He invited me," Barney whines as I help her into a seat. "He said I should come over...I thought it was okay."

It's my fault. If I hadn't wasted time with Kasili, I'd have been here in time to prevent this. With my hand on the back of her chair, I look around to see what I've dropped into. The natives here better beware. I won't wave a white flag. If they let Barney and me be, fine. If not, it's their problem because I'm taking no more crap today, not from anyone.

The faces staring back at me are so varied, it's like I've stumbled into a no-man's-land. I recognize the long-haired boy seated across from me. Neill—can't remember his last name—from the same English class as the Mite and me, so he has to be a junior or senior. Most of the others look like freshmen.

Neill looks me over like a general sizing up an opposing force. "You're David, right?"

"David Albacore." After seven months the name rolls off my tongue as if I've never been anyone else. Like Murhaselt was never a part of me.

"Second period. Never forget a face, especially one seven feet from the ground."

"David's only six-seven," Barney says.

Neill looks at Barney. "Still a big deal. And you're right up there with him. I'm Neill Mallory." He turns back to me and says, "Hope you're sure about sitting here. Most people consider getting too close to this table social suicide."

I'd never intended having a social life this year. "It's fine. I'm happy here."

I nudge Barney and she jumps. "I'm Barnetta Murhaselt."

Neill grins. "Big name, big girl."

"People call me Barney." She looks as if she's recovering. The social worker claimed to be thrilled about her resiliency. Me, I just hope she's not faking it.

The food's not as bad as it looks. As we eat, a couple of the guys introduce themselves, including a heavy-set kid named Carl seated next to Neill, and a tall, lanky Latino, Julian Morales, who's a sophomore. The girls immediately include my sister in a discussion on clothes and makeup, so maybe social death won't be so bad. And Barney's loving the girl-talk. She seems content, or at least more relaxed.

The room is filled with laughter, shuffling feet and the clink of plastic silverware against plastic plates. But there's no mistaking that rattle of beads. As musky perfume fills my nose, I turn to find the Mite standing behind my chair.

"I just wanted to say…sorry if we were…if I was—a bit rough before." Her eyes have trouble meeting mine.

I stand to make things even more difficult for her. "More than a bit," I reply.

She nibbles her lower lip. Why do girls do that? This one's got so much God-given everything, she doesn't need the extra advantage. From where I'm standing, the magnificent view inside her sweater's giving me a hard enough time already.

Maybe she's here to make friends.

She glances at Barney. "She didn't belong at our table."

So much for friends.

I turn my back on her and sit down. "And *you* don't belong here."

She leans over my chair. The combination of her warmth and perfume leave me squirming in my seat as she says, "My name's Yolanda. Yolanda Dare." Her head sweeps in a half circle, creating a string of soft notes from the beads and a hot thud from below my belt.

She leans even closer. "People call me Yoyo. And you can pull my string anytime you want."

My stomach performs an atomic bounce. Pull *her* string? As if she can't guess how the feel of her breath so close to my cheek jerks mine. This girl has a double dose of that thing girls have that makes a guy's legs shake and teeth clench until we're praying for relief. It takes everything I have to keep my hands to myself as I turn to stare at her face. For just a second, I let myself dream that the gleam in her eyes and her smile mean she likes me.

But I see her friends over her shoulder. They're all laughing and smirking. A sure sign she's only here to embarrass me.

"Obviously, anybody can pull your string," I say. "I'm not about to join your crowd of puppet-masters."

She straightens, and something washes over her narrowed eyes that's way stronger than anger. Her skirt swishes around her legs as she storms back to her table.

"You're an idiot," Neill says.

"Not interested."

Really. She's not even my type.

"Most guys would give a kidney for an invite from The Dare," Neill says. "Talk is, Yoyo graced most of the football team's offensive line with her favors last year." He points to the jock table. "This was supposed to be the defense's turn, but Malik stole her for basketball."

"Are you after an invite from her?" Barney asks Neill. By the way he stares at me, I guess his answer before he says, "I'd rather get one from your boyfriend." And I'm betting by the way Carl looks at him that they're a couple.

"You mean David?" Barney asks. She laughs. "He's not my—"

"Even if The Dare gave out lap dances, no one's got the guts to chase Malik's girl," one of the girls says. She turns to Barney. "Better watch out for Malik."

"Who's Malik?"

"The guy you were with over there. Malik Kaplan, son of the man who owns Kaplan's Body Shop. I don't know about his dad and cars, but Malik never met a female body he didn't want to work on."

"I know about his dad and cars." Neill shakes his head. "Don't go anywhere near his shop if you care about your ride."

Looking over at the group, I check out the guy who lured Barney to his table and started this mess. He's got a possessive arm around Yolanda's waist. He may scare the others, but to me, those drooping pants and the bandanna around his head signify gangsta clown with a capital C. He's probably never seen anything scarier than his own face in the mirror. I've met real thugs, the type you don't fuck with. They don't talk smack, and if you leave them alone you're fine; but if you cross them, you're an idiot and deserve whatever comes back at you.

He leans close to Yolanda, says something in her ear and she laughs. But her eyes stare at me across the room.

"He's got money and looks," Julian says. "And the hottest girl in school. He's got his own car and he throws major parties whenever his parents split town."

"If they've got money, why's he go to school here?" I ask.

Neill's voice goes all sarcastic. "Maybe his parents want to give all us poor, downtrodden inner-city folk an example of the successful black middle-class."

Julian leans his tall body across the table. "What magazine'd you get that from?"

"Or maybe they're not as well off as they pretend. Whatever," Neill says.

But Barney's still frowning at Neill. "What kind of invitation did you want from David?"

Before I can explain, Neill says, "Nothing. My boy Carl's the jealous type." Carl and Neill look at each other and grin. Then they kiss.

A scowling gray-haired cafeteria monitor walks over to our table. "Enough. You know the rules about public displays like that."

"What'd she mean by that?" I ask as she leaves.

"PDAs—public displays of affection." Neill turns to watch as she crosses the room. "Officially, none of us mere students are allowed to feel emotion toward each other. Unofficially, they jump on *undesirable* displays." His fingers trace quotation marks in the air. "But see those guys?" He points at the elite table where Malik holds court. "If he laid her out on the tabletop, someone *might* step in, but I wouldn't bet on it."

As if to prove the point, Malik begins playing skin the cat with his Yoyo. His hand moves up her skirt with no protest from the cafeteria monitor. No protest from Yolanda, either.

Means nothing to me. Nothing. But still, I can't look away. Can't move.

"She shouldn't be all over him that way," Barney says.

But she's not. She's just...letting it happen. Nothing more.

Finally Malik goes too far with Yolanda and the cafeteria monitor comes back. Malik's forced to bring both hands into view. When she leaves, Malik gets up and takes Yolanda's arm, but she shakes her head no and points at her full tray. Seconds later he frowns and stalks from the lunchroom. Two other girls from the table jump up and run after him.

Yolanda stares after him for a second. Then she squares her shoulders and looks down at her food. But she doesn't eat.

Why'd she let him go without her?

Not my business.

Julian turns to me. "Don't suppose you play basketball?"

I force myself to turn and concentrate on the people at my table. "No."

Julian sighs. "We could use someone like you on the team."

I should've known. With his height and build, of course he'd be a basketball player.

He lets out a huge sigh and his shoulders slump as he says, "You look like the type. And Coach's desperate for players. Desperate."

"Why's that?" I already know. I've read the stories about this worthless team. But I'll pretend.

The guys look at each other, and then all heads turn to Julian.

"Fine, I'll tell him," he says. "Last year the varsity bus crashed coming back from a game and almost everyone died. The Coach, the players—everybody. We got almost nobody left now."

"Yeah, nobody except Malik," Neill says. "He's this year's captain by default, only because he was lucky enough to have his own ride. That's why he wasn't on the bus with the rest of the team."

I look at Yolanda. Somehow she looks smaller without Malik at her side. If I hadn't seen her bossing the other girls, I'd swear she even looks lost.

"He claims he had a premonition," Carl says.

"Premonition hell," Neill says. "I heard the coach wouldn't let him on the bus—and that he was gonna be dumped off the team."

"Doesn't matter now," Carl says. "He's all that's left. Team sucked back then, so the replacements will suck this year. All except our Julian."

Julian frowned. "We won't suck. Coach Kasili says…he says we'll do fine."

But from the look on Julian's face, I can tell that the coach's psych degree isn't doing much to motivate this thrown-together team of leftover players.

"Aren't you a sophomore?" I ask.

"Yeah, but Coach moved me up to varsity this year."

"That's how bad things are," one of the girls adds.

Doesn't matter. I'm not playing.

Barnetta glances at me. "David, you could—"

"No!" I didn't mean to be that harsh with her, but no way will I ever go back to basketball again.

CHAPTER 3

The teacher in my last class of the day, The Sociology of Marriage and the Family, stares at me when I check in. I'm not expecting any more trouble from him than I've had from the other teachers.

"I expect commitment from the people in this class," he says.

His name's Henry Martin—short, balding, with nearly pitch black skin and steely eyes. I nod, not certain what else he expects. Students rush in trying to beat the bell, and hustle to their seats in silence. There's more than miles separating Grogan Hills and Farrington. I've seen restless, noisy students in my other classes in this school. But there's none of that going on in this room.

"Only twenty-two brave souls decided to try me this year until you arrived," he says, still looking at me. "I'll tell you what I tell everyone. You're expected to participate, but not disrupt. You behave, and we'll do fine. Otherwise, I'll just hand you your F now and you don't need to come through this door again."

"We'll do fine," I tell him. We have to. I need this class—the one I've been looking forward to most of all. I need some answers about what happened to my family and hope I can find them here.

I think back to the Murhaselt household in the old days, when Dad worked and Mom stayed home. We had a nice house, went on great vacations in the summer; it was all smiles and laughter, and weekends spent all together. I remember when the smiles vanished, too, replaced by tight faces and loud, angry words. A lot of drinking and cursing, and slammed doors. I knew my parents argued, but hell, my best friends and I did, too. One minute we'd be yelling and the next it was all forgotten, meant nothing. Afterwards, we all went on and did our thing, just like nothing had happened.

I was fifteen the first time I saw a bruise on Mom. I was so blind, so dumb. I believed her story about an accident. Ignored the dark, fearful look in her eyes.

Maybe here in this class, I can figure out what happened to two people who were supposed to love each other. Maybe it'll explain that what happened to us wasn't part of the Murhaselt blood that I can't drain from my body the way I threw off that name.

"Love makes you crazy," Mom said once. I was sixteen, and by then even I knew what was happening. She always had on heavy makeup and sometimes even wore dark glasses inside the house. But none of it hid what he did to her. I used to wonder what gave Antwon the right to hurt her and still call himself a man? He ran around claiming it was her own fault that he hit her—and that every problem, every single thing that went wrong, was always Mom's fault. How was that being a man?

I snap out of my memories when the bell rings to start the period and Mr. Martin points toward an empty seat near the back. Just as I turn, a last figure rushes through the door and I collide with Yolanda Dare.

Her notebook falls to the floor. I jump forward and kneel to grab it without thinking. When I look up Yolanda is kneeling beside me and I find myself staring into her eyes.

"My book," she says in a silky voice that leaves me frozen. I can't move a muscle.

"You're late, Miss Dare," the teacher says.

"Sorry, sir." There's something wary in her eyes as she takes her book from my hand, and she's careful to keep our fingers from touching. When she rises and turns away, the hem of her skirt brushes my face and I have to grab the edge of the teacher's desk to keep from losing it.

Yolanda takes a seat near the front as my shaky legs carry me to a desk in the back of the room. Yolanda keeps herself facing forward, leaving me to stare at the hair coiling down her back.

"All right," Mr. Martin begins. "Let's resume yesterday's discussion on the secrets of adulthood." He's walking around the room as he talks. "Society sets eighteen as a magic age, one that most of you have reached or are rapidly approaching."

Two more months and I'll be eighteen. Then David Albacore becomes real.

"Most of you think it's past time you get all your rights. But from the other side of the fence, people wonder if eighteen's too young for some things. So here's the question for you: is an eighteen-year-old really ready for the responsibilities of adulthood?"

"Adults don't ask themselves if they're ready." Yolanda says, like she's reading my mind.

I want to see her eyes again. Why won't she turn her head?

"It's an arbitrary number," someone says.

"Mostly." Martin nods. "It's something pulled out of a hat by modern-day American society. Less than two hundred years ago, many of you would already be married with families."

Turn. I've never believed in ESP but…turn!

Someone says, "We're ready by eighteen."

"Physically, yes. Biologically, the bodies of eighteen-year-olds are adult."

"We're superior to most adults."

"Making eighteen the pinnacle?" Martin joins in on the laughter. "But biology is only part of the equation. There's also an intellectual component, as well as behavioral, emotional and mental ones. It's a rare individual who's mature in all these areas at eighteen."

"Don't girls mature before boys?" a girl asks.

Amid male groans, the teacher nods. "In some ways, yes."

Yolanda's neck twitches. *Come on. Just a little more. Turn.*

"We're bigger and stronger. We're the ones forced to go off to war," one boy says.

She moves, *almost* turns. *More!*

"There hasn't been a draft in your lifetime, Mr. Jenkins.

If you're asking why eighteen-year-old guys get sent off to war, it's mainly because you're immature. That gives young men your age a crucial advantage when it comes to fighting. Does anyone know what that is? Mr. Albacore?"

I had no idea the teacher was standing right beside me. And this time there's no flashback to blame. "Yes, sir?"

"Perhaps you know the answer?"

What was the question? Something about war and being immature? "Uh, advantage, sir? Over women?"

"You might want to keep your attention focused on the lesson, Mr. Albacore." He continues walking down the aisle. "Can anyone tell me the advantage eighteen-year-old males have when it comes to defending their country?"

"They don't believe they can die," Yolanda says.

"Very good, Miss Dare. We old guys know the risks involved. So we'd need a lot more incentive before putting ourselves in harm's way."

I look up. She's staring directly at me.

When the bell rings, Yolanda leads the stampede for the door. Before I can follow, the teacher calls me over to his desk. "What made you select this class, Mr. Albacore?" he asks.

Should I tell him the truth? *Yeah, right.*

"Thought there'd be lots of honeys in a class on marriage," I say and laugh.

He doesn't. "Are you expecting this class to be a cakewalk?"

People think *cakewalk* means easy. But real cakewalks were difficult as hell according to my grandmother. They required endurance, balance and training, and only the best lasted until the end. Apparently my new teacher doesn't know this. Back at Grogan Hills, my classes were easy— what Martin would consider a cakewalk—thanks to my so-called tutors there. But no basketball at Farrington means I won't get the star treatment I used to rate.

"No sir." I reply. "I'm sure you'll work our asses off."

"My class is legendary for shaving more than a few butts. I don't give a lot of tests and quizzes, but everyone works. Next month there's a major paper and oral presentation due on a research topic of your choice. The research represents seventy-five percent of your grade for the marking period. As a newcomer to the school, you didn't know what you were walking into when you signed up for this class. So here's a one-time offer: you want to change to another class, I'll pave the way with the office."

I should be smart and take this offer, but I don't *want* another class. I need to know. Marriage. Family. What went wrong for my family?

I glance at Yolanda's empty desk. "I'll stay." *Even if I have to put up with The Dare.*

"I'm glad. I think you'll be a real asset in this group. I had that feeling." He leans back in his chair, sizing me up. "Your shirt's tucked in, your pants actually go up to your waist, and they fit, too. I'd say you're here to learn."

He stands, takes his briefcase and heads for the door. "By the way, you'll need to get your topic in to me by the end of the week, Mr. Albacore."

Crap! I have no time to even think about it. "How about the secret of life?" I ask, half serious. I used to think there was this Big Secret, something all adults knew. The one piece of knowledge I had to figure out. And once I did, I'd be welcomed into Adult Society. *The old folks kept tight locks around that secret*, I thought. Like young King Arthur, we had to prove we were worthy before we could enter the magic kingdom of adulthood.

Martin pauses at the doorway. "The secret of life? That's been way overdone. Besides, living in the adult world is just as scary as childhood. There *is* no secret. Nothing except…acceptance."

Just what I've learned—accept suffering, accept responsibility for my misdeeds. Even if that means giving up everything I've ever wanted.

CHAPTER 4

Back at Grogan Hills, we strolled leisurely in and out of the doors of the school, casual and safe. Here at Farrington, students line up to pass through airport-style metal detectors just so we can go through the one unlocked door, where stern-faced guards stand ready to wand you if the alarm gets set off.

Did Antwon spend a single second considering what he was condemning us to when he pulled that trigger? Did God, when he let the bullet rip open Mom's chest? David Murhaselt sure didn't, not when he took those painkillers, dropped his head on the pillow and slept through everything that followed.

Now David Murhaselt, the Grogan Hills drop-out, has been erased. Since I refused to play ball for them anymore, Grogan Hills didn't much care when I vanished. Now I'm David Albacore, a nobody from California, just another new student at Farrington. The money I spent to have my records changed was a good investment. If not for Coach Kasili and the Mighty Mite, today would have been good—quiet and anonymous.

Students and teachers have bolted from the halls during my talk with Mr. Martin. The echo of my steps down the second-floor corridor is the only sound I hear until one last girl runs past and races down the stairs. I stop to stare through the staircase window at the outside world and see that I'm not the only one who thinks real life doesn't start until we get outside. Nobody wants to be in this place unless they're forced.

From that window, I watch as fire-colored leaves drop from the trees around the school. They scatter and swirl through the air, then drift to rest on the browning grass and sidewalks. Freshmen run through the piles of leaves, dragging their feet and grabbing colorful handfuls for mock snowball fights or to crumble in the air. Laughter and wild screams show they've forgotten they're no longer in grade school. Upperclassmen look at them and laugh. And the seniors—you can always tell who we are because we like to act as if everyone else is invisible and just ignore them.

I see Barney outside in the park across the street, talking to some girl. Then I take a second look and change my mind. In spite of the stringy, shoulder-length black hair, I think that's a guy with her. Or half a guy, anyway. His head barely comes up to Barney's shoulder.

He looks harmless. I'd bet he's only a fourteen-year-old-freshman, still waiting to grow into his hormones. But Barney's younger than her years or appearance, so I have to worry about any guy who gets too close.

Yolanda and Malik stand outside, halfway down the front stairs. He's talking with a couple of other guys and sharing a cigarette with the red-striped girl. Yolanda's just standing there, probably too sure of her power over Malik to worry. Why shouldn't she be? Even from this distance, even through the glass, I can feel her power.

She finally moves between Malik and the other girl. Malik grips Yolanda's shoulder, they kiss, and then he pushes her away. My hands form fists out of the same rage that makes my heart pound. I want to hurt him. Maybe it's not my business. But...still.

The other girl laughs as Malik and his friends walk down the rest of the stairs. The girls stare at each other as I leave the window for my locker. It only takes a few minutes to grab my coat and head out the front door, into the blast of crisp October air. But in that short amount of time, the scene outside has changed.

Malik and his crew have crossed to the park. He points to the boy standing beside my sister and yells, "Where's my money, punk? Hand it over."

"I-I forgot." The kid's voice squeaks.

The wind carries Barney's voice: "Leave him alone."

I taught Barney to be brave; I taught her how to fight. But I never expected her to take on three hulks in defense of some puny stranger. She's over there, putting herself between her new friend and the kind of fake toughs who won't hesitate to push a girl around.

No way. Never again will I stand back and let someone I love get hurt.

As I run down the stairs, Yolanda weaves through traffic on the street to get to her man. Before I reach the curb, Red Stripe steps in front of me. "This ain't none of your business," she warns.

"Move." I don't know if I could knock a girl down without my mother's ghost blasting me, but the girl jumps aside so I don't have to beg Mom's forgiveness.

Traffic forces me to wait for cars to pass as Yolanda grabs Malik's arm. "Come on, this is dumb," she says.

He turns to face her and yells, "You calling me dumb?"

Yolanda blinks rapidly, as if she's fighting back tears. I'd watched Mom do the same thing for months, before she finally packed us up to leave.

"Not you," she says to Malik. "I-I didn't mean—"

The long-haired boy takes off running into the park. The other two guys go after him, with Barney at their heels. Malik turns to follow them, but Yolanda's got hold of his arm, almost like she's trying to stop him from going after the younger kids.

Just as I reach the other side of the street, Malik curses and punches Yolanda in the ribs. As he turns to join the pursuit, her foot slips against a rock. Her arms flail and she falls backwards. I shift directions mid-stride and catch her before she hits the ground. She's soft against my chest and one arm falls around my shoulders. Suddenly I'm rock hard and aching. My skin's so hot, I wish I could throw it off like a snake sheds in the spring.

I help her back on her feet, asking, "You all right?"

She nods, so I have to let her go—even though everything inside me screams to pull her back and hold tight. But Barney's being chased. I know where I need to be.

By the time I reach them, the long-haired kid's on the ground with a bloody nose. Barney's fist connects with one guy's chin and it drops him to his knees. I taught her that right cross, and for the first time in years—since she began growing in seventh grade—she's holding herself tall and straight. She looks proud of her size.

Malik stands smiling at her, almost as if he's amused.

Barney turns to him. "You'd best stay back."

The amusement vanishes from his face. "No girl tells *me* what to do, sweetheart."

"Then *I'll* tell you," I say and I've got Malik in a head-lock before I even finish the sentence. And no surprise, the would-be gangsta howls and slaps at my hands, just like the baby I thought he was. I tighten my arm around his throat until he wises up and stops fighting.

Malik's friends look like they're not sure what to do. The skinny kid jumps up, and instead of running off, he moves to Barney's side. His hands are in fists and he stays next to her, but he keeps throwing glances up at her, as if he hopes she'll take the lead. I wonder who's defending who?

"Who the fuck you think you are?" Malik snarls when I loosen up on his neck.

A man you don't want to mess with, that's who. "You stop bothering Barney, got it?" I say.

"Lemme go, dammit."

Man's got no sense.

I tighten my grip again until he's gasping. "Not till we have an understanding. You don't mess with these kids, got it, dickhead? Only one right answer keeps your face outta the dirt."

He nods.

The other two back away, but I don't care about them, or about Yolanda, who stands off to the side in silence.

When I release him, Malik coughs and goes to Yolanda's side. "You don't know who you're messing with. I *own* this school," he tells me, brave now that he's out of my grip.

I laugh. "Nice meeting you, Nadia."

His eyes bug wide and he sputters, "What the fuck?"

When Yolanda laughs, too, he turns and stares her into silence.

"You said you owned the place," I reply as he turns back to look at me. "So I figured you for the principal. Not exactly how I expected an old lady principal to look."

"David," Barney says, in that tone she uses when she thinks I'm being foolish. "You *know* who Malik Kaplan is."

"Yeah, I know who he is. And now *he* needs to know something." I step forward until our faces are only inches apart and he's forced to look up into my eyes. "*I'm* David Albacore," I say quietly. "And this is Barney. You hurt her, I'll hand you your ass."

"Barney and I are friends." Malik throws a crooked grin at her.

She smiles back.

Girls.

"You and *I* are not," I say.

"I'll take my orders from the lady. Did I hurt you, honey?"

"No. He didn't hurt me, David."

Well, I'm itching to hurt him. And it isn't all just about Barney.

Yolanda's not smiling. She breathes heavily as she stares at her man. She's shaking as if she expects an attack. Probably scared of me and what I might do next.

"And pull your damned pants up," I tell Malik. "Those baby-stripes look like a sign you're searching for a new kind of friend."

His jaw drops. "What the fuck you talking about?"

Yolanda clasps her hand to her mouth, but not before I catch her snickering. For a second our eyes meet and we share the joke that's flown right over Malik's thick head. I'm probably wrong, but something like approval seems to flash in her eyes.

I turn to Malik. "Stay away from Barney, away from me…and away from that kid."

Malik frowns. "Reyes owes me money."

"Choose. Eat the loss or eat my fist. Your call."

Choose the fist. Please.

He stares at me and a silent message passes between us. I'll be watching my back from here on in.

"Sorry, Princess," Malik tells Barney. "That thug of yours is bloodthirsty. Better be careful with him." Then he takes Yolanda's arm and struts off, as if he's won some kind of victory.

I turn to the little guy who started all this. "Who *are* you, anyway?"

He swallows and looks like he can't tell if I'm any less dangerous than Malik. "I'm Tyrone Barrows Reyes," he sputters.

"He's in the band," Barney says, sounding almost proud.

"I can tell." His "Band Geeks Do It on Cue" T-shirt is a dead giveaway.

"*Gracias*," he says, with a little bow to Barney.

But there's no time for courtesy. "We've gotta get moving," I tell my sister.

We're halfway down the block when I hear Tyrone's voice. "*Un momento*. Hold up." I'm tempted to try that eye-rolling thing of Barney's. When he catches up to us, Tyrone's got a stack of books in his arms and a light in his eyes. "You dropped these, *chica*." His stupid grin widens when Barney giggles.

"Oh yeah, thanks."

When Barney reaches for her books he says, "No. I will carry them for you, *chica*."

I hold out my hands. "I hold her books. You—get lost."

The band geek gulps. He may be love-struck, but self-preservation helps him control his tongue. "Yes, sir," is all he says.

I bite my lip to keep from laughing until he's run off. The four books are heavy and the ugly backpack she's wearing looks full. I'm still appalled at the tie-dyed design she picked when I took her looking for school supplies— yet another sign she's still just a kid. She'll be making different choices about a lot of things by next year. I'm already feeling a little sad about that.

"I can carry my own books." She said the same thing when she started eighth grade. I ignored her then and do the same thing now.

"Barnetta the Amazon," I say, as I settle her burden under my arm. She ducks her head, but I lift her chin until our eyes meet. "Don't. You did good."

"Yeah, but...it hurts." Bruises already darken the back of her hand.

"Ice'll fix that," I say. At least she's no longer walking with her shoulders hunched, as if she were trying to swallow herself. Maybe that therapy really is helping.

"How was school today?" I ask.

Her eyes roll. "Way easy. I already know the stuff they're teaching."

She's the brains in the family. Mom should have concentrated on Barney and college, and let me go my own way. But she was always after me to fulfill her dreams. I never found a way to tell her how I felt about school when she was alive. Now it's too late, and I'm forced to do a juggling act between school, my own homework and my job, not to mention dealing with our little sister, Linda. At least I get to enjoy my job.

"What's with all these books?" I ask her. "You sure have a lot of homework. Why'd you bring so much stuff home?"

"I had to. I couldn't figure out how to open my locker," Barney admits.

The whiny note in her voice makes me laugh. She drops a scowl on me and sticks out her tongue. Barney's so big, it's easy to forget she's still almost a baby sometimes.

"I'll show you how to handle the locker monster tomorrow at lunch."

" 'For the love of God, Montresor, for the love of God,' " Barney says, and strikes a pose with one hand on her chest.

I frown down at her. "What was that?"

"Poe. We're reading him in English. 'A Cask of Amontillado.' You'd like that story."

"Like it? Me?" *Not sure I could even pronounce it.*

"It's all about vengeance and retribution for imaginary insults. Full of irony and—"

"What makes you think I'd care?"

She gives me this long look and then sighs. "It's about construction, David. A guy gets bricked inside a wall."

"Masonry? Cool." After shifting her books to my other hand, I rub the top of her head. "That's in one of these books?"

She nods.

Just then, a plane's roaring engines drown out the traffic noises. I wonder if it carries escapees from Chicago's approaching winter, or if it's full of new arrivals with no idea what they're in for. I wonder what it would be like to just climb aboard an airplane and fly away from the past.

When the engine noise dies down, Barney asks, "Did you have to be so rough with Malik?"

I have to stop and stare at her. "Rough? He was beating up your little friend, and looked like he was getting ready to punch you, too."

"I know, but still…" her voice trails off.

I've seen this before, with girls. Malik's cute, so he gets a pass. Barney was ready to deck him in the heat of the moment, but now all she's remembering is his looks. And Yolanda gives him a lot more than a pass. He'd almost knocked her down. But he's her man, so all is forgiven.

I don't want that for my sister. Don't want Barney hurt or being used. Or any of the things I've done to girls that I shouldn't have. A year ago, none of that mattered. But my priorities changed.

"That stuck-up witch Yolanda Dare," Barney says.

For some reason, this bothers me.

"You like her, don't you? Better than me—don't you?" Something flickers in the back of her eyes, something like sad resignation, and my heart aches.

"No way," I say.

"You can tell me the truth, David. Guys always like pretty girls better than their own sisters."

"That's not true." I'm not giving her yet another reason to think life's not worth living. She's still too fragile for that.

A few minutes later we reach Aunt Edie's apartment, the one that wasn't roomy to begin with, when she lived in it alone. Now it's nearly bursting, with me, Barney and Linda all crowded in with our aunt.

Officially, I don't even live here with them.

"I still can't believe you got away with pretending to be someone else," Barney says.

"You doubted me?"

She rolls her eyes. "I guess not. You can do anything, David."

Anything. Except the one thing that really counted.

After handing Barney her books, I lean forward and kiss her forehead, just the way Mom used to. She even kissed me like that until I got too old—too foolish—and refused that loving gesture of hers.

How could I have been so stupid?

43

CHAPTER 5

The sun's nearly gone down and floodlights illuminate the yard when I get off the bus near my job. The construction site's dirty, noisy and dangerous. It's also my home, the place where I'm among the people of my chosen tribe.

I've known this place since they brought in the excavators and dug out the foundation for the first of four buildings we're putting up. I used to come up to this fence after school and stare at the men and women working the machines and carrying equipment. I envied the way they controlled the earth. Envied their strength and power and the way they made something from nothing. The first day I joined them left me blistered and shaking with fatigue. It also left me proud as hell.

That first day convinced me they weren't looking for a flunkey, which is what being a *day laborer* normally means. Technically I'm an afternoon laborer, since I start second shift after school. But I work side-by-side with these people doing all the same jobs, which makes me more of a full-fledged construction worker. If they didn't want me around or felt I couldn't cut it, Sanderson, the crew boss, would say so. He's not shy about showing his authority.

We're working on the last building now. I've dug trenches, laid rebar, carried rolls of wire and sacks of cement, and stood on a scaffold with the wind in my hair and a trowel in my hand. The master plan has grown into something real before my eyes—and with my help.

As I walk through the gates and onto the site, one of the guys says, "Oh lordy, break out the scuba gear, we're swimming with the fishes," teasing about my last name. "I'd share my tuna fish sandwich, but I guess that'd be too much like cannibalism, huh?" says another one of the guys.

Unlike the fish-face comments from the smart-alecks at school, these jokes leave me feeling good, and accepted.

"Watch yourself, Harvey. We're reading Poe in class," I tell him.

Harvey frowns. "What the hell's that supposed to mean?"

As I clock in, Sanderson shifts an unlit cigar around his mouth. "Means watch out he doesn't decide to brick your ass up inside the wall if you keep disrespecting him."

At least the days when the crew boss dogged my heels and checked my every move are long gone. Still, like the other guys, I'd rather he ignored me. So when he calls me over, I wish I could pretend to be deaf.

He points to a man standing at his side and talks about him as if he were retarded. "Pea-brain here can't decide which end of a hammer's which."

The guy frowns and corrects him, saying, "Peabody," like some kind of idiot.

Sanderson's eyes narrow and his clipboard slaps his knee. "What?"

The slap's a dead giveaway and I know enough to keep my mouth shut. Pea-brain's either as crazy or dumb as he appears. Physically, he's not much older than me. Mentally, I see that he's barely past kindergarten.

"My name," he says. "You made a mistake. It's Peabody."

"Just get your *body* over there and let Albacore show you how to nail wood together the right way."

"But he's just a kid."

Now Pea-brain's got me about ready to take the hammer to his skull.

Slap goes the clipboard. "And?" Sanderson says.

"Why have *him* tell me what to do?"

"Because he's a fucking master of woodwork, while you're just a master fuck-up. Any more questions?"

Pea-brain's shaking by the time I lead him away.

Unfortunately, he's still dumb as a rock and the boss wasn't exaggerating. He's got no idea what to do with a hammer and doesn't act like he wants to learn.

"Listen, kid—" he says, after destroying a dozen nails along with his thumb in his attempt to attach two pieces of wood to each other.

"The name's Albacore. Use it." Even the boss stopped calling me *kid* months ago. Building wood frames helped rebuild my arm once it was out of the sling. I've moved through a lot of jobs on the site since I started, but the hammer and saw remain my favorite tools.

"So what's wrong this time?" He points at his most recent attempt and I shudder. The nails are crooked and wouldn't withstand a harsh look, much less hold a wall together.

"The joint's not solid."

"So? It's gonna end up inside a wall, for Christ sake. Who'll ever know?"

I'll know. And he should care. I shrug and point with my chin. "There's the gate. You don't want to do the job right, then get off the lot. You work with me, you're going to do things right."

"My Uncle Walter's the boss here. You can't make me leave."

So I'm the one who's slow and never guessed. I'm stuck with Pea-brain because he has connections. I put my hammer back into my belt and leave him standing with his chin almost dragging on the ground.

Sanderson's sitting at his desk in the construction trailer when I slam the door on my way inside.

"Why'd you sic your newbie nephew on me?" I ask him. Forcing me to put up with Pea-brain means I'll have to do both of our jobs. I can't let that dimwit's idea of good enough become part of any building I'm helping to construct. And I can't even send him running, because he's got connections.

"You're still a newbie yourself, David. You should remember what it was like." Sanderson pours two cups of coffee and hands one to me. "Besides, anyone else would've already used a few power tools on him by now."

It sounds almost like a compliment from the man who dogged me for months, waiting for me to make a mistake. I take a sip from my cup; it's the first time he's invited me to have coffee with him. We both drink it black and strong.

"He's hopeless," I admit, feeling like I'm disappointing the man. "Trying to teach him to hit a nail straight is like trying to teach oil not to be greasy. Worst part is, he doesn't even care."

Sanderson sighs and drops into his chair. "I know. But he's my sister-in-law's kid. Which means my wife's after me to give him a job."

"Meaning I have to put up with him?" I lift the cup to my mouth to hide my anger.

"Meaning I'm depending on *you* to run him off."

With that, my coffee goes down the wrong pipe and he laughs while I choke.

"Just so your wife won't blame *you*?" I gasp.

"Exactly. Make sure *he* decides this isn't the place for him, so leaving's *his* choice."

"What if he doesn't scare off?"

"Hell, David. That grim look you get on your face scares *me* sometimes. Real work terrifies that spoiled, lazy nephew of mine. Consider yourself VP in charge of ridding the boss of obnoxious relatives."

"Add that to my new title, master of woodwork, and I should get a raise." *Pushy, but I got to try. We need the money. My sisters need so much that I don't know how to give them.*

"Hah. Good one, David." Sometimes Sanderson acts just like every other adult. "Now get out there and run Pea-brain off."

CHAPTER 6

I watch the ball leave my opponent's hands with only one eye. The other's looking at her. That Flexible-Flyer cheerleader. She's promised me a private party after the game if Grogan Hills wins. There's twenty seconds left on the clock and the win's a sure thing. Something in my head tries warning me, "Just let the ball go." But I just have to show off. This dream has to go like all the others. Once again I jump, and block the shot.

Then my tired legs collapse under me and I hit the ground.

◆

Wake up, David!

In the morning my muscles feel like I've done a century on a chain gang. Dressing for school is the last thing I want to do.

Barney feels the same way. "Can't I just stay home for one day?" she begs.

"You don't want to miss your friends."

"Look at me, I tower over everyone. It's hard to make friends. I wouldn't be so big if I could help it."

She's in that ninth-grade funk I'm grateful I left behind a long time ago. I remember those days, when I wanted a kid's freedom, but still fought to be an adult—even though I feared the responsibility. Her age isn't Barney's only problem. I can't even guess what being so much taller than all your friends does to a girl. But she developed early, too, and I've watched the looks in guy's eyes when they see her. Had dealings with a few of my ex-friends about that while she was still only in eighth grade.

"It's okay for you, giant guys are the rage. You get whatever you want. But not me—people laugh at me. And boys! What if I never have a boyfriend?" Barney bites her lip, then says in a rush, "David, what if no one ever wants me?"

Mom would know what to say. My sister's question makes my insides squirm and I feel like a worm on a hook. Barney's not really worried about the kids at school. And I can't let her depression win. Not when the social worker keeps talking about taking her away for her own good.

When the Department of Children and Family Services descended on us after Mom died, they split the three of us up. There was an uncle in Wisconsin all set to take me to help with his business. Everybody knows relatives are supposed to work for free. And Aunt Patricia was happy to take Linda to live with her in Jamaica. She's a nice lady, but she hates coming to visit the States and I knew we'd never see our little sister again if she went to a whole other country. Still, at least somebody wanted her and me.

Nobody wanted Barney.

She was headed for some foster home—*if* DCFS could find someone to take in a six-foot-tall fourteen-year-old girl with a death wish her therapists are still trying to tame. That's why I had to learn to grovel.

I grip Barney's shoulders as I say, "I want you."

"You're my brother. You *have* to say that."

"No I don't. You get on my nerves, I'll tell you. And I'm telling you this: I'll always want you. Once these kids get to know you, they'll like you, too."

She shakes, like butterflies are dancing in her stomach. "Even if they find out I'm crazy?"

"You're not crazy. You were upset and depressed, that's all. And you had a real reason. Nobody better call it anything else."

I feel her muscles relax and she giggles like my old Barney. "Or you'll beat them up?"

"Whatever it takes." She looks okay again so I finish getting ready.

"You don't need to dress up like that every day, David," Barney says.

Mom always insisted I dress properly for school. Even after the divorce left us with so little, she expected me to keep up appearances. Now, after seeing how the kids at Farrington dress, I totally understand why.

"Yes, I do."

"Because Mom said so?"

"Because some things have to stay the same." I can feel Mom's hands on my chest when she first taught me to knot a tie for church, and hear the pride in her voice as she said,

"You are such a man, David." She never knew I tore off the sport jacket she made me wear when I started high school as soon as I was away from the house. Now she's gone and I'd feel bad walking out the door for school without dressing the way she wanted me to.

"The world changed too much too quickly." Barney's voice trembles. "I thought we were all happy, David."

"I know."

"And then suddenly everything went wrong."

I see it in her eyes. She's looking inside her head at the same time machine that sits in my memory. Back to the days when Antwon was still Dad, when we all had good times with Mom and Dad. When we all still laughed.

"Did he love her?" Barney asks. "Ever?"

He said he did. Said he loved all of us. But I remember that look in Mom's eyes when he came home. A muscle in her jaw would twitch and her eyes would go wide, as if she was watching something that fascinated and frightened her at the same time.

"'Course he did. There's three of us as proof, right?"

"It's not the same thing and you know it. When they were fighting all the time, he said we were her brats."

He said worse than that in divorce court. I'm glad Mom didn't take Barney and Linda with her to hear that. Bad enough I was there.

"Everything went so fast," Barney says. "I lost my dad, then Mom, then my home. When they split us up, I thought I'd never see you or Linda again. I thought—just for a little bit—I thought it might be easier to be dead, so at least I could go be with Mom. *If* she'd have me. If she even wanted me."

Her words make my blood freeze. When I put my arm around her, she drops her head on my shoulder. I don't know what to say to stop her from hurting. *Of course Mom would have you?*

Instead I say, "It's easier to stay here in the world with us, dork. This is where we belong. Together."

Barney seems to relax and leave the sad spell behind as we head for school.

"Renata thinks you're cool," she tells me as we approach the building.

"Who?" I ask.

"David, what's wrong with you? She sits at our lunch table."

"Those two interchangeable girls? I'm supposed to know which is which?"

"She wears blue eye shadow and ruby lipstick."

"Yeah, right." *Like that helps.*

"She said she envies me. Not every freshman has a senior like you under her thumb."

I'm not sure I like where this is heading. "Neither do you."

"But I told her you were, like, mine. My guy."

"Then un-tell her. I'm your brother, remember?"

"But nobody knows that since you refuse to use daddy's last name anymore. And you don't have a girlfriend."

Mighty Mite flits across my brain. "No, I don't. And I'm keeping it that way."

Barney doesn't give up. "You could pretend. The girls already think you're my man."

"That gets straightened out the minute we get to school."

Her hands wave in the air and she looks like she's ready to jump out of her skin. "But if someone like you were my boyfriend, I could be important."

"You *are* important, sis."

She pauses and a strange look comes into her eyes. "Malik seemed to like me."

Unbelievable. "He was ready to smack you."

"He wouldn't really have hit me."

She didn't see him punch Yolanda. "Stay away from Malik Kaplan."

"You can't make me." She crosses her arms over her chest and looks at me like I'm walking dirt.

"You mean you're already out to betray your new boyfriend?"

Her eyes go wide and her hands fall. Suddenly the little sister who's also my best buddy is back. "You'll do it? Oh, thank you, David! Thank you!" The braid slaps her back as she jumps up and down. She looks like she's ready to throw herself on me, but I raise my hand before she reaches me.

"Rules: no kissing, no hugging, and absolutely no stupid, cutesy names. Got it?"

Her mouth gapes open like a startled fish. "Hand holding?"

Not in this life. "I'll carry your books."

"And buy me gifts?"

"No."

Her shoulders slump. "Then what good are you?"

Exactly. "Take it or leave it."

She sighs. "Dad used to buy me gifts."

Shows how little that kind of thing really means. But still. "Not everybody's Antwon," I say. "Look, why not pick on Tyrone to be your boyfriend?"

"The band geek?"

"He looked interested." *And looked like someone I can control.*

She sighs. "Maybe. But he's just a freshman."

"So are you."

Another huge sigh. "I'm shallow, huh?"

I bite back a laugh and nod solemnly.

She holds herself rigid for several seconds. Suddenly her stiff shoulders sag like wet cement as she says, "My therapist says it's okay to be selfish, since I've been through such a shock."

My therapist and I stopped talking fifteen minutes into my first session and I never went back for seconds. Barney and our baby sister, Linda, put on turtle shells after the—the incident. Barney's finally coming out of it, but Linda remains silent. She was never all that noisy in the first place, but I remember being eleven. At that age, Linda should be moving, doing, getting into all sorts of mischief. Instead, she ignores both Barney and me. Sometimes it's almost like she's not even there in the apartment. I want both my noisy, bratty, demanding sisters back the way they were before our lives went to hell.

I lean over and kiss Barney on the forehead. "Go right ahead and be selfish, okay?"

That makes her lift her head and her eyes sparkle. "So you *will* kiss me. Good! A guy should always kiss his girl-friend."

"Oh, no." *What have I gotten myself into?*

"You promised! Don't go pretending you forgot already. Besides, what can it hurt?"

More things than I can count. The same inner voice that told me to leave that ball alone the night I got injured screams in my head: *Back out. Now!* But I can't.

Even with disaster staring at me with wide black eyes, I can't say no to Barney. I don't want her to feel rejected. Not again.

CHAPTER 7

I lied to Harvey last night. My second-period English class isn't dealing with Edgar Allen Poe. Today the teacher wants to talk about Greek plays. Oedipus, the guy who kills his father and marries his mother—a family in worse shape than mine.

"I think the queen was grateful to her son," I say.

Yolanda sits behind me in this class, and if I turn my head slightly, from the corner of my eye I can tell she's staring at me. What's she thinking? That I'm a loudmouthed jerk, most likely.

"Go on," the teacher says. "Explain."

"I bet she didn't like her husband. Bet he was mean to her. She might have been thinking of leaving him. Or that he was about to desert her. Why else marry the man who killed him? It had to be gratitude."

I shift in my seat and sneak a glance at Yolanda in the back of the room. Even my tired eyes open wide as I gaze at the blazing red skirt that's just long enough to keep her from being thrown out of school. Her lush, caramel-colored thighs are so exposed, I'm glad I was safely seated before she walked into the room. When a student aide walks in and hands the teacher a note, I turn to look directly at Yolanda. I wish I could tell what's going on behind those dark eyes.

"David." The instructor's voice pulls me back. "They want you in the office."

Somehow I just know. The awful feeling that the world's about to collapse, that all hell's about to break loose, explodes inside me. I gather my books and follow the girl, preparing myself for the worst.

Malik's in the principal's office, too. With his pants actually pulled up.

"I've had reports of an altercation between you two yesterday," Mrs. Grayson, our principal, says. Her gray hair and sagging eyes make her look like a female Dumbledore.

Malik's eyes are downcast. He looks humble. Respectful. He's a true game player. I turn back to the principal, but stay silent.

"We don't tolerate violence on this campus," she continues. "Yes, I heard the report, that technically you were off school grounds. But I don't care about technicalities. This can't happen again, understand?"

"Absolutely, ma'am." Malik looks like someone's handed him an award instead of a scolding.

The principal turns to me, but I'm not playing this game. When I shrug, her frown deepens. "Make sure you both understand my position. Now, I want you two to shake hands."

Malik smiles and extends his hand. But I'm not moving.

The principal's fingers drum on the desktop as I remain motionless. "Mr. Albacore, that was not a request."

A vivid memory throws itself at me.

"It's called compromise, David," my mother said.

"It's being a hypocrite," I said.

She smiles and shakes her head. "No. It's finding the middle ground. You don't have to love someone to be polite." Her fingers brush my arm. "My oh so strong young man will never be a hypocrite. Just...don't make life tougher than it has to be."

My life couldn't *be* any tougher.

Sometimes I hate my life. Then I remember I deserve this. I screwed up and now she's dead. Work and school keep me busy and distracted, but it's not enough. I still wake up drenched in sweat. That shrink gave me a lot of forgettable advice the one time I agreed to see her. She did say the flashbacks would eventually stop. She just didn't tell me that eventually would take such a long, *long* time.

Malik and I touch fingers for a brief second. It's not a real handshake, and as our gazes lock I see his hatred. I'm not a hypocrite or a fool. Nothing changes with this little show. I'll still be watching my back.

◆

"You ever get used to walking through metal detectors?" I ask Neill next day as we enter the building. I can't believe how my skin crawls every time I have to pass through the metal arched monsters just to get inside.

Neill laughs. "Yeah, by about the sixth grade. Where you from, hotshot? Didn't they have them in your part of the world?"

I'm from another planet—one where I didn't walk past a half dozen abandoned buildings on the way to school. At Grogan Hills, torn T-shirts and jeans showing half your ass earned you a pass home and a phone call to your parents. The teachers would've shit bullets if they'd ever had to teach more than twenty students in a classroom.

Not that everything at Farrington's different. We still had the occasional whiff of weed in the bathrooms at Grogan Hills. The guys at both schools still have one thing on their minds and it's not school. The power plays are still the same, and your position on the food chain remains more important than just about anything else in school. I was top dog at Grogan Hills, where Malik's position belonged to me. I was hot and girls threw themselves at me.

All that used to be important. None of it means anything to me now.

Neill's funny, generous and smart. He'd give Malik some hefty competition if he weren't gay. But he makes no move to hide who he is or his feelings for Carl. Apparently some of the girls tried to change him last year. That's right up there with kissing the toad and expecting a prince to jump out of his skin. Neill keeps to himself, perfectly content to be at the outcasts' table with his guy. Maybe I'm envious, since here I really have nobody.

"Where *do* those girls get the money for their clothes?" Renata asks. (At least, I think that's ruby lipstick plastered on her lips.) "Just look at Nicole," she goes on. "It'd take me six months working at the Cookie Store just to pay for that blouse."

The smell of overripe cherries fills the air as Barney

pauses in the act of applying lip gloss, then says, "Forget Nicole. Just look at what Yolanda's wearing. Bet that's never seen the inside of a K-Mart."

Wherever they're from, Yolanda's clothes turn her curvy body into a pulse-pounding bundle. Today's blouse plunges so deep that when she lifts her hand to brush her hair, her breasts almost explode from the opening. Inside my pants, I feel myself stirring as she moves, and I'm ready to gasp as I stare at the girl in all her fineness. I watch as Malik grips Yolanda's arm as if he owns her. I want what he has—I want to call her mine.

When Barney leans across the table, I'm brought back to the here and now. Tyrone Barrows Reyes has joined our table today. He's been sitting across from Barney making googly eyes at her instead of eating. Either he worships my sister or wants to be near her for protection. Maybe a little bit of both.

"Stop staring at me or I'll rip your nose off, tear it in half, and stick the two halves in your eyes," Barney tells him with a snarl.

There's a second of silence, and then Tyrone belches and clutches at his chest. "Marry me," he says.

Seconds later, he looks at me and his olive skin turns pale. I almost bite through my tongue, trying not to laugh as memories flash through me of being a kid and struggling to find the guts to talk to a girl. My guess is that Tyrone's never had a Marybeth take him into the basement and show him how it's done the way I did. And he'll never find the guts to truly proposition my sister. He may know what he wants and may even feel the burn, but it'll be a long time before he stops having to take care of himself by himself. He's just that kind of geeky kid.

Still, I was once fourteen, so I'm taking no chances with anyone when it comes to my sister. I'll be keeping my eyes on him. As long as I let Barney talk me into this dumb fake boyfriend stunt, I'll keep using it to keep the guys away.

"Don't forget whose girl you're talking to," I remind the poor band geek.

Tyrone sputters and hangs his head.

"Where're your books?" I ask my sister when she stops giggling.

Her raised chin and attitude makes her look like a proud warrior queen. "They're inside my locker," she proclaims.

"You figured it out by yourself?"

"Yolanda helped me this morning."

"The Dare?" Renata's fork stops in midair. "She helped you?"

Barney nods. "She's really nice."

Nice? Maybe this really is another planet. Miss Cruel-and-Cold-and-Out-to-Wipe-Out-the-Competition disses Barney one day and becomes her BFF the next? I don't get it.

"She did everything but take a swing at you yesterday," the other girl at our table says—I think that one's name is Francesca.

Renata nods in agreement.

"She was only like that 'cause she thought I was after her man." Barney adds lip gloss to her lips for the fourth time since lunch began. Then she turns to me with a naughty grin. "A girl can't let something like that happen. You don't think I'd just let *you* walk out on *me*, do you?"

"Put that stuff down. You'll get addicted." I tell my sister. I'm not sure why her comment annoys me so much, but it does.

"It's not *stuff*, and everybody uses it," she says.

"I don't," Francesca says.

Barney sniffs. "Everybody who's anybody does. All the right people. We can't stand having dry lips. Nicole nearly panicked this morning when she couldn't find hers."

The right people? How will I ever be able to keep track of all the people influencing my sister? "Who's Nicole?"

Francesca frowns at Barney. "You actually listen to that girl who puts stripes in her hair?"

She can't mean Red Stripe, can she? But she does. Barney looks over at the table where that flashy crowd sits, then she points and waves at Red Stripe—who's sitting next to Malik. Who also waves at Barney.

◆

Maybe my report for Marriage and Family should be *Little Sisters Suffering for Your Mistakes*. "Seen your counselor yet?" I ask, as Barney and I walk home from school on Friday. Her transfer papers included the Murhaselt history and all about the murder, so she sees one of the school counselors once a week.

"I went this morning."

"She helping you?" I hope to God she does a better job

than some of those other therapists my sister's seen. Maybe I can talk with this one and see how things are working out for Barney.

"He. Mr. Kasili's okay, but—"

"Kasili?" How many people with that name could there be at this school? "Tall guy, brown eyes?"

"Yeah. He says I should call him Hakeem."

I'll just call myself toast. "What have you told him about me? About us?"

She frowns. "Nothing. Why would we talk about you?"

"What do you talk about?"

"Can't tell ya. It's private." She looks at my face and sighs. "Just what it felt like."

I wish I hadn't asked her. She doesn't talk much about those terrible days, but she has to be hurting. The shrink called my nightmares PTSD. Post Traumatic Stress Disorder. *How?* I never even got to see Mom's body until she was washed, dressed and tucked safely inside her coffin. What the hell stress did *I* suffer? If anyone's entitled to have blackouts it's Barney. Me, I slept while Antwon invaded our home and murdered the woman he once swore he loved. I dreamed my way right through the screams, the bullet and the blood. But Barney found the body; she had to walk through Mom's blood to phone for help.

◆

We're both quiet Saturday as we sit at the kitchen table and do our homework. My brain still won't come up with a topic, let alone a way to even start the paper for Mr. Martin's class. How do I write about my life, my family? The man gave me the evil eye when I rushed out the door at the end of class yesterday without giving him my topic. Should I write about the divorce? Almost everybody in school has a divorce story, except those who never actually had a marriage story to begin with. Maybe it should be, *"What it's like burying the mother you were supposed to protect."* Or maybe, *"Almost eighteen, and still crying myself to sleep every night"*? Or how about, *"Blame it on basketball"*?

"What's bothering you?" Barney asks. From the worried look on her face I guess she can tell I'm feeling more than just fatigue from work.

"I've got this paper to write." That much is safe to admit. "Having trouble getting started."

"So start in the middle," she says. "Always works for me."

The expression on her face reminds me of how I felt when my parents first brought her home. Even though I'd been told what was going to happen, I threw a hissy-fit at the sight of that screwed-up little brown face. What four-year-old really understands about a new baby? So I asked Mom to send her back. When Mom said that was impossible, I pointed to the toilet. That's where unwanted things that came out of you were supposed to go, and to my four-year-old way of thinking, it made perfect sense. When that didn't fly, I suggested they toss Barney out the window.

Antwon slapped me upside the head for that one.

"The paper's supposed to be about my life," I tell my sister.

"What's so hard about that?" She shakes her head and the dangling earrings she's begun wearing hit her cheeks. "I've always wished I was like you."

"Be glad you're you—you're so much like Mom."

Barney scowls. "I'm way bigger than she was."

"That's not the important part. You jump into life and feel so strongly about things, just like Mom. My pretty sister cares about people," I tell her. *Even me.*

"I'm too big to be pretty."

"Tyrone wouldn't agree with that. He likes you. Think how easily you could boss him."

"He's just my friend. Besides, he's a little…small. He may like me now, but he'll get tired and drop me for some girl who doesn't tower over him." *At least she didn't say she's too big.*

"He's gonna grow, Barney. He's only fourteen." I remind her.

"Maybe." Her eyes glaze a bit as she considers this idea.

"And if you weren't my sister, I swear I'd be chasing you for real."

I expect her to laugh, but instead she says, "I was thinking. Maybe we should stop pretending to be going together."

Thank God. I try sounding offended when I say, "I thought having a senior as your guy made you hot stuff."

"Duh, you're my brother. You scare people. I'll never get a real boyfriend with you around."

Duh, keeping horny guys away is the only reason I ever agreed to this in the first place.

PULL

"Why do you need a boyfriend anyway?" I ask her.

"I just want to be normal, like everyone else. That's why I have to have someone. A girl has to have a man or she's nothing."

Is that really how girls think?

She pauses, bites her lip, and then asks, "Do you think maybe that's why Mom stayed with Dad so long? Even after he got mean and said all those rotten things to her?" The words fall from her lips like water dripping from a slow faucet.

"Maaay-be" I say, dragging out the word. "And maybe that's why she let him in the house that night."

Half-way down the block from our aunt's apartment building stands an empty house with a FOR RENT sign on the front lawn and un-raked leaves on the ground. Every time I pass the front gate, I let myself dream that it's my house. The attic window leads to my bedroom, and we all live there together. Me, Barney, Linda, Mom...and even Antwon.

Once, he'd been Dad. And I wanted to be just like him. Once, I felt happy and proud being his son. But I hated the arguments, the dark cloud that sometimes filled the house and made it hard to breathe. At first I thought Mom needed to stop fighting with him and just give in. After all, he was the man of the house and should be in charge.

"You don't get it, Mom," I said. "It's hard being a man the way the world is today." Bet I even had a smug look on my fifteen-year-old face as I repeated Antwon's words to her.

She looked at me and seemed more tired than angry.

"Don't go using your father's tired excuses to me. Life is hard, period."

"Don't you love him? Don't you want what's best for him?"

"I love your father, and you and the girls. That's what makes everything so difficult."

By the time she packed us up and left Antwon, I understood. All I felt was relief. I was just glad the fighting was finally over.

Love makes you crazy, she'd said. I'd thought Mom was talking about her and Antwon, until she packed up and took the three of us kids out of the house. Until she said her kids were her whole world. She loved us all so much I could feel it, no matter how tired she was when she walked through the door after work.

Antwon said she'd never last without him. He claimed she was nothing. Mom put up with him for years because she believed that lie. Lived with his anger and abuse because she didn't think she had any choice. Then she grew strong and moved on to face the world without him. She still hated tearing us away from our father because she thought we still needed him. But I just thought about how proud I was of her.

That's the thing. I never got the chance to tell her I was proud of *her*. Proud that she turned her back on him and proved that he was a liar. Proud that she was beautiful and strong. Most of all, proud that she was my mom.

Murhaselt vs. Murhaselt wasn't the divorce case of the century, but it became a battle royal. I went to court with my mom and got a front-row view of the war. I even had to help the bailiff and security guards keep the once loving couple separated as the Jerry Springer–like courtroom proceedings went on.

Even after the divorce became final, Antwon kept threatening Mom. Familiarity breeds much more than mere contempt. But I didn't believe he meant his threats. I wonder if Mom did.

CHAPTER 8

"What's the benefit of marriage?" Mr. Martin asks.

"Do you mean for the husband or for the wife?" one of the guys calls out.

Zilch for the wife. That outta be obvious.

Mr. Martin joins the laughter coming from the other students. "I meant the benefit to society. But let's explore this direction for a bit. Mr. Grant, what is the benefit of marriage for a man?"

"Obvious. Regular sex, you get laid whenever you want," the guy behind me says.

A mixture of laughter and groans comes from around the class.

"Any other opinions?" The teacher turns to a student in the back who's waving his hand wildly. "Yes, Mr. Finn?"

"It means becoming normal. Doing what people expect. A man gets respectability when he gets married. He's considered mature."

"Let's hear from the ladies. What is the benefit of marriage for a woman? Uh, Miss Dare?"

"Well, I guess it still means regular sex." She pauses

while some of the boys snicker. "But it also means you get connected with someone who helps build you up. It gives you a home base. Marriage means connection."

Is that what she gets from tying herself to old drop-pants Kaplan? He may be the high-status guy, but take away the homecoming crown, car, money, and clothes, and he's just another nobody. Of course, that's a lot to take away. I wonder if she's like Barney, looking for someone to make her important. Maybe that's enough for a girl.

Mr. Martin nods. "Very good. Truth is, there are probably as many reasons for marriage as there are couples. But let's get back to the benefit of marriage to society, not just to the individual."

"There's no benefit to a woman," I say. "She just gets tied to some loser."

"Refreshing, Mr. Albacore. Most young men talk about how much women gain. Things like financial and physical security. Nice to see a man willing to look at the world through someone else's eyes."

Yolanda turns to me. "You're wrong, David. Of course marriage benefits women."

"Worst thing that can happen to her," I say.

The teacher laughs and sits on the corner of his desk. "I just love conflict."

"Look at the statistics on…on domestic disputes." I hate that phrase. Ranks right down there with family tragedy.

"Look at how single women are treated," she counters. "Especially single mothers."

"Marriage was only created because of property. And everything belonged to the man." My parents fought over everything during the divorce. Antwon wanted anything that held even a trace of value—everything except us kids.

"I'm aware of that." Her color grows darker and her voice deepens. "That's history."

"And you don't care that women were property? Men bought wives. I can't believe you're arguing in favor of something like that."

"At least it makes people feel like they're wanted and valued. That someone's ready to pay a high price because you're worth it to him. People guard the things they value."

She sounds as if no one ever valued her. Which can't be possible.

Her breathing gets deeper and her breasts press against her blouse. *God, don't let her lick her lips or I'll explode.*

The bell rings. Most people rush for the door and freedom. For some reason Yolanda moves slowly. My legs are shaking so hard, I'm still trying to get to my feet when Mr. Martin's voice cuts through the air.

"Mr. Albacore," he says.

Damn.

"Miss Dare," he adds.

She stops mid-step and the girl behind her almost knocks her down. Yolanda glares at me like I'm somehow responsible before heading to the teacher's desk. We stand there, side-by-side waiting to see what he wants.

After all the other students leave, Mr. Martin says, "I don't have research topics from either of you."

"Tomorrow," I say. The minute something bubbles into my brain. Maybe, "*Why people should run like hell if they even think about getting together.*"

Yolanda remains silent.

"No. Today. Since neither of you came up with something on your own, I'm assigning your topics myself. David, you'll write about 'The pros of marriage for women.' "

"Fine." That will be as easy as handing in a blank piece of paper.

"Miss Dare, you get the cons of marriage for men." He leans back in his chair and laughs. "And one more thing. Both your grades depend on both papers. Keep the debate going. I expect lots of fire and controversy—a masterpiece from each of you."

Great. Can things get any worse?

◆

When I get to the job site, Sanderson puts me up on the scaffold to work on the main building's exterior. I don't mind heights and love the feel of the cold air on my skin. But masonry's a killer job and the next morning, my tired muscles curse the alarm. Exhaustion kills my plan to get to school early and get started on the Marriage and Family assignment. That forces me to skip lunch—no real hardship there—and head for the library instead.

I see Yolanda sitting at a cluttered table hidden behind the stacks, right by the section I need. Her head is bent over the notebook spread before her, and there's a pile of books by her elbow.

Now what do I do? Leave? Say something? I move to the bookcase with my back to her and feel her eyes on me.

Right this second I bet she's licking those glistening lips and staring at me.

I turn to check. Her head's bent over her papers, but I know I heard her beads rattle. She keeps her head down as I move closer. I really want to see those eyes again, so I stop by her elbow and say, "You've got it, I should've known."

"What? What do I have?"

My stomach pitches and rolls when she blinks up at me. I can understand what Malik sees in her. *Now what?* I search the table and point to the book on top of her pile. "Emerson's book, *The Marriage Bargain.* I need it. You finished with it?"

I know she's not, but she shoves it toward me before bending back over her papers. "Take it," she says. A breathless note in her voice tells me she's playing that game girls sometimes do to put a guy on edge.

After picking up the book I don't really need, I take a seat opposite her at the table. The room feels hot and I see that she's sweating. I say the first thing that comes into my head. "You smell..."

Her head jerks up and she stares at me with narrowed eyes. "I what?"

Did I really say that? "...Nice. I mean you smell nice." *Like...mom's cooking, and summer, and the old days when life was still fun.* "Real nice."

Her expression softens for a moment. Then her attention goes back to her work. As her pen moves across the paper I stare at her. I don't understand what I'm feeling. I can't care about this girl. *Can't.* I'm just...curious. Yeah, that's it, I'm curious. It can't be anything more than that.

She stands up.

Now what? "What's wrong?" I ask.

"The period is almost over. The bell will ring in a minute."

I stand and follow her toward the door.

"David."

Her silky voice strokes my groin and I ache. "Um, yeah?"

"You've forgotten something."

"Me? Forget?" I can barely think straight.

"The book? That all-important book you needed so badly."

Busted. "Right," I mutter and run back to the table for the book I have no use for. By the time I check it out and turn, she's gone; lost in the sea of students passing the library on their way to their next class.

CHAPTER 9

When we were about to be split up by the Department of Children and Family Services, I made the rounds to everyone I could think of. My father's widowed sister, Edie, had shown no interest in us after her brother was convicted of murdering our mother. But I must have hit her at a weak moment because she suddenly agreed to take in three new mouths. I still don't know what made her say yes. Probably my promise to pay back every cent she spent on me and my sisters. I wasn't looking for a handout. I promised to take full responsibility if she'd just let us stay with her, together. And I'm doing just that.

My aunt can't enjoy housing us in this cramped apartment of hers. Dinners are especially rough. She wants us to eat together. She spends the time claiming my mother should have been a better wife. I grind my teeth and keep quiet. I can't tell her what I really think because I don't want to make her mad. With her, I can protect my family. Without her—well, there *is* no without her.

But gratitude's not enough to tame my anger at the accusation in her eyes whenever she gets back from visiting

Antwon. She's a lot like her brother, and one hundred percent on his side. I can tell she thinks it's my fault he's in prison. Like I don't know that if I hadn't downed those painkillers the doctor prescribed, Antwon wouldn't be where he is, and that the three of *us* wouldn't be here. That my mom would still be alive, and Aunt Edie could have this chintzy place all to herself.

"I'm going to visit your father on Sunday," she says as I enter the kitchen to grab some breakfast.

"I don't care, and no, I'm not going with you."

"He looks…remorseful."

Big whoop. I don't feel sorry for him or believe in his remorse. And I'm never going to visit him. "I said no."

Barney walks in and saves me from having to say anything more. She's wearing a colorful scarf around her neck. I don't know much about fashion, but that thing looks expensive. No need looking at the label to tell it's outside our budget.

I point at the scarf. "Where'd that come from? We have no money to waste on unnecessary things."

"Waste?" Barney's tone changes enough to show she's quoting someone. "That's sooo dumb. The right accessories are never a waste."

I don't need three guesses to tell who the originator of that quote is. Barney's been spending a lot of time running with Yolanda's clique these last few days.

"Where'd you get the money?"

"None of your business."

"Barney." I feel like the wicked parent cross-examining his poor, innocent child, but I have to know. Since my job brings in the money that got Aunt Edie to take us in, I have the right to question how it's being spent.

"It didn't cost you anything; my friend gave it to me," Barney says, lifting her head in a way that doesn't conceal her embarrassment.

"What friend?" Whoever thought he could give my sister clothes was about to get his attitude adjusted big time.

"Yolanda."

"Yolanda Dare gave you this expensive scarf? Why?"

"Because we're friends."

"I thought you said she was a stuck-up witch."

There she goes with the rolling eyes. "That's so yesterday, David."

More like last week, actually. *I'm so glad I'm not a girl.*

"What is it with you and the snob?" Okay, so Yolanda's like a nightlight attracting all the little insects with her aura. She's even pulling me in. But I can't let her trap my sister. Barney can't compete with Yolanda or the girls in her crowd.

"Don't call her that," Barney says.

"Call who what?" Aunt Edie asks.

She likes to pretend she's interested in us. She wears that same face she used with the social worker. The of-course-I-want-my-poor-misunderstood-brother's-children face. Very different from the embarrassed but greedy look I see when I hand her my paycheck. And I never forget she's only *his* sister. Not our mother.

"We're talking about a girl at school," Barney says. "David doesn't like her because she doesn't like him."

I should correct my sister, but it's not worth the effort. "I suppose the makeup's Yolanda's idea, too."

"So?" Now I'm treated to the hands on hip, side-to-side neck movement thing. "What's your problem with me looking nice?"

The *problem* is the dogs she'll attract. In a blouse cut too low and Yolanda-style dangling earrings, my sister's gotten way too attractive. Tyrone won't be the only one giving her looks I don't like. What's Yolanda Dare's motive for hanging around with Barney? It doesn't make any sense.

"Stay away from that girl. You can't hang with her anymore. I won't allow it. And you have to return the scarf."

"I will not. You're not the boss of me."

What I am is the guy trying to take care of her and make things right. With no thanks from anyone. "Just do what I tell you."

She turns her back on me. I reach for the end of the scarf and hear it rip as she tries to jerk away.

"Now, take that thing off." Maybe I finally understand parents, at least a little. 'Cause now I'm the one busting a nut trying to take care of her and she doesn't even care. "Go change, and wash that paint off your face before we're late for school. You're still only fourteen."

"You're not my father!" She spits out words that scrape across my skin. She can't mean them.

But she does.

"You're ruining everything for me and I'll never forgive you," Barney vows before stomping off to her room.

While Barney changes her clothes and washes her face, I move to the living room and sink onto the rug beside

Linda, who's staring at her PlayStation Devil Dice game. For the hundredth time I wonder if buying that thing was the wrong move. But it was either that or watch her stare at walls instead.

Her devil races around the grid, building chains of dice. Linda, the automaton, moves as if the devil on the screen is the one in charge, not her. She never picks her head up, even when I take the controls. Her empty hands just hang in the air, as if she intends to control the digital devil by the sheer force of her will. She sits there, even after I turn the machine off. In a way, it's a lot like me: a poor substitute for her mother.

"Time for school, squirt." She doesn't protest. She never fights my orders.

No, this isn't normal for a kid of eleven.

Girls of any age remain mysteries to me. How did Mom handle this?

I'll never have children. Especially not girls.

◆

Wednesday is warm for fall, and the gym teacher uses the opportunity to have us run on the track outside. The gray clouds filling the sky hold the threat of rain, but the air is clear. I'm leading the pack almost every step of the five miles he wants us to go, twenty times around the quarter mile track. A glance at the timing clock when I cross the finish line shows how slow the run was. I could've shaved twenty, maybe thirty seconds off my time if there'd been any competition. But I was too far in front of the pack to bother.

Kasili comes up beside me and I almost choke on the Gatorade I'm chugging. Haven't seen the guy since my first day, and I've let myself relax. The opening basketball game's two days away, so I figured I was safe.

"You've got speed," he says.

I just couldn't allow myself to be beaten. One of the last vestiges of being a Murhaselt I haven't stamped out. I shrug, toss the bottle in the trash and turn away.

"You never came for a tryout," he adds.

No shit. If he's after something, he should just come out and say it.

"Didn't want to make a fool of myself," I tell him.

"You can't expect me to believe that."

"You've seen me play."

Kasili's lips tighten. "No, I don't think I have. Not really."

"You've got your team." *Go away.*

"Have you thought about college?"

The unexpected question holds me. Mom was all about college. "Of course you have to go, David." Her words, always delivered in a soft, but firm, voice. She never believed me when I said I hated school. She'd made plans for my senior year. Plans that included scouts and me being recruited to some big prison they'd call a university.

But that was before Antwon lost his job.

Before *Murhaselt vs. Murhaselt.*

Before....

"High school's enough," I say. "I don't waste time on the impossible."

He sighs and nods, and I take that as dismissal. But

when I turn to go he says, "I hear you and Barnetta Murhaselt are an item."

I know she hasn't just come out and said "David's my brother and lying to the school." But this man seems like the kind who'd worm things out of you without you ever knowing what you'd told him. Unless you kept up your guard. Mine's not going down one inch.

"So what?" I say.

"Seniors and freshmen, it's usually not a good idea. Unless…"

"Unless what?"

"David, if there's ever anything you need to talk about, come to me."

As I head back to the other guys, I want to believe I've won something from that encounter. But I know that at best, we've only fought to a draw. At worst, it hastens the day when I'll have to fight to remain David Albacore.

CHAPTER 10

Apparently Kasili wasn't the only one watching me during gym. Malik's standing outside the locker room when I leave.

"You look like you're in great shape, champ," he says.

I keep walking.

"Come on, David. Bygones, right? Let's forget the old, okay?"

Not in this life. He may want to pretend we're friends now. But I know better.

"I'm having an after-the-first-game party on Friday night. Hell, we might even win. Come over. Oh, and bring that not-so-little girl of yours, too."

The hell I will.

He runs ahead toward the cafeteria. I detour by the study hall, the way I've done every day since I found out Yolanda has fourth period study. She's a junior, and upperclassmen can sign out of study hall and study—or pretend to study—anywhere they want. I see her through the window, sitting near the back with her head bent over her papers. If Malik's also free during fourth, why isn't she with him, instead of always in that room?

◆

The smell of game-day is so familiar, it hurts. Not even the aroma of buttered popcorn overcomes the scent of the court. The gym is only half-filled with mostly silent spectators. Farrington's never been one of Chicago's powerhouse sports schools, but I didn't expect to feel a pull when I entered the stands to watch the team's first game.

I'm a fool for being in the stands. Back when I played, I had Mom and my sisters sitting in the stands watching me. Now I'm here with Barney, to see a team I refuse to care about. Sanderson acted like I'd asked for his firstborn when I told him I needed a night off, but I insisted. Barney's eager to be a part of high school life. Since I'm supposed to be her boyfriend, I had to bring her to the game I'd much rather ignore.

The guys on the team are trying. They're running good plays, but their inexperience shows, and so does Malik's bad influence. Julian's got skills, but he and the other Farrington players act like the ball's a bomb and Malik's the only man capable of handling it. They pass the basketball to him the second it touches their hands. He's a good player, but one good player doesn't make a team. The stands around me erupt in cheers every time Malik scores. What people don't notice is how often his teammates ignore shooting opportunities to get the ball to him. But the other team catches on.

Julian tries for a shot that misses the rim. Malik yells "This way, retard," and Julian drops his head, looking as lost and uncertain as a stoner attending his first twelve-step meeting.

I jump to my feet.

"What is it?" Barney asks.

I'm sure my face reveals the confusion running through my head. I almost—almost—feel like running down on the court, snatching the ball and showing them how it's done. As I shake my head, I drop back into my seat.

Kasili calls time and substitutes another player for Malik. Sound idea, but a round of boos follow the new guy onto the floor. In spite of Mr. Motivator and his psych degree, the five men on the floor continue acting like the ball's a hot poker they don't dare touch, let alone try to shoot. The other team has a twelve-to-two run. When Kasili sends Malik back into the game, his replacement looks happy to exit the slaughter.

Our team's pushing and they move well. But by halftime, we're down by eighteen points. Malik's scored sixteen of Farrington's twenty-two points; but with his teammates shoving him the ball all the time, he should have scored twice as many. With time, practice, and that showoff Malik out of the picture, the guys on the court could develop their own style and have a good chance of winning their fair share of games. One glance at the coach shows him staring up at the stands in my direction, as if he's expecting something from me.

Minutes later I'm heading for the refreshment stand, following the smell of popcorn overloaded with fake butter. Barney loves that stuff and I want to make her happy.

Two men walk by dissecting the game. "Eighteen points behind and that fool coach takes Kaplan out? What the hell's he thinking?"

"That the team might learn to play better without him," I say. Not one of my smartest moves, but Kasili doesn't deserve blame. He took Malik out to give the rest of his players a chance.

"Who asked you?" one man says. "You know so much, why aren't you on the court?"

Unwilling to answer that question, I shrug and get into line. Amateurs never understand. I know how nervous Julian is. He's been thown into the varsity spotlight too soon and won't learn to rely on himself while Malik plays superstar. But that's Kasili's problem, not mine. I'm up here to get drinks, popcorn and candy, to take care of my sister's sweet tooth.

I'm almost at the counter when I see Yolanda, Red Stripe and a few other girls in the corner of my eye. As usual she outshines her satellites, wearing an outfit that emphasizes her thin waist and grabbable hips. I imagine my hands running over those curves. Soft and warm, all silky caramel. She'd smell as sweet, too. And her lips—

"Whaddaya want?" The old woman behind the counter yells so loud, I realize she must have repeated the question several times already. And now everyone's turning to look at me.

I place my order and hand over the money, then grab the food and drinks and head back toward the stands. People continue staring at me. Maybe they aren't all laughing at me, but I see their glances and it feels—

"David."

Icy drops of Coke splash from the cup and onto my hand as I whirl to face Yolanda.

"What?" Does she need something from me? Food, money—my body at her feet?

"You forgot your change."

"Oh. Thanks."

I stand there, looking and feeling helpless as she holds out my money. I'm not sure I could move my hands, even if they weren't full. Her smile widens, pushing up her cheeks. For a moment I feel as if some understanding flashes between us. She's definitely not laughing *at* me.

One of her friends calls, "Yoyo. Come on."

She turns and nods at the girl. When she looks back at me, her smile is gone. A quick step forward, and she thrusts the money into my pants pocket.

That sets me on fire.

She has no idea what she's doing to me. She can't, or she couldn't just stand there, staring up at me while my head, heart and cock wage war.

Toss everything, my head says. *Grab her, fuck her and get her out of your system*, says the other head. My next thought: *It's not that simple, and once won't be enough.*

My heart hangs back, saving up energy for the real fight.

Yolanda steps back and her eyes grow dark. Then she turns and half-runs, half-skips to the other girls.

I can't slow my breathing down. I'm frozen, stuck staring at the spot where she disappeared—until the horn blows announcing the second half. Then, turning on rubber legs, I go back to find my sister.

Kasili's machine sputters further in the second half, as inexperience and youth catch up with the team. We lose the game fifty-six to thirty-eight. Malik has twenty-six points and Julian just five.

After the game I take Barney home. Then I head to Malik's house—I don't know why. I'm not one for torture, and I don't care about being one of the guys.

Can't be because Yolanda will be there.

The smell of clashing perfumes and colognes, cigarettes, beer and weed burn my nose as I walk through Malik's front door. Someone with deejay ambitions abuses a turntable in one corner of what's supposed to be the living room. The overturned chairs and beer bottles leave me wondering what I missed. The music's blasting and the bass pounds my chest so hard it hurts. Gyrating bodies fill every open space, and dancing feet smash chips and candy into the expensive looking carpet.

Should have known Malik would live the garish life. Besides the cluster of bodies, the living room's filled with loud furniture and knick-knacks that remind me of the kinds of treasures you see at carnival games. If Neill's right, and he usually knows what he's talking about, Malik's dad makes his money with overpriced auto repairs using counterfeit parts. Apparently that adds up to a good living, 'cause if Malik's parents ever divorce, they'll have a lot to fight over.

I see no sign of Yolanda as I push through the crowded room. Just a bunch of skanks in neon glitter, or off-the-shoulder tops complete with artful cut-outs that leave nothing to the imagination. Body-hugging shorts—didn't anyone tell them it's October already—and low-rider "spank me" jeans complete the outfits. *I can't believe I used to love parties like this.*

Someone points me to the back when I ask for Malik. I wander through the dining room to the den. He's standing in front of a big screen TV showing a Cubs game with the sound turned off. In one hand he holds a beer bottle. His other arm is wrapped around a giggling Joelle.

Julian flashes a smile at me as I enter the room. Someone else trips and the beer bottle he's holding flies from his hand. The glass crashes against the mantle over the fireplace, and a framed photograph falls over as foam rains down on the floor.

"Sonofabitch. I ought a make you lick that up." Instead, Malik lifts the bottle in his free hand and turns to wave at me. "Hey, Davie, glad you came."

It's David, asshole.

"Someone get our boy some refreshments. How'd you like the game, Davie? You see that piss-ant coach take me out?"

Joelle presses against him. "I can't believe he'd do that to his best player."

"And all because I tell the truth." He releases her and looks around the room, the grin on his face widening as other heads nod. Only Julian and I stand motionless as he adds, "Why the fuck shouldn't I say what's on my mind? I told him off, who wouldn't? I'm the only real player around, and that shit-head coach better start acting like he knows it."

Julian draws in a deep breath, then turns and leaves the room.

Someone passes me a beer bottle that's so cold and wet, it feels like I stuck my hand in a tub of ice water. It's Budweiser—Antwon's favorite. I can't make myself drink it, not when I know how he'd laugh and say, "That's my boy, drink up."

"Where's that not-so-little girl of yours?" Malik looks around for Barney.

She's at home, where I belong. "I came alone," I say.

"Me, too. That tiny bitch of mine stood me up." An ugly laugh falls from Malik's grinning lips. He punches my shoulder like we're supposed to be friends or something, and I wonder again why he invited me. To show off? Show me up? I hate the way he talks about Yolanda. She's his girl and she's probably used to being called "tiny bitch" and worse. Who knows, maybe she enjoys it. But that doesn't stop me from wanting to use my fist to close that grinning mouth of his.

"Well, plenty of fresh meat all around," he says. "Go find something you like and enjoy yourself, Davie."

"I'm here, Malik." Nicole pushes past me to rub against him. In Yolanda's absence, her so-called friends are rushing in to do what girls do, claw past each other all the way up a man's ass.

"Yes, you are, Nikki." Malik gives her the same noisy wet kiss he uses on Yolanda. When her hand moves down to his bulging zipper, he laughs. Joelle's face twists into a pout.

"Come upstairs with me, Nikki. I got something you gonna like." He heads for the staircase. "Bring some beer."

Nicole snatches two bottles and follows. Joelle jumps after her. "Me too, Malik."

Nicole's face twists into a snarl. "Nobody needs *you*."

Malik stops halfway up the staircase and looks down. "I'm man enough for two. Come on up, ladies."

Joelle sticks out her tongue at Nicole before joining the end of the line.

More than the stench of this so-called party leaves me ready to puke.

"That man thinks he's some kinda god," a guy behind me says.

"I need parents like his," another one says.

"I need a stable like his," another laughing voice adds.

I need to get the hell away from these people. Now.

Pushing my way through the crowd to the dining room, I take a side door into an empty kitchen. Closing the door behind me shuts off the worst of the party's smells and it's quieter. Amazing. As I pour the beer into the sink and watch the yellow stream disappear, the sick feeling in my stomach grows. I toss the empty bottle in the garbage, then bend over the counter. And for a second I think I'm going to barf.

What if Yolanda had been in there with Malik? What if I'd had to watch him and his "tiny bitch" climb those stairs and disappear into a bedroom?

Get out. Get out, now.

Before I can move, the outer door opens. A blast of October air freezes my skin for a second. Then someone enters. A girl who makes my skin feel like it's bursting into flames. There's no trace of her figure inside the heavy woolen coat, and a dark brown scarf covers her hair and neck. But I know. Before she raises her chin, before I see cheeks glowing red-brown from the cold, I know who's just walked into the room.

Now I know why I had to come here tonight. And why I *cannot* leave.

CHAPTER 11

Yolanda's jaw drops when she looks up and sees me.

"Didn't see you earlier," I say. *Stupid.* I can't even slap myself because she's staring.

I want to tell her about lover-boy upstairs, sandwiched between her two friends. Want her to rage and storm, and then tell him it's over because he couldn't wait for the girl he's supposed to care about. Once she kicks him to the curb, I'll take her in my arms, comfort her, and tell her she's better off without him—better off with me.

Me?

Malik, a guy with money, a car, status—or *me*, one with nothing, not even free time to spend with her? A guy whose real name is tied to a murderer? How could I think she'd make a dumb-ass choice like that?

I say nothing because she knows what her man's like. Telling her what's going on would only make her cry, and what's the point of that? I've seen too many female tears already. And what if she rushes upstairs to make it a foursome? I can't bear either thought.

Moving carefully so we don't touch, and so I won't lose control, I help her out of her coat. As I throw it over the back of a chair, she blows on her hands to warm them. I want to grab those hands and rub them, to share my heat with her.

"You want a drink?" I ask, and start for the door to the dining room, ready to brave the crowd to get her whatever she wants.

"I'd really like something hot. Maybe a cup of coffee."

I've gotten to be handy in a kitchen, so I have the coffee pot going fast. When my nose tells me the brew's ready, I fill us each a cup. She takes cream and sugar, and knows exactly where to find both. I won't let myself think about what that means.

"I guess—" I bite my lip before forcing myself to say, "I should get back to Barney."

A noise like a baseball hit square by a metal bat fills the room when the cup falls from Yolanda's hands and shatters on the floor tiles. "She's here? And you left her out there by herself?"

"I came alone." Why does she care? Her so-called friends are bigger threats to her position as queen than my sister could ever be.

Yolanda drops to her knees to pick up the pieces of broken cup. After grabbing a hand full of paper towels, I kneel beside her to help clean up the mess. When we're done she starts to pour herself more coffee. But her hands shake so much, I take the pot and do it for her.

She looks up into my eyes. "I suppose my...Malik couldn't wait for me?"

"I don't know what you mean."

"Don't pretend, David. Who'd he take upstairs?"

Common sense tells me to lie. Once she knows, her claws will fly and I'm in the line of fire. "I really don't know."

She shrugs. "No matter. I'll find out on Monday, once she starts bragging."

"Doesn't it bother you? Malik and his other girls?"

Her lips twist. "I'm still number one. He's too much for any one girl. He wants me. I'd be a fool to expect anything more."

Yolanda's no fool. She's not one of those mindless girls who collect dicks like trophies, just because they can. I'd swear this is a girl who wants more. She's smart and thoughtful, and I know she deserves more.

The door bursts open and a couple of partygoers stumble into the kitchen. They don't look ready to leave anytime soon, and Yolanda heads for the back door again. I grab her coat and follow, draping it around her shoulders as we step onto the porch. I don't need a coat, not when *she's* this close.

"Does this happen often?" I nod back toward the house and the party.

"Whenever his parents leave town," she says. "Every couple of months."

"They don't mind coming back to find their house trashed?"

"His parents are pretty forgiving. It must be nice."

Her voice is high-pitched and wistful, and I imagine her parents must be really strict. Mom never went anywhere, but if she had and I dared anything remotely like this, I can't imagine the consequences.

"What about your folks?" Yolanda asks.

"Mom kept an eagle-eye on me."

For a long time, I believed my mom really did have eyes in the back of her head. Twenty-twenty vision, too. Mostly she had her spies. People watched out for the Murhaselt kids and reported back to her. And Barney's a born tattletale. I managed to put something over on Mom once in a while, and then lived in terror waiting for her to find out. No one terrorized me like Mom.

"She was pretty forgiving, too." That was most the important thing about her.

"Was?"

"She's...dead."

Yolanda places her cup on the porch railing and puts her hand on my wrist. My skin tingles as an electric current shoots between us.

I want her. Like I've never wanted any girl before.

Truth time: I did put a few things over on Mom. Marybeth and Patti and Sharon—no, she found out about Sharon. Handed me that "not-my-son" glare before turning me over to Antwon for *the talk*. Not one of those girls made me feel like I do now. Not even Marybeth, the college girl who was the first to pop my gasket. No girl has ever made me feel like holding her in my arms and making her smile and—

And nothing. This is The Dare. Malik's girl. And I can't let myself feel what I'm feeling.

She raises her hand and her fingers hover in the air. She takes a long slow deep breath and looks like a scrub that's just missed the game-winning free throw as she turns toward the door.

"I need to get inside and mix," she tells me.

I take her arm and guide her back into the kitchen. Thank God it's empty again. Some slow song is playing and soft music flows through the room. Instead of letting her go, I say, "Dance with me."

Her breath catches. She stands motionless, like she's waiting for an echo.

So I try again. "Dance with me."

The coat drops to the floor and she moves into my arms and it feels—right. Usually I dance with taller girls, girls who rest their heads on my shoulder or kiss my neck while we slow dance. Usually there's no head against my chest, right where my heart beats. And usually I don't feel this tightness in my body. Not just the boner. Yeah, that's getting painful and needy, but there's something else going on. I want more. Even though going after more of her could destroy what I have right now.

I pull Yolanda tighter, and breathe in the scent of her hair. My heart pounds like a pile driver when she looks up at me. Her lips are so close, full and red. If I just bend a little more...

She suddenly stiffens. Her eyes flare when she pulls herself from my arms and steps back.

I feel like part of me's missing. Like I have only the tiniest part of what I need. How could this happen? She's all wrong for me. She's Malik's Dare.

I thrust my hands in my pockets to keep them from shaking.

This time when Yolanda heads for the door to the dining room, I let her leave.

Antwon's voice streams through my head. *No real man lets a woman tear him down.*

My teeth clench and in my mind I scream, *Shut the fuck up, Antwon.* But his words remain and I know I can't be a real man. Not and let myself be torn this way. I don't know how it happened. But I'd do anything, give *anything*, just to keep Yolanda Dare with me.

I've got to get out of this place.

The kitchen door opens before I can move and in walks Malik. He looks loose, as if his bones have turned liquid, or he's too sated to hold himself together. He's changed pants and his shirt's unbuttoned.

His nostrils widen when he comes close. "Why you out here by your lonesome, Davie boy?"

"It's just too busy out there."

I can't help wondering if something about me reveals—what? That we danced and I felt—I feel—something for his girl? Can he smell my need for her the way I detect the unmistakable musk of sex on him? Does he know that I want—that I ache for—his Dare?

He reaches for my arm. When I pull away, he frowns. "You think you're too damn superior to hang with me?" he asks.

Before I can answer, he looks down. Yolanda's coat still lies on the floor by the back door. "So that's how it goes, eh, fish-boy?"

Pushing down a feeling that's part guilt and part envy, I correct him. "My name's David."

"Right. Davie."

Music blares as the door opens again and Yolanda walks in. She crosses to Malik's side. I know she too smells the sex funk on her boyfriend, and wish I could keep her away. But she already knows what he's like. Worst of all, she's probably already forgiven him. That's what women do.

She places a hand on Malik's arm. "I have to go."

"You. Just. Got. Here." The threatening growl in his voice makes me take a step closer.

"My parents called," she says in the voice a mother uses with an unruly two-year-old. "My brother's sick and they need me back home."

As she picks up her coat, Malik says, "And I need you here. You come late, spend a few minutes and then leave? How's that make me look?"

"Don't pretend you'll be alone."

"I won't. Ain't a bitch in here I can't have."

"Then you won't miss me." Her fingers curl and she looks more likely to hit him than kiss him goodbye.

When she turns to leave, Malik steps between her and the door. "Be careful, girl."

She shivers. "I have to go, Malik. I'll make it up to you."

"Yes. You will."

The door closes behind her and the air in the room grows cold.

"Bitches," he says, like we're buddies or something. "Gotta love 'em."

Then why doesn't he love Yolanda?

I push my way through the dining room. The party's jumped up a level, from busy to frantic. The room's filled with pulsing bodies and I hear shrieks from girls playing at being coy, along with laughs from those unwilling to pretend. Foul smells go with the sucky music.

Malik grabs some girl and begins grinding. Joelle and Nicole look on with wicked frowns. Outside the living room window, I see Yolanda's unmistakable form walking down the block.

She's not even hurrying. By the time I grab my jacket and run from the house, she's barely at the end of the block. I run after her. It's late, I tell myself. I wouldn't let any girl walk through these streets alone at this time of night.

I catch up and reach for her arm. "Wait up," I say just as she whirls. I hear a hiss and a white cloud fills the space between us. Suddenly my throat burns and I realize I've been hit. It's pepper spray.

"David? Oh, my God."

Everything's on fire—my throat, my eyes.

The canister clangs as it falls to the ground where I'm bent over, struggling to breathe and choking. She grips me by my shoulders and holds me steady, saying, "I'm sorry, David. I didn't know it was you."

I can't say much with my throat in flames and I'm wheezing so loud I must sound like a monster movie. Mighty Mite's well trained and ready for trouble. She might have killed me if I wasn't so tall.

"Why did you follow me?" She asks as she helps me sit on the curb.

"Couldn't leave you…alone…late at night. Thought …you'd need protection," I gasped.

"I think maybe you're the one who needs something right now," she laughs that soft feathery note that ruffles my spine in spite of my pain. "I know how to take care of myself."

"So I see."

Damn, this hurts. I'm sitting with my eyes shut tight and my mouth hanging open to try and suck in some air. Worst of all is having Yolanda Dare see me like this. I cover my face with my hands as I try to hide from her.

"Good thing I'm so short," she says as she drops to the curb beside me. "I couldn't reach your eyes."

"You came close enough." My eyes still burn from the mist, but most of it hit the lower part of my face and neck. I try to laugh, but the most I can manage is a croak. If my eyes felt the way my throat does, I'd probably be rolling on the ground.

"David, you're choking." Alarm fills her voice as she pats my back.

"I'm...a little better."

"It won't last forever."

I force one eye open. "How long?"

"Maybe half an hour. That's what the brochure said. I've never actually sprayed anyone before."

A different scent drifts into my nostrils as the spray begins to clear. Yolanda's perfume fills the air and the fruity scent reminds me of Mom's peach cobbler. I wonder...what if I kissed her? Could a slap feel as bad as this burn?

When I start to stand up, she grips my shoulders and pushes me back down. "I think you better rest a little longer."

No problem.

I'm almost sorry once I can see and breathe clearly again. When I finally get up to continue walking to her home, she throws me a look. "You don't need to stay with me. I walk home alone all the time, Mr. Albacore, day and night."

"Well, not tonight, Miss Dare." So she doesn't need me to protect her? I don't care; I'm still going to see her all the way home.

She stares at me through bottomless brown eyes and licks her lips. I want to join her tongue with mine.

She stops at the gate of a house that looks like so many others. Small, with one tree growing beside it whose leaves are scattered on the ground. Two stories, plus an attic. Just like the house I grew up in.

"What's wrong with your brother?" I ask.

She looks confused. "What's wrong with whom?"

"Your sick brother."

"Oh. Jerry...I'm sure it's nothing. Mom exaggerates sometimes. Anyway, you can go now. I'm home." She stops on the sidewalk outside the house.

There's a lot of things I can do. But leaving her now isn't one of them. "If I walk a girl home, I take her the whole way."

We turn up her walkway and climb the stairs to the porch.

Then the door opens and living room light floods the porch, making my still sensitive eyes blink. A white boy who can't be more than ten comes out on the porch and laughs at Yolanda. "You're gonna get it. You know you can't bring guys here."

I look at the blue-eyed, pale-skinned little snot. "Is this your brother?" I ask.

"Foster brother," the kid says. "And the old lady's gonna kill her for bringing you around."

He's got to be exaggerating, but her shoulders slump as if the Mighty Mite has been transformed into a helpless child.

I step closer to the kid and ask, "What'll it take to keep this between us guys?"

He looks me up and down. He's not a bit scared, just evaluating the larceny potential. "Ten bucks," he replies.

"Jerome," Yolanda says in that exasperated, motherly tone I heard so often when I was his age.

Me, I smile at the little businessman. "Five now, and ten more if Yolanda gives me a good report about you on Monday."

Yolanda protests, but I extend a five-dollar bill. He whips the money from me with greedy fingers and runs back into the house.

"He doesn't look all that sick to me," I say, when he disappears.

"No, he's not sick," she says. "I lied. I just didn't feel like staying at that party tonight."

"Neither did I." Her eyes gleam in the moonlight. I wish I had the right to kiss those quivering lips.

"Your foster brother, huh? Nice of your parents to take in a foster kid."

She steps through the door. "Not my parents. His."

She closes the door without turning around. Suddenly nothing in the universe feels secure. I pause when I reach the sidewalk and look back. There's a light coming from that attic window. Somehow I knew that'd be her room: at the top, looking down at the world.

She's outlined against the window and I wonder. Is she looking at me? Thinking about me?

CHAPTER 12

Late Sunday afternoon I go for a walk, hoping the cold will force an idea of what to write about for this term paper into my head. I pass the church our Aunt Edie claims as hers, although I haven't seen her attend. It's late, but the service is still going on. Singing and clapping pour from the entrance and cars line the streets.

I feel sorry for the kids trapped inside. Mom was a regular churchgoer. For as long as I can remember, I sat beside her in the pews every Sunday. Our service seemed to go on for days when I was little. I'd stare at the floor, not understanding half the things the man up front was saying. My prayer was always the same: *Please make that man lose his voice so we can leave*.

Today I have an equally impossible prayer. Make things go back the way they were. Make me little again, and have all my guilt and responsibilities disappear. Let me just lie back and be able to depend on my parents for everything for a little while longer.

Along the street, people are out raking up dying leaves

from their lawns. Men and their sons, mostly. They're smiling and sometimes playing in the piles. When did it all change in the Murhaselt house, I wonder. When did we stop chasing leaves and being a family?

I hear the sounds before I reach the corner and turn to see a small park. As I approach, the grunts and yells grow louder. There's an old woman sitting on a bench beside a long-haired dog. Scattered papers blow in the heavy breeze. A rundown basketball court lies behind a chain-link fence. The dog barks as I approach and the old lady looks up from her knitting and eyes me. She apparently decides I'm harmless and shushes the animal. It lies back down with a relieved sigh.

Several kids lean against the fence, watching a pick-up game on the court. I once was one of these kids, standing behind a fence, watching the big guys playing with a ball that moved like quicksilver. Those players ran and sweated, grunted and...flew. I remember begging God for the invisible wings of those giants on that court. I had no idea back then the kind work it took to actually grow those wings.

Cracks run through the blacktop and the lines painted on the playing surface are fading, but the guys on the court don't seem to care. My curiosity turns to interest when I recognize Julian. Tired as I am, I slow down and stop to watch them play. Julian's good—much better than he seemed during the game. When he stops being afraid of the ball, the kid has real skills. Another year, a few more inches, and the absence of a know-it-all on his back, and he'll be a great player.

He and his opponent collide. Julian jumps up quickly, but the other guy comes up limping. Julian sees me and trots over. Its cold, but the sweat on his forehead reflects the lights on the court.

"Yo, David. Want in?" he asks.

I say no, but I'm already heading through the gate and onto the court.

The last time I touched a ball, there were less than twenty seconds left in the game. Only seconds on the clock and a twelve-point lead. Grogan Hills was about to win. I'd already scored eighteen points, ten rebounds and blocked five shots. But the cheerleader on the sidelines who'd promised me that sweet reward if we won was blowing me kisses and I wanted her to see me fly up in the air one more time. I jumped high for block number six. But my tired legs couldn't hold me up when I came back down.

I take the place of Julian's injured defender and Julian moves fast, takes a pass and rushes the basket. He scores almost before I'm in position. I'm about to congratulate him when he gets this stupid look on his face, lifts his chin and makes a checkmark in the air in front of my face.

The boy needs a lesson.

The next time the ball's in his hands, I steal it so quickly, he's left staring as I drive for the basket. And my legs—my wings—reject gravity and lift me high as I dunk the basket for an easy two.

All eyes are on me when I land.

"Dang."

"Dopest player I've ever seen."

Julian stands silent.

In minutes I have him falling over his feet in the struggle to keep up with me. The guys on my team and the growing crowd at the fence all scream and applaud. I don't care about the score; just the ball and the press of bodies, the court, and the basket. I pass to one of my guys, who misses the shot. I rise up and tip the ball into the net.

As play stops, I lift the bottom of my t-shirt to wipe sticky sweat from my eyes. When I lower my shirt, Yolanda Dare's standing at the opening of the fence.

The world…stops. She's looking at me the way a hungry lion stares at a wounded gazelle. Me, I can't even think. I can barely breathe.

A memory of my mother fills my brain.

"The way a girl looks is no way to tell what she's like."

I didn't want that talk with Mom. I couldn't explain that Marybeth Nagle made those words over a year too late.

"This isn't easy for me, either," she said. "You'll make mistakes, David. Girls will fool you."

"Not me. Nobody fools me."

She laughed. "I can't remember being that young and sure of myself. But trust your feelings, not your hormones, not your—"she waved her hand, "—you know." Mom's cheeks darkened. We both knew what she meant.

I want to be close to Yolanda. I want to believe there's something more in her. That no one who makes me feel such an aching pain and need can really be cruel enough to hurt someone just because she can. *What do I do, Mom? What do I say? You taught me so much, what do I do now?*

Julian and some of the others come over and surround me. "That was awesome, man."

There are faces all around me and guys are patting my back. Someone suggests we head out for something to eat. By the time they accept my need to leave, Yolanda's already gone.

I'm pulling on my jacket when Julian comes over to me. "Why aren't you on the team?" he asks.

"One pickup game means nothing."

"But the school needs you."

"You're talking school spirit? I'm putting in my time, marking the days on the calendar until June. That's all." Since Mom can't be there, I don't even plan on walking up the aisle to get that meaningless piece of paper.

Julian looks like he's on the edge of tears. "But, David…"

"Don't. If you're gonna be my friend, don't push me."

He looks hurt, but shrugs. "Fine. But your moves— you're unbelievable."

"So are you." I smile. "At least once you stop thinking so much."

"I have to think to remember what to do."

"Not in a game. Eyes open, stay ready. Then let your body do its thing. Just like you did out here."

"This is different. Nothing depends on this."

"That's the secret. Nothing depends on a game, either. When it ends, it ends."

CHAPTER 13

I can't tell my English teacher Kanye's my favorite poet and everything else belongs in the garbage. Especially not a teacher who thinks *everyone* can write poetry. So I had to put something down on paper. Mom might have listened to the words I wrote. Might have told me they were all right. But I won't answer the teacher's call for a volunteer to read their work out loud. I don't have rocks in my head.

Besides, Yolanda's sitting in the room. No way will I act the fool with her around.

"Anyone want to share? Anyone at all?" The teacher's smile grows tight. For once the classroom's almost silent.

I hear a rustle behind me. Someone's getting up, and I don't even need to look to know who it is.

"This…it really sucks." Yolanda's voice sounds shaky and uncertain, like she's forcing herself to sacrifice something important. "But…I'll read it anyway."

When I turn in my seat, I see her hands are shaking and her eyes are fixed on the paper. She doesn't look up when she begins.

*"If what we had included love
Our loved ones peer down from above.
Asking us to laugh and love."*

My heart jumps. Does she? *Mom, are you there? Looking down? Do you see me? Forgive me?* And somehow, suddenly, I see her. Hear her smiling voice. Feel her lips pressing a kiss on my forehead. As if I could ever deserve to be happy again. If I'd acted like a man instead of a weak, sniveling baby, she'd still be alive.

*"Nothing ever will replace
A lost touch, a smiling face."*

Yolanda looks up. She's not smiling, but something in her face pulls me, calms me. I almost feel forgiven. If only Yolanda would touch me, maybe then I could believe. God, I want her to touch me.

*"If you listen you can hear
Real love cannot disappear
Now they fly beyond our sight
But in the end we'll all unite
Inside God's unending light."*

Her voice is strong. The last words sound almost like a promise. I glance down at my paper, where I've written my own poem. It's a prayer for amnesia. I crumble the sheet in my hands. I don't want to forget. Not any more.

As Yolanda drops back into her seat, chuckles and smirks go around the room. Some wise-ass says, "Yup, that sucked big time," and I'm ready to strangle him.

Her head's bent over her desk. She's breathing so heavily my chest grows tight. I want her to know that her words spoke to me. Suddenly I'm standing and clapping. She looks up, licks her lips and smiles. A bone-melting wave surges through me. Legs that scramble over scaffolds, that once lifted me through the air to reject the shots of enemy players, now threaten to leave me limp on the classroom floor.

Real love cannot disappear. God. I wish, I hope, I pray that Yolanda's right.

◆

"The party was great, but that Malik. Ohmigod, I was like, bleeding everywhere." The red-striped head bobs as Nicole shoves her way through the hall.

Hell of a thing to overhear on the way to lunch. Red Stripe doesn't seem to care about anyone around her. It's almost like she's boasting. *Kaplan fucked me hard. Whoopee.*

"Yeah, that's messed up." There's no sympathy in her companion's voice. More like admiration. Maybe even envy.

Nicole's shrug is slow and heavy. "He's selfish, but what man isn't?"

"At least you got something out of the deal."

Nicole extends her arm to reveal a gleaming bracelet. "His selfish ass needed to get me earrings, too. It wasn't even like he's all that big—"

She says this while I'm holding the door open for them. I feel like quick-drying cement holds my legs in place. No way will I stop listening now. Nicole mutters an absent-minded thanks before continuing,"—it's just that he's so rough."

So that's how Malik does it. He gets these fine sisters to gather around him like he's a half-priced shoe store by showering them with expensive gifts. I wonder what Yolanda gets for her efforts? What would she be wearing today if she hadn't been late to the party?

What made her late, anyway?

◆

"You want to tell me why I'm the only girl in this school who didn't know about the party?"

Christ. The set of Barney's shoulders should have warned me before I dropped into my seat at the lunch table, but I'm still shocked by her anger. "Party?"

"You know, the one you *didn't* take your girlfriend to. I had to stand there, looking like an idiot, when Tonia asked me for details. You're supposed to be my man. Why didn't you take me?"

"Not at lunch, Barney. Later."

"How about never? I'm...I'm breaking up with you."

I'm thinking *Thank God*—I never wanted this anyway. Still, visions of guys surrounding my sister whirl through my brain. "I thought I made you hot stuff."

"Not hot enough." She stares across the cafeteria. "I'd give anything to be at that table."

"Never happen," Neill says. "That's exclusive territory for seniors, with a few special juniors allowed in by invitation only."

"That Yoyo tramp moved over as a sophomore," Renata says and I want to punch her. "But never a freshman."

113

Malik's arm rests around Yolanda's shoulders and his hand's too damned close to her breasts. A girl that smart could do better. She should do better.

I wish she wanted to do me.

"He already likes me," Barney says.

"Who?" What did I miss?

"You're not even listening to me." A growl rumbles in her throat before she jumps up and runs out of the lunchroom.

She's right. I can't hear. Can't see. All I can do is—feel.

Neill frowns and then leans across the table toward me. "Don't want you mad at me, big guy, but you need to keep an eye on that girl."

He almost looks scared. We've only known each other a few weeks and, while I enjoy frightening my enemies, Neill won't ever be in that group. He's funny and smart, and could give Malik a real fight for popularity, if he was willing to conceal his feelings for Carl.

"I know you like the Dare," he says.

I hope my shrug looks casual. "She's just a girl."

"And Perez Hilton's just a guy. Whatever. But that group doesn't let just anybody hang with their crowd."

"What are you saying?"

"Barney's running with The Dare and her girls," Neill says.

That's what worries me. The paths of freshmen and upperclassmen seldom cross outside of lunchroom. Even I seldom see Barney in the halls. Yolanda Dare plus my sister equals *trouble, big time.*

"I wouldn't let Yolanda get within spitting distance of anyone I cared for," Renata says. "Girls like that only take a freshman on for sport."

I risk a glance at Yolanda. "Maybe she just wants to be friends."

Renata laughs. "That's like expecting a panther to let a puppy last longer than it takes to gobble him down." She looks down at her tray. "Okay, bad image."

"Still, Rennie's right," Neill says. "Your Barney—no telling what she'd have to do to fit in. If they're dragging her into their group now, it's to set her up for something. You want to keep her safe, you better break her away from them. Big as Barney is, she's still a little young, if you know what I mean."

I know what he means. Mom said she'd grow into her skin someday, but finding Mom in a pool of blood on the kitchen floor probably set my sister back several years on the emotional growth curve.

"The Dare rules the girls in that clique," Renata says. "My money's betting that she's got something planned for Barney."

"Something?" I ask. "Like what?"

"They crushed a lot of girls last year," Renata insists. "One girl failed her initiation into the group even after she agreed to play sandwich with two of the guys."

Francesca's lips curl. "Lots of sharing among the in-crowd."

Had Malik been a part of that deal?

"Just a month ago, a girl trying to break into the group found herself arrested for shoplifting," Renata says.

I have to swallow before I can speak. "You're saying Yolanda's responsible?"

Both girls nod. "Look at what they wear," Renata says as envy makes her lips curl. "Those girls have to dress so they're accepted, and Yolanda sets the pace. I know you don't notice, but she's wearing a several hundred dollars right now. They have to be lifting stuff. Yolanda hangs around at the Tribal Expressions boutique at Ford City all the time." Renata would know—she works at the Cookie Store at the Ford City mall. "They've lost a lot of stuff there; I've heard the employees talking."

I think back to the scarf Barney said Yolanda gave her. This can't continue. I'm glad Barney's been happier these last few days and I'm glad she has friends, but it can't be with someone who'll hurt her or get her in trouble. I don't want to believe Yolanda would do anything like that. But what's her motive in hanging around with a freshman? Does she intend to hurt and humiliate Barney? Or worse?

I risk a glance at Yolanda. Nicole's saying something and hanging on Malik's arm. At least he's not groping Yolanda. If anyone ever looked at me the way Nicole's looking at Yolanda, no way in hell I'd call her a friend. Yolanda's got to know what those other girls think of her. The fancy clothes—is her foster father King Midas? Are they proof she's a good thief? Or is it all just payment for putting up with Malik?

I make myself remember the fire in Yolanda's eyes the first time she saw Barney at her table. I want to believe that's changed, that her motives are different now. She can't be evil—not the girl whose poem gave me hope. *Not my Yolanda.*

Thing is, she's not *my* Yolanda. I have to remind myself that as the bell rings. She belongs to Malik, and she struts through the crowd without even glancing my way. I want to believe in Yolanda, but what if I'm wrong?

What I want doesn't matter. I have to protect my sister.

CHAPTER 14

After our last class, I follow Yolanda to her locker. She's wearing gold and silver beads in her hair today and they glisten under the hall lights. I raise my hand, aching to bury it in those coils and trace the curve of her shoulders. The clang of metal echoes through the hall as she slams her locker shut, turns and runs right into me. My arms automatically tighten around her.

"David." Her voice is a paintbrush stroking my skin, coloring me in shades of eager and painful longing. "What do you want?"

You.

"We have to talk." I'm having trouble remembering what I need to say.

Her eyes widen and my chest tightens in response. Mighty Mite has the muscles to go with the name, but she's still a nice, soft bundle. She steps out of my hold and licks her lips, breathing fast. Her plunging neckline skims the dark mounds of her breasts. I look down and down and down.

"Any trouble Friday night?" I ask. Anything to delay the confrontation.

"No." She smiles. "The brat kept his mouth closed."

Blood red lips smile, and I swallow hard. I release her and step back. "I called him a businessman, didn't I? And, since he's an honest one..." I hand her a ten.

"Call him greedy. David, I can't give him more of your money."

"Take it. Unless you want me going over to pay the man myself."

She looks around as if she's afraid someone's watching before slipping the money into her pocket. "He doesn't deserve any of this."

"It's okay. I like a guy who keeps his word."

The hall's hot and I'm steaming. It's not just the way she looks. Not just the way she stares at me, as if she sees something she likes. There's something more I want from Yolanda Dare. Something I need. Something I don't even understand.

"Did you—" She pauses and looks around the hall again. "Did you tell anyone? About...you know, my...family?"

"No." Her eyes flicker and I step closer to whisper, "I'll never tell anyone."

She turns to leave and it's like I'm losing Mom all over again. I have to ask, "How did you lose them?"

"Lose? I didn't lose anything."

"Your poem this morning. That was about your parents, wasn't it?"

"Those were just words." She shrugs. "Teacher wanted a poem, so I tossed some words on the paper. They're meaningless to me."

Nothing that spoke to me the way those words did could ever be meaningless. I understand that kind of agony. And I want to know Yolanda's pain.

The love I felt from my mother. Why did I let myself get too old to be tucked into bed? Too old for the goodbye kiss? Too old—but still young enough to act like a baby the one time it counted? My love for Barney, the sister I never wanted until I suddenly realized I couldn't remember life before her or deal with life without her. And Linda. I was so thrilled about her arrival I almost felt she was mine. I remember every minute of her life. If the three of us had been torn apart—our love wouldn't have vanished. *Real love cannot disappear*. And the comfort that comes with the memory of Yolanda's words pushes down on my pain.

"What about—" God, I can't even talk. The sounds of voices and scurrying feet die down around us. The halls are emptying fast as students hurry to catch buses or race home. I lean close, clear my throat and whisper, "What were your parents like?"

The sound of her books hitting the floor makes a passing student jump.

She kneels to retrieve them.

I get down beside her and see tears on her cheeks. "They left a long time ago. I barely remember. No big thing," she says as she rises. "I didn't lose anyone. They threw me away, okay? Now please get off my case."

I want to kiss her. I fight the need to hold her and comfort her. She has no one, and I want her to be mine. "Maybe it's none of my business, but—"

"If something's none of your business, then it's best to

stay out of it." Something descends over her face. It's a combination of fury and sorrow that darkens her eyes and leaves her jaw clenched. "Don't you have a girlfriend you're supposed to be with?"

"Barney." No getting away from it. I have to warn her off Barney. After that...there is no after that. I push back the dream of her body against mine and say, "Yeah, that's why we need to talk."

"Has something happened to her?" Her eyes widen.

"No. And I want to keep it that way."

"I don't understand. What do you want with me?"

"I just—you have to stay away from Barney."

She shivers as if I've just dumped a bucket of ice water over her. "Stay away from her? Why?"

"Take this back. Any gifts she gets, I give her." Yolanda doesn't reach for the scarf I pull from my pocket. I'm left with the soft cloth waving like a flag in the air between us. "She doesn't need anything from you. The stealing you and your friends do is an open secret. You can't toy with her the way you do with other girls. Lead your pack into whatever shit you want, but you can't take my...you can't take Barney with you."

I expect a curse, a slap, or even a laugh. But not the way her breath catches as if I'd struck her.

"I? Lead? You think I'm a thief? And a skanky ho, too, I bet."

I don't want to, but I don't dare trust my feelings. They cost us our mother. Now I owe Barney protection, even if she's never going to be grateful. I grit my teeth and say, "Like I told you, just stay away from Barney."

"Barney, Barney, Barney. That girl knows how to take care of herself."

I wish she did. Wish I didn't always have to act like a parent. Wish I could tell Yolanda I believe in her.

"Just keep her away from me." Yolanda turns toward the staircase. "If you can."

Move, hands. Don't let her leave.

I ignore my brain's frantic orders and can only watch Yolanda's beautiful body as she walks away from me. She stops at the end of the hall and points toward the window. "Looks like you're not quite *all* Barney has."

When I get to the window and look, Malik has an arm around my sister. She's giggling like a sixth grader by the time I'm out the door and down the stairs to the sidewalk where they're standing together.

"Let her go," I say.

"Relax." Malik smiles, but his eyes look empty. "I'm not hurting your girl. Count yourself lucky. You've got one sweet treasure."

Barney giggles louder.

"Let. Her. Go. Now!"

He takes his arm from her shoulders and looks up at Yolanda, who's still standing at the top of the stairs by the door. "Maybe this pretty girl doesn't like seeing her man hanging around another woman."

"Then you've got nothing for her, not with a girl in every class and two on the weekends."

He smiles. "I leave them all satisfied."

"That's not what I hear."

His rat-eyes narrow and he looks over my shoulder. I

turn to watch Yolanda descend the staircase. The evening rush hour hasn't officially begun, but the horns of impatient drivers already fill the air. The street sounds aren't loud enough to cover the sounds of her heels on the stone stairs.

Malik crosses his arms over his chest. "I'm not satisfying you, Yo?"

She swallows. Her eyes remain fixed on his face and she looks afraid.

I step toward Malik. "She didn't. It wasn't Yolanda who said—"

"Guess I'll just have to work harder," Malik says. "You won't need to complain again."

Yolanda's lips twist into a smile. "Good to know, babe. Now let's get away from this giant you've been toying with."

"Giant?" Barney sounds hurt. "You don't—you don't mean that, Yolanda. We're friends."

"Sure we are. That's why I didn't say clown. Don't look at me like that. You're just a freshman. What can we have in common?" Yolanda puts her hand on Malik's arm. "My man likes his women to be women, not tree trunks. He wouldn't know what to do with someone like you."

The lines in Malik's forehead grow deeper, like he's trying to decide if Yolanda's words are praise or if she's dissing him. Me, I'll bet on the insult, which means she's playing a dangerous game.

No matter what, Barney's been dissed and she's certainly going to hate Yolanda.

"Stay away from Malik," I tell my sister as Yolanda and Malik walk away.

"Why? You're mooning after that awful girl of his all the time."

"Not true." I don't even know what's going on inside me.

"Please, its sooo obvious."

I turn only once to look at Yolanda before Barney and I turn the corner. I have to let the girl go. I have no choice, I owe this to Barney.

CHAPTER 15

I can't catch up with Yolanda after English class ends the next day. She's silent all during the period, keeps her head down over her books and then rushes for the door almost before the bell rings.

When gym class ends I shower quickly. As I do every day now, I head for the study hall. It still seems odd that she's always there in that room when she could be outside with Malik. My steps slow as I reach the door, where I see her with her head bent over a book. She's wearing a turtleneck sweater and her hair hides her face.

Someone comes and stands next to me. I don't even have to look to know its Malik. My guts know, and I automatically twist my hands into fists.

"Saw you falling all over your ass in class again, Davie boy. Kinda useless, ain't you?"

He's no mind reader. Otherwise he'd be running as fast as those legs could carry him. Instead he hangs beside me as I take a last glance through the window. I'm about to turn away when Yolanda lifts her hand to turn a page.

There's a dark purple bruise on her wrist.

Something solidifies inside my lungs and I can't talk as I struggle to suck in air. Why do girls let that happen? Is going out with the Homecoming King really worth all the pain? Doesn't she understand what happens next? Someday there'll be more than a bruise. Mom claimed she still loved Antwon all through the separation and divorce. Maybe right up to the moment when he pulled the trigger.

"I'll be glad to give you some pointers," Malik says.

The day I need pointers from that cruel prick...

Yolanda raises her head. As our eyes meet, I see another dark bruise on her chin.

Malik steps closer to the window. "You're really interested in that little bitch? She's getting a little well-used, but if you want, you can try her out. Since I got nothing against big girls, why don't you and I just switch?"

He waves his arm and all I can think about is that he used that hand to grab Yolanda, to hit her.

Almost before I know what's happening, my left connects with his jaw. A satisfying shudder runs up my arm, and then I nail him with a right uppercut under the chin. This sends him staggering back against the door, which swings open and he falls to the floor. Girlish screams cut through my ears, along with male voices shouting as I throw myself on Malik, who struggles to stand. Then I grab his arm and twist, and he begins to yell.

The proctor and a security guard jerk me away and slam me against a wall. When the guard twists my arm behind my back, I grit my teeth and remain still. No point fighting that hold. Instead I turn my head, look through the mass of staring students and find Yolanda.

Eyes that would freeze molten steel meet mine. Like that congealing metal, my guts thicken into a heavy, useless slag. I'd forgotten the mystery of the female mind. Forgotten how they love their tough guys. The thugs, cruel, but cool, are always surrounded by adoring women. A few bruises don't matter to her. I've downed her honey, the school's number one high-status guy, and now she's pissed at me.

Why did I ever imagine Yolanda was deeper than other girls?

As the bell rings signaling the end of the period, I'm left sitting on a wooden bench in the school office, waiting for the principal to arrive and decide my fate. The security guard leans against the wall, thumbs tucked into his belt, waiting—maybe even hoping—I'll try something. He's definitely not Officer Friendly. But I've done enough stupid things for one day. Now I have to think of some way to save myself.

Mom made me promise to graduate. I can't keep failing her. Still, if I have to beg to stay in this place I hate, can I even do it? Will begging be enough now?

During the change of classes bodies rush through the hallway while I sit in the office on display. The wall between the office and hall is glass for a reason: just like at Grogan Hills, the administration wants to embarrass us. Everyone stares at me through the glass as they pass.

Students wander through the door into the office. Some have official business, such as Devontae Scott, one of the school nerds who spends fifth period helping out in the office. He sends me a sympathetic shrug, then settles at a computer to take over as a secretary leaves for lunch. Other kids drift through just to get a closer look at the fool waiting to be handed his head. They giggle or give me a smug look, but nobody looks me in the eye. I can just imagine what they'll be saying in the cafeteria, what Barney's going to hear about all this.

Almost the entire period passes before they call me into a conference room. It's the little things that surprise me. The principal's seated at a table that fills the room. Once again I'm faced by this robot with gray hair and perfect posture. And she's not alone. Coach Kasili sits beside her.

The principal waves me to a seat, but I'm not dumb and I don't fall for her gracious act. A smiling executioner leaves you just as dead. I know I'm supposed to believe she's my friend, but she's an even worse liar than Barney. She's got the "I own you" gleam in her eyes that official types use when they know they've got you cornered.

"I'll stand."

"Sit down, David." This time I hear the edge in her voice.

For a moment I consider fighting. Or maybe I could just yell and rush at them. But I need my energy for whatever's coming, so I slide into a chair near the door. My heart beats against my ribs and the room feels like a desert. I can taste my sweat but they both look cool as can be.

"How many days?" I ask, hoping for a simple suspension.

The principal glances at Kasili before saying, "You know the school rules about fighting on campus. We've had this discussion before."

Oh God, Expulsion. And this wasn't even a fight to save my sister. "I know I have to work on my temper." I say.

The principal folds her hands on the desk and gives me the smile people use on small children. "I don't tolerate violence," she says. Meaning she has no idea what really goes on in the halls and bathrooms. "I'm old-fashioned enough to believe fighting has no place in my school. Neither do students who think violence is the answer to any question."

"Why attack Malik?" Kasili asks.

"He hurt her," I mumble.

"Has he done something to Barnetta?"

"No." *To Yolanda. His girl, not mine.*

Coach Kasili stares at me as if I were some kind of puzzle he can't quite solve, while he says to the principal, "This is a special case. Maybe we can make some compromises."

"Hakeem, you know how I feel."

"I know, but still, this could get pretty ugly."

"You think I'm worried about this coming out—" She snorts, but I see her breathing change and her lips tighten.

Kasili continues, "I think we need to talk this over a little more. Privately. David, would you wait outside?"

Another question that isn't.

Barney's in the outer office when I head back to the bench. She runs over and puts her arms around me. "It's all my fault, David," she says.

I guide her head to rest on my shoulder. My sister blames herself for too much, for most everything. But this wasn't about Barney. Just a girl who doesn't even care.

"It's okay," I tell her. "Get back to your class."

Instead she hugs me tighter. Just like the old days, once I stopped telling Mom to get rid of her. I kiss her icy forehead and she sighs.

When I look up, I see Yolanda and Malik passing by. He's got a large bandage on the side of his face. Then Yolanda's eyes meet mine and she stumbles. Malik says something and laughs, then keeps walking while she kneels to pick up something she dropped. Then she stands up and hurries on down the hall. I stare at the back of her head, hoping she'll turn and look, knowing she won't.

The bench is hard against my butt as I sit with my arm around my sister, waiting for the official end of my high school career. She doesn't ask any questions, just remains at my side until Coach Kasili opens the conference room door and says, "David, come in, please."

Barney gets up to follow me inside.

"No, Barnetta. I just need David." He stops at the desk to write her a late pass. "Get back to your class."

His voice seems to calm Barney, who takes the pass and glances at me. "It'll be okay, David."

I nod. "Nothing to worry about. Get going to your class." She's still standing in the office when I look back from the conference room door. I give her a final wave, complete with a smile meant to show confidence I don't really feel.

At least once I'm kicked out of this place, I can work full-time. Maybe get in some overtime pay, too. Rent us a house. Do a better job of supporting Barney and Linda. Maybe I'll find some good in all of this, someday.

The conference room is empty except for Kasili and me. "Where's the principal?" I ask.

"Sit down, David. Mrs. Grayson and I came to an understanding. You're getting one final chance, as long as you agree to a few conditions."

Adult-speak for do-what-I-say, or else.

He sighs like a big solid bear. "You know, it was a sad day when I heard David Murhaselt dropped out of Grogan Hills."

"Cried buckets, did you?"

"When I learned Barnetta would be coming here I hoped her brother would show up, too."

"Guess you were wrong," I say.

"Yeah. No David. At least not David *Murhaselt*. 'Course, there *is* David Albacore. And he's *not* from California."

I hate being toyed with. "Meaning?"

"Legally, you're still David Murhaselt. Correct?"

Fuck *legally* and fuck the dumbass for asking a question he already knows the answer to. How did he find out? What did I miss? I pound my fist on the table as I say through clenched teeth, "Who told you about me?"

"Don't blame your sister; she never said anything to me about you."

Christ, is he worrying I'll do something to my sister over this? Even if she spilled everything, none of this is *her* fault.

"You fucking bastard," I say, enraged that he'd even think that I'd hurt Barney. Mom would slap me upside my head for talking to a teacher like this but I'm too angry to care.

"I'll chalk that up to stress, David. But why Albacore? Because it's your mother's maiden name?" He says that last sentence like he's discovered some ancient secret. "Why is it so important for you to make it yours?"

"A tribute to my mother." My aunt refuses to give me permission for a name change. She believes I'll change my mind or forget about it. But that's not about to happen. Not now, not ever.

"A tribute, or…"

"It keeps her alive."

Kasili smiles like a crew boss picking up an on-time performance bonus, and I know I've been manipulated again. "How'd you change the records?"

I'm not giving Devontae up.

"Go fuck yourself," I tell him.

He ignores my command.

"Of course, using an assumed name isn't a problem," he continues. "After all, you're not a criminal. You haven't killed anyone."

At least he blushes when he realizes what he's said.

I know he doesn't remember the details of a shooting from seven months ago. There's more than a murder a day in Chicago and I had to search all the way back to page ten in the paper to find the tiny paragraph about Mom. Domestic disputes don't make the front page unless a celebrity's involved. A devoted mother and nurse didn't qualify.

"Just don't ever call me *Murhaselt*. Or there *will* be a killing."

"I'm sorry, David. I'm not out to reopen old wounds. I see this means a lot to you. I can only imagine your pain."

He *imagines* nothing.

"Why are you doing this to me?"

"I do what I must to help my clients."

"I'm not your client and I don't want your help."

"But Barnetta is. And *she* needs my help. Just think what your expulsion would do to her. To use a cliché, you've got potential, David. You need some direction. What you've engineered is beyond what most men twice your age could manage. That kind of talent moves worlds and needs to be nurtured. If you agree to a few conditions, it *will* be both nurtured and encouraged."

I force my breathing to slow down. If I didn't have sisters, I wouldn't have to put up with this—or him. I'd walk out of this place right now. But he's right about Barney—and Linda.

"What kind of conditions?" I ask.

"I've told Mrs. Grayson about your family tragedy, and she's agreed to offer you counseling."

Agreed to consider me a freak is more like it.

"I won't do counseling," I tell him.

"That's non-negotiable, David. You've been dealt a trauma. You need an outlet. One period a week. What could it hurt?"

"Not with you." I will *not* talk to this man.

"Agreed—" He says it so quickly, alarm bells go off inside my head. It can't be this easy.

"—And you'll join the basketball team. That, too, is non-negotiable."

Something inside me wants to jump at the idea, but I push that urge aside. He wants me on the team because he expects David Murhaselt to ignite a miracle. Or else he wants to do some undercover counseling. Or maybe it's both.

"No."

"I think you need the game."

"I think you just care about winning."

"Who are you angry at, David? Basketball, or yourself?"

That last game. The shot I jumped above the net to block. The cheerleader and her promised reward. The fall and the pain as my bone cracked. The emergency room doctor and those wretched pills—to take "as needed." Pills to kill the pain I had no business feeling. But like some sissy baby, I took them.

I was supposed to protect Mom. I was the man of the house. I was all she had. Instead, I went to sleep.

"Quit dicking around," I say. "David Murhaselt's never gonna play again. I'll just take my suspension."

But Kasili shakes his head. "The only alternative is expulsion, for the safety of the student body. Frankly, the principal still wants you out."

"Okay. I'll clear out my locker." *It's over.* I rise on shaky legs.

"She's also mortified by the fraud you put over on the school—on her. She'd like that part handled quietly."

So I wasn't the *only* one being blackmailed. In spite of my anger, I'm impressed. His skill at manipulating the principal is right up there with the way I manipulated the school records. *But still.*

"I won't be blackmailed into playing. I'll leave first."

"Seven months before graduation? Not very wise."

I fucking hate Kasili!

"I won't lie, it'd be fun to win a couple," he continues. "The students would like that, too. But that's not what I'm after, here." He leans closer. His eyes darken as they stare into mine. "I'm offering a way for David Albacore to graduate."

And a way to make my mother's dreams to come true.

You have to graduate, David. This divorce doesn't change that.

I'm trying, Mom.

Don't just try. Do it. Promise me, David.

"*If* I let you blackmail me."

"Blackmail's a harsh word. I'd rather call this opportunity. One we can both benefit from."

And rat droppings by any other name remain a pile of shit.

"The team has problems. You have problems. Maybe the two problems can fix each other."

"As long as I agree to join your ratty team."

"You get to stay in school." He smiles as if he thinks he's already won. And unless I don't plan to set foot inside this place again, he has.

"I'll see you on the court for practice after school today," he says.

Something inside me stirs in anticipation. My legs quiver like two traitors, ready to start off on their own. But I have to tell him the truth. "I can't."

His eyebrows rise. He's so sure of himself, he makes me want to puke. "Sorry to hear that. I'll let the principal know you're leaving."

A snake slithers through my stomach. "I can't come today. I have responsibilities I need to take care of first."

His eyes narrow for a second, and then he nods. "Agreed. Take care of things over the weekend. I'll see you at Monday's practice."

He stands and extends his hand, as if he expects me to shake and forgive. As if he and I have just made some bargain.

As if I have a choice.

The bright side? Malik's face when I show *him* a few pointers.

I step back and shake my head. I've reached the door when he says, "One thing more, David."

What now?

"No more fighting. Whatever your beef with Malik, it's over. I can't hold the principal off your ass if there's a third strike."

CHAPTER 16

I have dreams. A house, like the one we used to live in before everything fell apart. A bedroom on the second floor, with a place for everything. And a window where I look down on the street and pretend I'm a king.

Some king.

I don't know how I'm going to cram everything into my already overfull life. A day only has twenty-four hours. School takes up the daytime. Work fills up the evenings. Practice and games? I don't know how I'll manage. An angry voice inside me yells that I can't take on anything more. But I don't dare listen.

I was never a cartoon-lover as a kid, paid no attention to Bob the Builder. I always liked looking at heavy machinery, but construction was never part of my plans. Only now that I'm in it, it's awesome. I've helped haul debris from the trench and lay rebar stakes to reinforce the foundation. I like the feel of the equipment belt on my hips, and the hard hat and steel-toed boots are as familiar as my Keds. I want this life for my future. I completely love my job. Love the idea of turning a hole in the ground into something real. Maybe someday I'll hear people say, *Albacore made that. Without him nothing would be standing here.*

I remember my first day. I walked right into the yard, stopped in front of Sanderson and said, "Hire me. I'll do anything." I don't think he really believed me when he handed me gloves and a shovel. The first few weeks he was at my back every time I looked around. Waiting for me to fuck up, and maybe drive a spike through my foot or add too much water to the cement mix.

I don't remember exactly when that stopped. I just know I admire the guy, feel something for him I never felt for Antwon. Sanderson taught me everything. Hammers and mortar, and safety on scaffolds in twenty-mile-an-hour winds.

The world on the site is more real to me than school. No one tries to screw me over here. The crew members have jobs to do and want things done right. Got families they love, just the way I do mine. I carry my weight and that makes me one of them. I want to keep doing my part in getting the job done.

Tonight I have to talk to Sanderson, and ask him for something extra. I've gone over it a hundred times in my head but it always ends the same way. He tells me to get lost, just not that nicely. A couple of the so-called thugs around school could take serious vocabulary lessons from my boss Sanderson.

Just before the shift ends I head for the construction trailer. Sanderson's standing at the door.

"We need to talk, boss," I say. No point dicking around.

Something grim passes over his face, and I wonder if he also reads minds. "Okay. Step into my office."

He waves me inside, although I'd have preferred talking out in the yard. The background noise of earth-movers, hammers and co-workers' voices might have helped me make him understand. Here inside the trailer, I hear only the beating of my own heart.

Sanderson settles behind the cluttered desk and lights a cigar. "My old lady'd yell if she saw me smoking this, but a man needs a few vices."

In seconds the cramped trailer smells like the woods and brings back memories of a camping trip in Wisconsin when our family was still whole. I think about things I used to have but won't ever have again.

He leans back in his chair and stares at me. "What about you, David? What's your vice? If you could have one thing in the world, what would it be?"

"The Dare."

I don't realize I've said that out loud until his eyebrows pull together in a straight line. I quickly recover and say what I would have only a few weeks earlier. "Your job. That's what I meant. I'd dare go after your job."

I wait for his laugh. I can't believe I've said this to the man whose approval means so much to me.

"Let me give you some advice, kid." He doesn't seem offended. He looks solemn, as if he's speaking to his own boss. "Aim higher."

I feel that same fierce surge of pride as the year before, when I hefted the trophy after being named MVP. "You really think I can?"

"I know you can. You pick up shit faster then anyone I've ever seen. You get the work, took on everything I threw at you. And you've got brains. You understand risks and timetables. I say the words *critical path* and some of the jokers who've been around five or six years roll their eyes. But you actually get it. You put in six hours and do more than a lot of the chumps out there manage in eight. You're dedicated. And you care."

Hearing him say that only makes things worse. What I'm about to ask for will make him tell me to get lost from the world I want to stay with. I force myself to say, "I need to ask for something."

"I'm not resigning." He laughs.

"No. But—you might want me to, after I finish."

His eyes narrow. "I thought you liked it here. What's up, Mr. Albacore?"

Great, I've already ticked him off. He knew Antwon, so he usually calls me David because he doesn't like the idea of me changing my name any more than my aunt. "I need to cut back my hours."

His fist slams on the desk. "I knew it. Always happens. Your girlfriend giving you a hard time? You lasted longer than most. I never expected to see your sorry tail again after it dragged off the lot that first day."

"My tail wasn't even sure it'd last all the way home," I say. As bad as things are, his words make me remember that day and I have to laugh. I'd sweated blood and walked out on feet filled with blisters and bruises all over my body. Lost a fingernail, too, and was damned glad my finger wasn't smashed, too. I don't think anyone expected to see me show up again the next day.

"This isn't about a girl," I say. "It's school. I'm joining Farrington's basketball team."

The cigar falls from his mouth. As he fumbles to find it, I can almost hear his thoughts. *Of all the bumble headed reasons. Basket-fucking-ball. Knew you were a kid and kids just can't be counted on. Outta my sight and don't ever bother coming back.*

Just let me stay. I'll do anything, remember?

"Basketball, eh? You prefer playing a game to honest work?"

"Not exactly."

"Basketball," he says again. "You any good?"

"Better than good."

He leans back in the chair and blows a smoke ring. Perfect. Like most everything he does. Like he expects from the people working under him. "Confident, ain't ya? Suppose you think you'll center for the Bulls someday."

"Yes, I'm confident." And at least smart enough to know the difference between good and elite. I don't dream dumb dreams. Only impossible ones.

"You're already part time," he says as he opens a desk drawer and pulls out my check. "You're good, dependable and you know what you're doing. You stand on your own two feet, don't beg, don't expect favors, even when you're knee deep in mud. Reduced hours, eh? How much could you do?"

"We have to practice after school. Maybe...four hours a day. Unless there's a game that day."

His lips move, probably cursing me. "You really good? Will that sorry-assed team finally win something?"

"I'll make us win."

He laughs. "That's why I like you, David, you know what you can do and you won't let yourself be less than the best. I put in some time at Farrington back in the day. A couple in the W column will bring back memories. Just remember, I'll only pay for actual hours worked, understand?"

My pulse races like an out-of-control jackhammer and I'm so nervous the check flutters from my hands. I have to dive to the floor after it. "Thank you, sir. You won't regret this, sir."

"You call me *sir* again and I'll regret this right now."

"Sorry, si—sorry. I'll be here every day right after practice. Unless there's a game. And once vacation starts, I'll be here every day, all day."

"Yeah, well, about that..."

"What?" Something in his tone puts me on alert.

He points at his computer screen. "Tell me what you see."

I've seen the project management software before. I stare, checking out the charts and graphs, and the red line that marks the project's critical path. And the dates. "It's ending?"

"We're ahead of schedule, in part thanks to you. Which means your job was gonna end soon, anyway." He points out the window. "Another month and its all interior work. I'm looking for my next gig, myself."

Interior work means skilled carpenters, electricians, plumbers...all things I can't be a part of. The ground's still gonna collapse under me. "I'll learn. You know I pick things up fast."

"I know. I'd make book on it you'd be the kind of apprentice a master dreams about having. But right now, people around here aren't looking for untrained help."

"If you hear of anything…"

He nods but doesn't look hopeful. "I hear anything I'll call you. But work is drying up in these parts. I don't know where I'll go myself."

I stare at the magic date. A few more weeks and I could get stuck with a fast-food job after all.

◆

Now I need to tell my aunt the bad news.

It's almost midnight when I get back to the apartment and I'm surprised to find her awake. She's sitting at the kitchen table, holding a cup of coffee and staring at the clock on the wall. She barely moves when I come into the room. When she looks up, something about her face looks wrong, as if one of Linda's devils has leapt from her game and chased her around.

Does she expect something more of me? Whatever it is, I have to do it. I can't complain or say anything that'll make her send us away. No matter what the law says, my sisters are my responsibility now. I have to take care of them, even if it costs what's left of my pride.

"Are you really serious about giving up the family name?" she asks. "You really want to make this permanent and erase your past?"

"Dead serious." My mother gave me the name David. Antwon's name wasn't a choice. I accept my mother's gift.

Antwon and everything that goes with him can rot in hell.
I can't rip his DNA out of my body, but I'll never again bear
the name of my mother's murderer.

"I know things aren't easy for you. I know my brother
made some mistakes."

"Mistake?" The divorce, where everything from the
silverware to the broken chair was fought over—everything
except the children—maybe she could call that a mistake.
What happened after that goes into a whole other category.
"It wasn't a mistake," I say.

"I visited my brother today. He regrets what he did."

Regret. Hah! He kept saying how he loved her, loved
us all. Linda and Barney visited him and came back with
his gifts and money, and sob stories about how lonely he
was. Barney swore he was so sorry about hurting Mom that
he cried.

Antwon was sorry, all right. So sorry he broke into the
house and put a hole through my mom's chest.

"You should visit your father."

I should slit my wrists first. Or better yet, slit his. Father, hell. To me, he's just the fucking sperm donor.

"I'm not going. End of subject."

"He's sorry for what he did."

"*What he did* was murder my mother." I leap to my
feet and my chair falls to the floor. If I went to see him, they
wouldn't have enough guards to prevent me from doing
what I should have done long ago. Aunt Edie's never going
to believe her little brother's anything but a martyred saint.
I have to get away before I say something that gets us
thrown out of her home. "I know he's your brother. You
have to love him. But he killed my mother."

I head for my room, a space little bigger than a closet. Barney and Linda share a bedroom, but I'd rather have privacy in here than bunk on the sofa out in the open.

She calls my name and I stop. "You're so much like your grandfather. Dad showed his feelings by what he did, not what he said. Good thing, because I think he hated ever having to say more than two words at a time. I can't expect you to be anything except who you are, David. I still think its wrong, but, since you insist on changing your name..." She extends a piece of paper toward me.

My hand trembles as I take the paper from her and realize what it is—a name change form from the State of Illinois, signed and notarized. My heart pounds against my ribcage.

"You agree?"

"Mr. Kasili was right, I guess."

This stops me in my tracks. "Hakeem Kasili?"

"He came and talked to me two days ago. Said you really needed to do this."

Two days ago? Before the fight and the meeting with the principal? What game is Kasili playing? What does he really want with me? No matter. I got what I wanted. This paper gets filed, and soon I'll have the legal right to bear the name *I* chose. Looks like I'll also owe that man.

"You know he expects me to play for the basketball team?" I ask my aunt.

She nods. "I'm glad. He said you need time for fun."

"Basketball's not fun anymore."

"Your arm's fine now, isn't it?"

The problem was never my arm. The blocked shot

made no difference to anyone—except to my mom. *Don't blame the game, Dufus. You were the fucking showoff.* In the end, all my excuses are meaningless.

"I'd like to see you play," Aunt Edie says.

So she's actually interested in something more than the money I turn over to her?

Money! How could I have forgotten? After fishing the crumpled check from my pocket and placing it on the table before her, I say, "I'm afraid next week it'll be much smaller. In order to play, I had to cut my hours."

"The good Lord will help us find a way." She closes her eyes for a second and seems to have trouble catching her breath. The bags under her eyes look darker, and I could almost swear her hair turns a bit grayer as I watch.

"What's wrong?" I ask.

"Nothing."

"Tell me." Whatever her problem is, it's my problem, too. She's not my mother. But she is kin after all.

She puts down her coffee cup and rests her chin on one hand. "The timing could be better, David. My hours just got cut back at work. I'm a part-timer, too, now."

Oh, shit. "That's it then. I'll go back to the boss and keep my hours. Maybe I'll go full time." At least for a few weeks. And then what?

She shakes her head. "That's not necessary. My supervisor says this is temporary and in a few weeks—a month tops—we'll be back at full production."

She takes another sip from her cup and continues staring at the wall. I don't see how she can be so calm. Or maybe I do. If things don't get better, she'll just turn those hangdog eyes at me and remind me I'm the reason she's burdened with three extra mouths.

Get off your tail and do something, David Albacore, or Murhaselt, or whatever you want to call yourself, she'll say. *Fix this mess you helped cause.*

CHAPTER 17

On Sunday I try explaining to my sisters how life has to change. I don't want to scare them, but if we're going to manage, we'll all have to pitch in. I need to make them understand and accept our new situation. They've been through so many changes this year; I wonder how much more they can take, especially Linda.

My little sister still buries herself in that stupid video game. Since we all got back together I've fought to put a smile back on her face. But so far it's not working. She obeys orders, does homework and chores. But the loving little girl who still crawled into my lap to plead for a story hasn't come back to us yet. The docs told us to just give her time, and that soon she'll work things out. But sometimes I just want to shake her, or hold her tight. But I'm afraid to do either one—maybe it'd just make things worse.

Right now, my baby sister looks like she wants to find a hole to jump into and pull down on top of her. I remember when Linda was born like it happened yesterday. There's a picture of me holding her on my lap, with a smile on my face that says I'm the man and she's totally mine. I mean, I love Barney. She's my best buddy on earth. But my Linda—she's my baby—she's mine.

"Will Aunt Edie divorce us?" Linda asks, her wide eyes stare at me.

"No, silly," Barney says in her fake grown-up voice. She's sitting on the edge of her bed, knees drawn up under her chin. "She's not married to us, so she can't divorce us."

"I don't want to go to Jamaica." Linda says quietly.

"It's nice and hot there all year long." Barney's voice sounds wistful.

Linda's eyes fill with tears.

"No one goes anywhere, got it?" I say. "I got us back together, didn't I? We're staying together. We'll just have to be extra careful about money. Got it?"

They nod, but Barney looks sullen.

"We should start making our lunches," I tell them.

"I can't," Barney says. Her voice is so loud Linda jumps and whimpers. "Only dweebs do the lunch bag thing."

"And the cell phones have to go, too." Might as well ask my sister to slit her throat.

"I can't live without my phone," Barney says.

"Do you want to live here? Or end up like—"

"Like what?"

I almost said end up like Yolanda.

"—Apart. Do you?"

She shakes her head. Linda shivers and I know I shouldn't have revealed how close we are to the edge. As I watch, Barney runs to the closet. She pulls a jacket and blouse out and throws them on the floor. The dangling earrings and a pin follow, along with the cherry-flavored lip gloss.

"Where'd this all come from?" I ask.

She frowns at the pile on the floor. "Yolanda. *She* gave them to me. I don't want anything from that bitch."

"Don't, Barney."

"That's what she is. You were right! We need to stay away from her kind."

Tell me to walk through fire, no sweat. Swim to the bottom of the ocean, I'm there. Even rip my hammering heart out of my chest, go ahead, knock yourself out. But tell me to stay away from Yolanda Dare? I don't know if I can. But that's not what I tell Barney.

"I'm stuck working with her. It's the teacher's fault. We have a class project thing."

Barney puts her hands on her hips. "Do you have to work with her, of all the people in school?"

"It wasn't my idea," I insist. "The teacher's making us work together."

Accept that. Please. "Sorry. Don't like it myself."

"You poor thing." Barney frowns. "Just tell her, she messes with you and she's messing with both of us. I'll be happy to kick her fancy ass."

Well, it wasn't a total lie.

◆

Monday morning and I'm up almost before my head hits the pillow. It's been a long time since I was eager to get to school.

The fourth-period bell rings and I walk past the gym. I go inside the study hall, instead of just staring at Yolanda through the door. I feel her eyes on me as I check in with the proctor.

He's not happy to see me. "No trouble, right?"

"No trouble," I assure him.

He continues frowning for a few seconds, then turns back to his newspaper.

Yolanda stares at me as I pass. She's one girl that doesn't need to worry about those fashion magazines Barney and the girls drool over at our lunch table. The Dare beats everyone on those pages every single day. Today her blouse sports a scene from an African safari, with a lion's head covering her breasts.

Yolanda watches me drop into the empty seat behind her, pull out a book and pretend I'm reading. I just need one last minute to practice my speech. I'll charm her and then...

"What are you doing here?" she hisses.

"Studying. Guys on the team don't have to take gym class."

She swivels around to face me. The bruise on her chin is fading, but the outline's still there. "The team? You're on the basketball team?" she asks.

"Starting today."

I wait for her to look impressed. Instead she turns back to her desk. The clock hands crawl for most of the period and she stays bent over her papers. But I'm big enough to see over her shoulder. She's working on algebra, marking her paper, crossing things out and shaking her head. Ten minutes before the period ends, I close the book I'm not reading, get up and stand at her side. The newspaper rattles as the proctor looks up and starts to say something, then shrugs and lowers his head.

"Exponentials," I say. "A real pain in the ass."

She looks up. For a second I'm scared she'll tell me to get lost. Instead she says, "You understand this stuff?"

In construction we use math every day. Samuelson's showed me about figuring scales from blueprints, calculating volumes and square footage. But who knew those hours I strained over algebra last year would ever be this useful? I kneel by her chair and go over the solution with her. "See, logs are just another way to write exponents. You multiply like bases by adding exponents. Multiply logs the same way." I smile, as if I didn't have to sweat blood learning that one.

She licks her lips. "Thanks." I feel so good I could die happy.

Now's the time. I clear my throat. "I thought…"

"Yes, David?"

My tongue sticks to the top of my mouth and now I have to lick my dry lips, too. Swear to God, I had this speech all ready. It worked when I practiced in the john. The mirror showed an irresistible smile and my voice was as smooth as her blouse. *Yolanda, I thought you and I could work together on the report. We can spend study hall and our lunch period together in the library. In the back. Together. At our table.*

What's wrong with me?

"We have…this stupid-assed…the paper. You know, we're partners."

She frowns. "You mean the Marriage and Family paper? I'm working on my half." After a moment she turns back to her math.

"We could...I mean, I thought..." *I can't even think around this girl.*

"What?" She raises her eyebrows. Any second and she'll be yelling for the proctor to haul the crazy guy away.

"The project. We could do something."

"Something? You mean work?"

I nod.

"Together?"

Yeah! That's it. "Not here. Library." The air's heavy. I feel sweat on my face and taste salt on my lips.

"You're asking if we could work on the project together? In the library?"

Without all these people around. "Yeah."

She nods. "That's a good idea. We could meet this afternoon after your practice."

"Can't." *Damn that job.* "Tomorrow?"

She's thinking.

I'm praying.

"Okay," she says, and I start breathing again. "I'll meet you tomorrow, fourth period, by the stacks at our table."

Our table. Oh, yeah. Only the bell ringing keeps me from falling at her feet.

She says nothing as I follow her through the hall to the cafeteria line. She stays silent when I help her get her milk—skim, and dessert—lime Jell-O. Then she moves to the cash register and I tell the guy, "I'm paying for her lunch."

He nods, but Yolanda says, "No. I pay my own way."

I don't understand her resistance. "It's just lunch," I say. What I really don't understand is my own reaction. Why should buying her lunch be so important to me? I don't have money to throw away.

One look at Barney's face when she plops down in the seat next to me has me struggling to figure out what I did wrong this time. After rolling her eyes at me, she turns her head away. She and the other girls start talking. Like always, I try ignoring them, until the gossip crew starts in on their favorite topic—Yolanda.

"Just look what The Dare's wearing now," Francesca says.

"That group's got a dress code," her friend Renata says.

"Yolanda is the dress code. She gets something one day and they all have to have it the next."

Is that why the girls at that table claw each other to get at Malik? To keep up with Yolanda?

"I'd swear that top came from the African boutique," Francesca says. "You know, that one up at Ford City. What's that place called?"

Barney and Francesca look at Renata, who says, "It's called Tribal Expressions, and it's expensive as all hell. The Dare hangs around that place all the time. Me, I couldn't afford a hankie from there."

"She's got good taste," Barney says. "She must have a lot of money to be able to pay for stuff like that."

To me, it's money well spent. Looking at Yolanda makes me hungrier than ever. I can't help wondering how her underwear tastes. Maybe I should ask Malik.

Oh, God. I have to get that image out of my head.

"Who says she pays?" Renata asks as I stuff something into my mouth and chew, head down. "Criminal chic, I'd bet. A lot of stuff just walks away in those mall stores."

"Why would she have to steal?" Barney asks.

Malik leans over Yolanda and says something that makes her shake her head. He throws back his head and laughs, as if her refusal means nothing to him. Her hand closes over her Jell-O dish and I pray she'll throw that green slime into his face.

"Do it," I say, hardly knowing I've said it out loud.

"Do what?" Barney turns from her friends to ask me.

"Nothing," I tell her. Not one damn thing. Yolanda gets up and leaves her table. Meanwhile, Malik's still laughing.

As The Dare walks past, Barney yells, "Steal anything good lately, Yoyo?"

Francesca hides her face in her hands. Renata hugs herself and snickers. I bite my tongue to keep from snapping at my sister.

Yolanda's lips twist into a smile, but her eyes never move. I know she's not joking when she says, "I don't touch things that aren't a whole lot better than good."

"God that bitch has nerve," Renata says as Yolanda leaves the cafeteria.

"Yeah, that bitch," Barney says.

I grab my sister's arm and lean close to her ear. "What's wrong with you, Barney?"

"Wrong with me? What about you? I thought we were cutting back. So why'd you buy that skank's lunch?"

Maybe 'cause I work my ass off and I should be able to spend a little of that money any way I want.

"No biggie," I say. "She wouldn't let me pay for her anyway."

"But you wanted to. You tell me I should bag a sandwich, but you're ready to waste money on the girl who hates us both. That's so bogus."

Bogus? She lusts after a low-life like Malik Kaplan, and she calls me *bogus*? I go out every night, bust rocks to pay for her needs, live in that tiny closet that is not now and was never a bedroom, just so she and Linda can have a place of their own, and *I'm* bogus? She may be a freshman, but she should be old enough to show some gratitude.

The dry bologna sandwich I'm chewing feels like a wad of cotton. My chair scrapes the floor as I push away from the table.

"David, where are you going?" Barney asks.

"Out."

"Why?"

Because I can't stand being with you right now, is what I want to tell her. Instead I clamp my teeth and hold back the thought until I'm far enough away and can scream my rage in peace.

The first thing I see when I step past the metal detectors and out the front door of the school is Yolanda. Her hands are shoved deep in her coat pockets and she's staring at the sky. Although I try being silent, she must hear me because she says, "Go away, David."

I ask the same question I asked my sister. "What's wrong?"

"Why do you care? You're a guy."

"Is that a sin?"

That makes her turn to face me. The tight look she displayed to Barney is missing. "Nothing's wrong. It's just...sometimes I feel so tired."

Be tired of Malik.

"You could try something new," I say.

Something electrifies the space between us and I swear her eyes grow darker. My breath catches in my throat.

"I don't think so," she says. "Like my grandmother used to say, you're better off with the devil you know. Right, Barney?"

When I turn, I find my sister standing behind me. Her eyes are just as dark as Yolanda's.

The two girls stare at each other. Something's happening between them, as silent messages rush past me, leaving me feeling like a blind man at a deaf convention because I have no clue.

Their stare-a-thon lasts long enough for Yolanda to take three deep breaths. Then she nods. "I may steal, but I don't poach."

Meaning there's a girl code and I just witnessed its power. Maybe it's a good thing Barney's pretending to be my girlfriend. Keeps me from doing something totally stupid, like grabbing Yolanda and holding her to keep her from leaving.

CHAPTER 18

Farrington's basketball team played its second game on Saturday, the last one before I'm one of them. They lost again, too, this time by a whopping twenty-four points, and I refused to watch. Now I'm standing in Kasili's office, about to join them. He should be smiling—he won the battle—I'm here.

Instead he has dark circles under his eyes. I've seen them on Mom and on my aunt. There's no reason for him to be tired or worried. This school and this team can't mean that much to him.

"The kids out there are inexperienced," he tells me. "I don't expect miracles, but they need something after two bad losses. They feel like they're letting the whole school down."

"You're the shrink. Teach them to live with disappointment."

"I'm the *coach*. I'd rather teach them what winning feels like."

A surge of agreement roars through my body, surprising me as it energizes. I guess I've been at this school too long. Somehow I'm feeling a part of things.

He rises from his chair. "Suit up."

"What about Malik?" Does the dingus know I'm coming? Kasili frowns. "I need you two to overcome your differences."

Malik stays away from Barney and I stay away from him. End of difference.

And Yolanda?

I turn toward the office door, pause and force myself to speak. "My aunt signed the name change papers. Am I supposed to thank you or something?"

Coach nods like he's pretending nothing matters. "Being that it's you...no. You got what you wanted, and I had my own reasons for talking with your aunt. Someday you'll realize in the grand scheme of things, Shakespeare was right about roses and names. But for now, I agree. You need to be Albacore."

Shakespeare my ass. Names matter. I ask him, "Which would you rather see on the menu, blue cheese or sour milk laced with gross-out mold?"

He shudders. "Neither. They taste the same—shitty. Now get dressed and out on the floor. You, David, are going to oil my rusty machine."

Grunts, yells and the sound of dribbling balls and running feet greet me when I leave the locker room and head for the gym. This isn't the playground, it's for real. I stand at the door and watch the scrimmage. The guys look as tight as they do during games. Just as scared of the ball, too. Kasili glances up and gives me a raised eyebrow. As I watch from the sidelines, Julian runs for the ball, dribbles two feet and then throws a pass that slips through Malik's fingers.

"Asswipe." Malik sneers, then jumps, waves his arms and yells like a rodeo clown taunting a bull. "If we had any *real* players you'd have bench blisters on your ass."

"Real players know the receiver uses his head and his hands to catch the damn ball," I say.

Heads turn and jaws drop as I cross the court. *Don't blame me*, I almost say, *this is all Kasili's idea.*

"Let's give your new teammate a warm welcome," Kasili says.

So that's what a psychology degree gets you? Maybe he expects those pitiful words to work, but I don't, so I'm not disappointed when everyone remains silent. All I hear is the sound of one guy palming the ball against the hardwood like a fifth grader. At least Julian grins like he's happy to see me.

"So fish-face plays roundball," one of the guards says.

Even Malik scowls at the speaker, who ducks his head and takes two steps backward.

"We don't need another scrub," Malik says as he turns back to me.

"David's no scrub," Julian says. "He's good, you'll see."

"Why's he even here?" Malik continues. Without warning, he snatches the ball from the dribbling kid and jets it toward my head. As the ball zips through the air my arms tense and fingertips tingle in anticipation, eager to feel the rough leather surface.

I catch the ball one handed. The weight is familiar, the dribbling, natural. The sound of the ball striking the floor is as well-known as my own heartbeat.

Everything comes back to me.

Pivot. Shoot.

Everything.

As the ball leaves my fingers I feel the perfect connection between me and the basket. I don't need to look. I just know. The ball sails through the net with only the softest swish, audible only because everyone on the floor has gone quiet.

"Sweet," the coach yells. White teeth gleam in his face as he laughs. "Can't help it, I'm old school."

Standing beside Malik, I hold myself as tall as possible. Petty, but it feels good. If he wants to engage in dick measuring, he'll discover I top him there, too. And I don't leave *my* women bruised or bloody.

The problems I saw from the stands are more obvious at ground level. A lot of these guys know they'd never have made the team under normal circumstances and they're unsure of themselves. And way too used to looking to Malik for direction. Back at Grogan Hills, Coach Anderson believed in finesse, precision plays, timing and fast moves. Maybe Kasili would have done the same thing if he had experienced players. With this group, their only chance is the grinding, no-nonsense style he's teaching them. Nothing fancy—just drive for the basket.

Malik throws an elbow at me that Kasili doesn't see. It's always that way. Coaches and officials never see the blow that starts things, only the retaliation. Unless you're smart.

I'm smart. And I never forget.

Ten minutes later, I flatten Malik with my forearm, all behind Kasili's back.

Oh yeah, I love this game.

CHAPTER 19

Tuesday is another one of those cold, gray days when the alarm clock is my deadly enemy. Rain pours through the air in sheets that should make me glad to be indoors. Problem is, I'm stuck having my first meeting with a new shrink in the therapy part of Kasili's deal package.

I'd rather be in the bottom level of hell than this office. Bad enough I'll have to sit in this windowless room once a week with this woman they've stuck me with, until the end of the school year. Worse is knowing that sooner or later, someone will see me coming or going. Then it'll be all over school that Albacore's a crazy loon.

Now, I expected an old therapist with gray hair in a bun, thick glasses and bad breath, but instead I got this hot brunette in a blue dress that matches her eyes. Wonder if Kasili put us together because he thought Miss Could've-Been-A-Model would distract me enough to make me talk. He doesn't know that when I compare her to Yolanda, she doesn't measure up.

If this shrink says, "Tell me about your mother," I swear I'll walk out right now and take the consequences.

162

What does she want to hear? That Mom was beautiful and strong? That she was more than my dad deserved? More than I deserved?

"Let's talk about why you're here," she says.

I shrug. "I've got a temper. Big fat hairy deal."

"What's going on in your life right now?"

"You mean, other than being forced to waste an hour of my life in this place? Nothing much."

Do I really have to put up with this chitchat crap every freaking week?

When will that bell ring?

◆

It's fourth period at last, and there's no place I'd rather be than here at our table. Well, maybe one, as long as Yolanda could be with me in my closet of a room at home. Here in the back of the library, it's quiet and I finally have a chance to get to know her. As I stare, I see that makeup covers the last traces of her bruise and she's wearing a necklace that reflects the light into my eyes with every breath. Her gold hoop earrings fall against the curves of her cheeks, and a bunch of bracelets dangle from her wrist. I wonder which one was the I'm-sorry-I-smacked-the-shit-out-of-you gift from Malik? The necklace? The earrings and bracelet, or all of it?

She's smiling and looks almost carefree, but I've seen that pretend smile before. Mom smiled that same kind of smile every time she forgave Antwon.

"Earth to David! Where *are* you?" Yolanda looks annoyed and I guess I missed something.

"Right here. Don't pretend you're blind." *What's wrong with me? Why did I say that?*

"Did you at least read the book?"

I don't need a book, they don't give real answers. I'm supposed to be in favor of marriage. Just another sign of how useless school can be. I've got eyes. I've seen how bad marriage is for women. Guys who have any sense will run away from the altar, too.

"Why don't you just explain why girls want to tie themselves to a guy?" I say to her. But *How tight are you tied to Malik?* is what I want to know.

For some reason, that question makes her hands tremble. "People don't want to be alone. Having no one is the worst."

"Guess battered wives oughta feel lucky to have husbands?"

"Don't be stupid. The right man, one who'll give anything for the woman he loves—"

"Dream on." *Anything?*

"When two people care about each other, they want to be close."

"Fairy tale."

She sighs. "We're never going to agree, are we?"

I'm so afraid she's right. "Never."

"Don't you believe in love?" she asks. It's like she's trying to make me believe that she believes in it herself.

"It's just a fantasy," I tell her. A stiff willie's a stiff willie, nothing more than that. Right about now, mine's full of quick drying cement. "This isn't about love," I say. "'Sides, aren't you supposed to argue the opposition's part?"

164

She gives me a look from the corner of her eyes as if she's checking to see if I'm mad. "It's a joint assignment. I'm free to look at all sides of the question."

"Not a lot of sides, it's a simple question. What do women get from marriage? Besides the obvious?"

"The obvious?" For a second something hard and cold flares in her eyes. "Since you don't believe in love, I guess you must mean regular sex?"

"I mean the guy's wallet."

"It's the twenty-first century, David. Women can take care of themselves. It's all about finding the right person."

"How do girls know? When they've found the right man, I mean."

I don't know what made me ask that. I just pray she answers.

She bends forward a bit and clasps her hands together, like a kid who's saying grace. "Mostly we hope a guy picks us."

What if I just say, Tag, you're it? If I open my heart and ask her to take it—and she runs and tells Malik what a fucktard I am.

"Like I said, it's a fairy tale. Waiting for some loony prince to wander into Chicago's south side. What if he's no prince? Just some ordinary nobody?"

Her fingers tighten on the edge of the table. "When you have no one, you make do with the frogs and the snakes and the spiders."

It's hard to breathe through the band that's tightening around my chest. Was I the snake or— "If there were, if someone wanted to be with you—"

"Are you offering yourself to me, Mr. Albacore? Barney not enough for you?" Something cold fills her voice and she looks at me like she's looking at a roach.

◆

It's almost midnight when I get back from work and I'm ready to drop.

Barney's still awake. She comes to the door in her faded yellow flannel pajamas, looking like a grown-up girl with a little one's sad eyes.

"I didn't mean to make you mad," she says. "I shouldn't have said those things to you. It's just—at first I wanted Yolanda to be my friend. Then she showed me what a horrid person she was, and I can't help how I feel about her now."

"Nobody blames you." Barney's noisy, bratty, always-in-the-way, and I can't imagine life without her.

She needs someone she can talk to. There's Kasili, but is he going to be there when she just needs a hug? To talk about her problems with boys? Or how much she misses how life used to be? My sister deserves someone who understands the things that go on inside a girl's head. I can be her big brother, but it takes a girl to be what she needs most right now—a best girlfriend. Girls don't do well without them.

But she's stuck with me so I have to do my best. My dirt and fatigue don't matter. We head into the kitchen and I pour two glasses of milk for me and my best buddy while she talks.

"I guess I understand. Renata told me how boys like bad girls, and Yolanda has it all. She's always happy and she has the best clothes, the best guy, the best everything. Everyone looks up to her and wants to be just like her. So when she became my friend, I was so happy. I wanted to be like her, and I really, really thought she liked me. We talked and laughed, and I thought the others were wrong about her."

"I know. I was worried about you and her."

"You don't need to be. I'm not really like her at all. I've never stolen anything. You do believe that?"

"I know you wouldn't." Then I take a deep breath before going on. "Maybe Yolanda didn't either."

"Renata says she's guilty as sin and just too smart to get caught."

"What do *you* say?"

She stares at the wall for a few seconds, then shrugs. "That I guess I'm really dumb. 'Cause I still want her to like me."

We have way too much in common, Barney and me.

"Renata's right about one thing," Barney goes on. "Malik's too good for her. If he leaves her, when he leaves her, maybe he and I could—"

Barney and Malik Kaplan?

"No!"

"But think. The two of you could become friends."

"No way," I tell my sister. Malik and I will never be anything remotely resembling friends. I know too much about guys like him. I should—I used to be one of them.

At Grogan Hills, I was the man. Guys wanted to hang

with me and be just like me. When I was there, I'd have mocked guys like Neill and the other kids at our table—if I even noticed them.

Girls threw themselves at me at my old school. They were pawns, like Tamika Baker, the shy girl I stole from the chess nerd on a dare. That was seven months ago—plus thirty miles, one divorce, a murder and a lifetime. Things that were once so all-important, like having a harem, winning the game, and being number one don't even count anymore.

It's funny how I see the same face in the mirror every day, shave the same chin, even say the same things. But no way am I the same guy. And it's not just the different last names. Broken eggs aren't the only things that can't be put back together again. People break, too.

Once I let a game become more important than the people who depended on me. I can't let that happen ever again. Certainly not over a girl. Not even if she might be *The One*.

◆

Things look like they're back to normal the next day. Yolanda's back in study hall, and back to being groped by Malik. Just as well, I guess. My list of worries is a mile-long already, without adding on The Dare.

Still, I grab her arm at the end of the day as we're leaving Marriage and Family—just to be sure she's all right.

"Don't worry," she says. "I'm working on the stupid report."

"But how are you doing?" I ask.

"Who cares? I'm a thief, remember?"

I hear myself say "No, you're not."

She looks as surprised as I am. I didn't expect to say that right here, or now. But I realize how much I believe it.

"I know you're not a thief," I say.

"Everyone knows I'm guilty," says The Dare.

"I'm not everyone."

This look comes into her rainbow-flaked eyes, like she's found that pot of gold.

But then she says, "You better think again—about your precious Barney. You were right keeping her away from me. I'm much too dangerous."

CHAPTER 20

After spending Saturday at the construction site doing masonry, a job I swear Sanderson put me on as punishment, I'm looking forward to my day of rest. And so are my shoulders and back. But my aunt has other ideas.

She has me spend the day helping her fill a box with crap she no longer wants. Me, I believe junk should be left for the garbage man to chuck. But she wants to donate the stuff to that church of hers for its once-a-year rummage sale.

I'm thinking about tossing in that PlayStation I so regret buying Linda, and Barney throws in the scarf and other gifts from Yolanda. She's doing what I can't do—she's throwing that girl out of her life.

"Now we just need to get this over to the church," Aunt Edie says. Meaning she wants one of us to cart the box of junk over to the place. I haven't been inside a church since Mom's funeral, and Aunt Edie's giving me her devil's-gonna-get-you look but I don't say a word. Then she turns to Barney. "Could you take this to the church for me, honey?" I'm not surprised when my sister turns up her nose and whines, "Do I have to?"

In the end I volunteer, which is probably what my aunt wanted all along. So why go through the pretense of asking? I'd really like to just lie in bed and rest, but can't take a chance denying our *beloved* aunt. I'm tired, it's cold, and I have to fight the urge to let out a whine myself as I pull on last year's winter jacket and head for the church.

The brick building housing the Heavenly Wind AME church is barely a tenth the size of the awful place our mother used to drag us to every Sunday. I suspect if my aunt actually walked through that church door, she'd be handed a visitor's badge or get the same raised eyebrows they give me when I walk in carrying our box. The large man who stands at the door looks tired, and I can't understand why he'd want to be in a church on a Sunday afternoon any more than I do.

"Delivery," I say, and he frowns.

"Now? We're having our service," he says.

"If you want me to just toss this, I'm game,"

He's not, and points me towards a set of stairs leading down to the basement. Then he says, "Quiet now, we're in the middle of the reverend's sermon."

So I hear. The minister has a voice that carries, and he's deep into hellfire and brimstone. Preaching fear the devil or face the wages of sin, or some other such thing. Almost every step I take is followed by someone screaming "Amen."

Mom's church had a gentler approach. But now, nothing could make me sit through a church service ever again. I was forced to sit in a pew every Sunday as a kid, wearing a shirt and tie, with my hands crossed in my lap. I didn't want to be there, listening to the minister, the choir or those people who jumped up to tell how they were saved, while I was just praying it would end so I could get outside. Barney never seemed to mind, but I always felt like I was sitting on a nest of fire ants. I can still hear Mom's orders clear as day: "Don't fidget, David. It's the word of God."

Mom was the one who believed. While Antwon buried his head in his pillow every Sunday, she had the three of us up early to make sure we got to church on time. She filled the whole house with smells so good, I only pretended I didn't want to get up. She knew the smell of fresh baked cookies or pies could get me to do whatever she wanted and took full advantage of it.

And that's how I remember her—happy to stay home. She was willing to go out and face the work world when she had to, but always made time for us, no matter how tired she was. Mom was always finding excuses to touch me—my arm or my hair. I started to be embarrassed as I got older and told her to stop. I forgot to tell her how much I really loved it, despite what I said.

I'm sorry I never got to tell her how proud of her I was, proud that she broke free of Antwon. Proud that she was *my* mother.

I'm not a believer myself. I mean, what kind of God would let something so terrible happen to her? No, I have no use for any of this.

The sounds of the sermon chase after me until I'm safely down in the basement. I place my aunt's box on a table as directed and see that the table is already filled with other assorted boxes, and bags, whose contents I don't want to know about.

One thing I don't need to guess at—there's a kitchen down here and someone's baked fresh cookies. The aroma of chocolate chips floats in the air with the voices of little kids. But it's another voice that tickles my skin and that voice doesn't belong to a child.

I follow the sounds to an open door where I see ten or twelve little kids, some at a table and others playing with blocks and toys.

Running the show is a short older girl, dressed in a plain white blouse and long black skirt. It makes her look like an usher, this girl with the long, beautiful braids streaming down her back—Yolanda.

She's kneeling beside a pale-skinned little girl who is sitting on the floor and she's helping her dress a doll. A million tiny pins stick my skin as I watch Yolanda's slender fingers and red nails. Those elegant hands smooth the blue and gold dress on the doll's body and brush the doll's hair.

Even dressed in a plain outfit like she has on, Yolanda looks like a queen. Electricity flashes through me. I want to grab a trowel and bricks so I can build her the palace she deserves.

The little girl grabs the doll from Yolanda and gives it a big hug. Then she looks up at me and says, *"Mira!"*

Yolanda jumps to her feet and whirls. The smile on her lips fades, and just like that I feel worn out all over again.

"David. What are you doing here?" says The Dare.

The little girl runs to me and holds the doll out. She's saying something my two years of Spanish fail to translate.

"It's nice," I tell her, my eyes still riveted on Yolanda.

"Vaya tenga una galleta, Carmen." Yolanda puts her

173

hands on the girl's shoulders and turns her toward a table where a bunch of other kids sit having snacks. If I was one of them, would she put those hands on me?

"You don't belong here," she says

I'm being dismissed, but I can't leave. "What is this place?"

"The church nursery. We watch the kids while their parents go to the service."

"Aren't they supposed to be listening to God's word or something, too?"

"They're little, David. We talk to them, tell them stories, let them play. No one expects them to listen to Reverend Fair. Believe me, Sunday service is an all-day event with him. He'll be spouting the end of the world for another half hour, at least."

I look back at the faces of the kids in the room and ask, "No Jerry?"

"He's at home with his parents." She shrugs. "My foster family isn't big on church."

Yolanda comes here when she doesn't even have to? I have to ask: "Are you pretending you believe in God? Maybe expect him to send you a miracle or two?"

"Of course I believe in God," she says, her voice so like Mom's I swallow to push down the lump in my throat. "I just don't believe in miracles," she adds.

"So why aren't you upstairs in a pew?"

Her lips twitch and she says, "I'm right where I want to be."

With a dozen kids, all younger than Linda? There's even a baby in a walker, and only two other women here to help watch them. Then a high-pitched shriek and the sound of a metal chair slamming the floor sends Yolanda running across the room, where two kids are tussling over some toy. The boy's grip on the head separates it from the body in the girl's hands, and she drops to the floor in tears with her half of the broken toy. The little boy tosses the useless head and turns away, but Yolanda takes his arm and pulls him back.

As she smoothes his curly blond hair, she says, "That's not how you should behave, Peter. Now apologize to Haley."

Oh yeah, that'll work. I wait for him to start yelling, but somehow her voice and gentleness coax a stumbling apology from the boy. Then Yolanda releases him and pulls the still crying Haley into her lap. She reaches for the girl's chin and says, "There. See, he's sorry, honey."

"He broke my doggie." Haley extends the toy to Yolanda. "Fix him."

Yolanda examines the head and body. "I don't think I can, sweetie. I'll get you a new toy."

"No! I want my doggie!"

Yolanda wraps her arms around Haley in an embrace so sweet, just watching it makes me catch my breath. As Haley continues crying, Yolanda looks as heartbroken as the little girl.

I kneel and take the head and body from Yolanda, and say, "Let me see."

She looks at me through lowered lashes, then asks, "Do you think you can do anything?"

I will. I have to.

The break isn't even, but I've dealt with worse disasters fixing toys for my little sisters. Five minutes, some superglue from the office and a little bit of duct tape later and I'm handing the toy to a still sniffling Haley.

"Just be careful. He's still hurt, so don't remove his bandage," I say as she grasps her repaired treasure. Yolanda looks pleased and I don't remember ever feeling this proud.

"How'd you do that?" Yolanda asks me as another helper takes the girl and her bandaged toy to join a group sitting on the rug.

"Not my first repair job. I have two sisters. Uh, real little sisters," I quickly add.

"No wonder you understand kids," she says.

What I don't understand is girls. Or why the queen of the school is down here on a Sunday afternoon in a church basement, handing out cookies to a bunch of kids, or playing peacemaker. Who'd guess she lets her man walk all over her from watching this little scene.

"Don't I…get a reward? Or something?" I'm going for a kiss. Or maybe a caress from those graceful hands. I'll settle for just a smile, but what I get is a cookie. It's still warm and tastes good with the glass of milk she hands me after leading me to the table.

"You here every Sunday?" I ask as we sit down together.

"Yes. I love kids." Her face lights up as she speaks. It's the same glow I saw in them the first day at school.

"Does Malik come around? Does he help you out down here?"

The shiver runs through her so quickly I might have missed it if I'd blinked. "You can't expect Malik to have time for something like this."

"Because your man's so important?" Which makes her important, which shuts me out.

Her face tightens and I barely hear her voice as she says, "You need to stay away from Malik. Keep your girl away from him, too." Her lip curls as she speaks and I feel like she's torn through my flesh and muscle, ripping right through my heart.

Her true feelings show from behind the mask of pretend friendship. It'll be off with Barney's head, unless she keeps away from Yolanda's man. She'll protect her territory, no matter what. At least she wants what I want—Barney a safe distance from Malik.

There's no reason for her words to leave me feeling so empty. No reason at all.

Just then, a woman announces story time and the kids run to sit around her chair. Yolanda gets up and clears the table. While she's out of the room, I feel a tug on my leg. It's Carmen at my side, her smile is as bright as the gold fabric covering the tiny baby doll she holds. I've got no real idea what to do with kids, and just enough Spanish to realize she's asking for my name.

"David," I say, hoping she won't ask me anything else. While I look around for Yolanda, Carmen tugs at me again. This time she points to her own dress—it looks just like the clothes on her doll.

"*La Señorita hizo esta ropa para mí.*"

My brain struggles to translate. "Yolanda bought that dress for you?" She's really generous with her foster parents' money.

But Carmen's English is better than my Spanish and she shakes her head. "*No. Ella lo hizo.*"

While I'm wrestling with my mental dictionary, Yolanda comes back into the room.

She says, "*Carmencita, va a Lisa. Ella leerá el libro a ustedes,*" and points to the young woman reading to the kids at the other end of the room.

Hizo, comes from *hacer* meaning *to make.* Carmen runs off just as I finally have things figured out. "You made that? The kid's dress and the doll's?"

Yolanda shrugs. "She doesn't have a lot. Relax, I'm not about to lead that child down the path to ruin." Yolanda turns away but I grab her arm to keep her near.

"I didn't mean it that way. You must know that," I say.

She shrugs again, like it's no big deal. But I feel her arm relax.

Then I ask, "What else do you make?"

Yolanda tenses again and lowers her eyes. "I have to get back to the kids."

I look at her hands. Hands that can do so much. "You make your own clothes, too. Don't you?"

"No, of course not." Her voice is a husky murmur, and she looks so miserable that I know the truth.

"You do! Why'd you let me think you were a thief?"

Why make me hurt so much inside?

"Would it have made any difference?"

No, because my guts never believed you stole a thing.

"You should tell people the truth. Let them know what you can do. I've heard them talk. No one can tell the difference between a Yolanda Original and all that designer crap."

She has talents—makes beautiful things. I'd give anything to build something wonderful. To be able to say, *Hey World! Look, here's a genuine Albacore original.*

"You mean tell Barney and get laughed at?" Her lips form a tiny smile, but it quickly vanishes. "It's bad enough I'm a charity case, a girl with no family. You don't know what that's like."

What is life really like for girls? They seem to have it all, and a string of guys they control with a few smiles and hip switches. But they think dumb things like labels and makeup and clothes are what's really important.

My own shirts barely fit since my chest has grown so much from working in construction. Do I care? Hell no. And I don't care what Yolanda's wearing. I'd take her in rags.

"Clothes aren't important," I tell her. "Besides, you always look really…" Awesome, beautiful, the hottest girl ever.

"Let me guess, you'd prefer to see me naked."

Yeah, that would work, too.

"You prefer having people think you steal?" I ask her instead.

Yolanda just gives that little head shake and says. "People look up to me. And they judge me on how I look and dress. If people found out I wear homemade clothes, they'd laugh and wouldn't want to be around me."

"People? You mean that stupid clique you hang out with?" Girls who think the more lipstick stains they plant on Malik's dick, the higher their social standing? The same ones who've made stealing an art form, and think jail time's a badge of honor?

"They need to look up to see a snake's ass." I tell her. Probably not the smartest thing to say.

I realize a second too late that she could think I'm insulting her. The words hang in the air between us. I can't do anything to pull them back.

"You don't know how hard it is just to hold on and try to belong," she says.

"You're the queen at Farrington," I tell her.

"I'm only something because Malik is, and because he has eyes for me. He's the puppet master you talked about."

I wish I'd never said that. "So get yourself a different guy."

"I've *had* different guys. They're different, they're all the same. I guess I'll just stick with this one. Until he gets tired of me."

"How does anyone get tired of you?"

She hangs her head. "I guess it's not that hard. Even my parents did."

She blinks a couple of times and goes on. "Look, just don't tell anyone, okay? And I know I shouldn't keep asking you to hide the truth for me. You're so honest; keeping secrets like this must really bother you."

Honest? Me? Lying is the least of my sins.

If I spread the word, her friends drop her, Malik tosses her, and she's available to me. Then I can go after her. But then she's also miserable. And I can't have that.

"I won't say anything," I say.

"Not even to Barney?" Her bottom lip quivers.

"No. Not to anyone." She acts like she's more afraid of Barney finding out than any of her friends. But she pushed

Barney away, and deliberately turned my sister into an enemy. Suddenly I need to know why.

"What made you call her a giant, anyway?" I ask.

Her lips curl into a snarl. "That's what she is. Sorry if the truth hurts."

"That's not the reason you did it. Don't you lie to me."

She draws in a deep breath, tosses her head and laughs. "Shows how little you know. I truly hate that girl."

"Thank you," I say, grabbing her hand as she tries to walk around me.

She stumbles, saying, "What?"

"I *know* why you said it."

She doesn't look at me. "You don't know anything."

Maybe I don't, but I believe.

Before I leave the church, I fish out the scarf she gave my sister from our box of donations, then stuff that Yolanda Original into my pocket.

When I try telling Yolanda she looks nice at school the next day, all I earn is a frown. But this time I understand.

I spend the day watching the people around her. Nicole's dark, narrow eyes prove that Yolanda's right. Her "friends" are searching for weakness, making Yolanda a prisoner of her position on top of her throne. She's surrounded by jealous girls who'd gladly snatch away her place, the one she's fought so hard for.

And if there's one thing I understand, it's fighting to keep what's yours.

181

CHAPTER 21

Gameday. I step onto the court and my body knows practice time is over.

Muscles, get ready to make me fly. Where's that whistle?

No caged tiger was ever more ready for release. *How the hell did I ever give this up?*

My enemies stand before me, clad in green and white—sissy colors. My fingers itch for the ball. I'm ready for battle. *Blow the whistle, Ref.*

The opposing center eyes me. I won't pretend or smile. Sportsmanship? Mercy? Hell no! We're enemies.

He thinks he has a chance. He should just surrender now. That ball belongs to me.

It's mine.

Blow the whistle, Ref, or I'll blow it my own damned self.

That kid's not touching my ball.

Finally I hear the whistle. Time stops. The world narrows and there's only me, my opponent and the ball, flying into the air.

My legs are jet afterburners, defying the laws of gravity. I grab the ball and send it hurtling towards my teammate. Adrenaline burns my throat as I race for the basket, turning to wait for the pass.

Malik has the ball and he sees me. Then he shoots.

The defender's outstretched hands deflect the ball. Both teams turn and fly to the other basket.

By the time we're down ten to four—both baskets scored by Malik—I realize that nothing's changed. He made nice in practice, but today's real.

The other guys have also fallen back on their old bad habits and keep passing Malik the ball. They won't even let me touch it, except when I block a shot or grab a rebound. Malik has my teammates mounting a four-man offense and every bit of their confidence in practice the last few days is gone.

Here, with the heat and the lights, and the crush of bodies filling the stands, the noise of the shouts and boos of a game, the team's muscles are too tight, their wrists too rigid and they make one mistake after another. The other team notices and adjusts; they concentrate on Malik. And closing him down effectively shuts out our offense.

Coach returns my look with a raised eyebrow. I consider hoofing over to the bench, sitting down and letting him deal. But my sister's in the stands watching me play.

And Yolanda's watching, too.

The smile on Malik's face makes my decision easy. I have six enemies on this court. The next time Malik has the ball, I foul him.

The crowd falls silent, like no one's ever seen a man

foul his teammate before. The official clearly hasn't as he watches Malik hits the floor. The ref blows his whistle, then stands frowning, uncertain how to handle the situation. As the silence continues, the ball's fading bounces sound like boulders falling down a hill.

The officials run to where I stand over Malik's prone form. Kasili joins them as they try to decide how to handle the situation. Then Malik gets to his feet, ignoring my outstretched hand. Then he turns away. After a few minutes' deliberation, the refs shrug and resume play.

The other team scores.

Malik calls time when I flatten him again. This time, laughter runs through the stands and the officials just signal play on. By the time I amble over to the bench, Malik's roaring at Kasili, "Get him off the court."

That's no way to handle an old guy. Especially one already weary of you thinking you're the boss. Not even the spit spewing from Malik's mouth makes Kasili blink. "Albacore stays," is all he says.

"I'm the captain," says Malik.

"And I'm the coach. I set the lineup. He stays. Now if you want to take yourself out, feel free."

I have to admit I almost admire the man.

Malik growls. His hatred's real and I can almost see flames jumping from his eyes. And he doesn't take a seat.

Coach slaps his leg with the clipboard and turns to me. "Looks like you had a few accidents out there."

"Sorry, Coach. I was being ignored so much, I wasn't sure which team I was supposed to be playing for."

He smiles and says loudly, "I'm sure they'll *all* act like they're your teammates from now on."

Three heads nod.

Farrington's up by three points at halftime. Tyrone and the other band members move onto the court to play while we head for the lockers. As his saxophone blares through the closed door, the guys throw glances from Malik to Kasili to me. I can see they're happy—this is the first time we've had a half-time lead all season.

Kasili acts like everything's normal, pointing out weaknesses, making changes—typical half-time locker room stuff.

Malik drops into the seat beside me. "You superior bastard," he mutters when the coach moves to the other side of the room.

"Yes, I am." And I've enjoyed showing him why.

"Nothing changes between us," Malik snarls.

"That's right. Nothing," I say as my back tightens. I can almost feel the knife he aches to insert into me and twist.

As we leave the locker room, I grab Julian's arm to hold him back. "The tip," I say. "I'm sending the ball to you."

His face twists. "Uh...okay."

"You go straight for the basket and score."

He stumbles. I reach out and keep him from falling. These guys need to believe they're free to shoot and good enough to score. The first half was still all about me and Malik. Kasili's rah-rah words weren't enough to convince them of that fact. But I trust that Julian's basket will be.

"What if I miss?" he says as we jog onto the court.

"What if you don't? Look, Jules, you've got all the

skills you need. It's like the playground. Just don't get sloppy. Take your time, get in position. And make the damn basket!"

The other team has shifted their attention to concentrate on Malik and me. I'm betting their half-time pep-talk reinforced that. Julian's defensive man won't expect him to do anything but pass. Julian should be able to get the shot off before he can react.

Their center tries to take the ball away from me, but no way will I let him anywhere near my ball. Then it becomes Julian's ball. He turns and dribbles and my heart nearly stops. From just outside the three-point line he jumps and the defender is barely checking him. By the time he catches on to what Julian's pulled off, the ball arches through the air and swishes cleanly through the net.

"Everybody scores," I shout to my teammates as the crowd roars. "Everybody! And nobody passes to anyone else if you have a shot. Got it?"

Our opponent team, the Screaming Eagles, got sent home tonight by their prey, and they're screaming, all right—but in pain. We win, sixty-eight to fifty-nine. I walk off with eighteen points and the knowledge that my three-point shot remains just as sharp as ever.

Coach congratulates us. "Loved those snappy ball moves. You guys had more fire than I've ever seen in you before." The guys are jumping, laughing and high-fiving each other as students stream onto the court. Then he hustles us into the locker room.

Malik frowns. Like I care. Nothing quenches the fire in my guts—not his attitude or the shower.

The other guys dress quickly and Julian comes to my side. "After a game, we usually head to Frank's Place for hot dogs and cokes. Tonight'll be special. The owner promised the team free dogs if we ever won a game."

I pause from buttoning my shirt. Malik was in a big hurry and is already gone, but the rest of the guys are looking at me and I think they really want me to come. But the last thing I want is to sit in a crowd, eat a greasy hot dog and rehash the game. If I have to spend more time in Malik's presence, I'll puke.

So I beg off, saying, "I'd love to, but I gotta get home. Promise I'll go next time."

Julian nods but looks disappointed. As he picks up his gym bag and follows the others to the door, I call to him, "Hey, hotshot, twelve points. Nice work."

Teeth flash in a huge grin and he almost floats to the door. I haven't forgotten what it's like being an unsure new player. For a sophomore, Julian's great. Once he believes in himself, Kasili will have another leader on his hands.

Now I'm alone in the locker room and I take my time getting dressed. I've given Tyrone permission—make that an order—to walk Barney home, so there's no need to hurry. I'll have the walk home to wind down, and then it'll be off to the comfort of my own bed.

My steps echo in the darkened hallway. There's an old guy mopping the floors who salutes me as I pass. Pausing at the side door, I pull up the collar of my jacket. Temperatures drop fast this time of year, but the game's done such a job of pumping my adrenaline, I may not even need my coat.

Some kid—maybe nine or ten years old—and his dad are waiting just outside the door. They want my autograph. It's hard to tell which of them is more enthusiastic. Only a few people and cars are still hanging around outside in the parking lot. There's laughter and shouting, and someone's even setting off firecrackers. The smell of beer wafts through the air, proving again how little the principal knows about what happens on school grounds. There'll be more than a few hookups tonight and hangovers in school tomorrow.

I'm cutting through the parking lot when I hear Malik's voice: "You think I didn't see you in there?"

Great. Just great.

He's standing under a light beside his car, a few feet away. His form's unmistakable.

So is Yolanda's, and she says, "I'm just happy the team won."

"The team? Or Alba-fucking-core? I'm not blind, bitch."

"I don't need this," she says, then turns and takes two steps before he jumps in front of her.

"You been almost wetting yourself over that bastard since the day he showed his fish face in this school."

Can that be true?

"I just don't want to be with you anymore, Malik. It's got nothing to do with David."

"You don't drop *me*, bitch."

"Then just tell people it was your idea." Her voice sounds more resigned than defiant, like a prisoner facing a firing squad.

"Who the fuck said you could go? You're nothing. There's plenty who'd snap up your spot in a second."

"Then maybe you should grab a couple of them. Try that biatch Nicole. Bet she'd be happy scratching those crab-filled balls of yours."

Malik's jaw falls open, like he's hearing a corpse recite the Gettysburg Address. "Bitch, just get your ass in the fucking car."

A sour note fills my throat as I remember: the arguments, the fights. The angry voices coming through the door of my parents' bedroom. Those hate-filled words in low, grating tones, like a dull saw cutting through concrete. For months before Mom filed for divorce, it was all I could hear—nothing but sniping and anger. A domestic dispute between the school's royal couple isn't my business. But I can't move or even close my eyes. Not this time.

He's behind the wheel before he looks up and notices that Yolanda hasn't moved.

"Dammit, move your ass, bitch," he says.

She takes a step backward, shaking her head. "Not tonight. I don't want to be with you."

He jumps from the car and grabs her arms. "You don't want to? Nobody gives a flying fuck what you want." His fingers tighten on the sleeves of her jacket. I don't need to hear the hiss of her breath to know he's hurting her. Mascara-stained tears streak down her cheeks and make my blood boil.

"She said no, asshole," I growl.

Malik jerks around to look as I step into the brightness of the street light, then drops his hold and steps back.

"That's not how you treat a lady. Apologize."

"A lady? You mean that ho'?"

I grab him by the collar and lift him a few inches off the ground with just one hand. "Apologize for that, too."

"Fuck you."

I slam him back against the side of his car before leaning in close enough to smell his tobacco and alcohol and fear. "I've beaten the shit outta you twice already. You ready for a third round?"

Sheet metal groans and a grunt escapes his lips. Then he whispers, "I...I'm sorry."

"Can't hear you. Try saying it again—louder."

"I'm sorry."

"I'm sorry, Miss Dare."

"I'm—I'm sorry, *Miss* Dare."

I release him and step backward. "Just you and your hand tonight, Malik. Give yourself a tug for me."

I'm waiting—hell, I'm begging—for him to try something, anything, so I can pound him into a pulp. But even his thick, caveman skull still contains a few working brain cells.

Our eyes remain locked as he rounds the car and scrambles into the driver's seat. As he steers the car toward the road, he rolls down his window and yells, "You want the worthless ho'? I was getting tired of her anyway. You can have her, Fish Face. We're through, bitch. I'm dropping you back into that sewer I pulled you from."

Brakes squeal and the smell of burning rubber fills the air as he peels out of the parking lot, narrowly missing an old Chevy parked between him and the gate.

Obviously, my brain cells are the ones missing because I expect a little gratitude when I turn to Yolanda. But she's standing there with her arms crossed over her chest, head high, eyes pure steel, proclaiming nothing's wrong, even though her quivering chin says the opposite. Then her tongue spits fire.

"How dare you?" she says.

"I was just trying to help."

"That was a private conversation. I didn't need your help."

Yolanda's sunk her teeth in me and it hurts.

"You're always getting in my business, David. I never asked you to interfere with Malik and my problems." Her breath makes clouds in the cold air. "I suppose you expect me to demonstrate my gratitude now, right? You want it here, or are you taking me back to your crib to be paid for 'rescuing' me?"

The thought of me and Yolanda together in my broom closet bedroom makes me a little dizzy. "I...I..."

"I, I, what?" Her voice is getting shrill.

"Nothing. That's not why—not what I want—" The words tremble on my lips.

But I do want her. Right here and now, or anywhere else I could get her. But I do what any smart guy does when faced with a rabid girl. I lie.

"There's nothing I want from you."

CHAPTER 22

Because I have to follow Yolanda—at a distance—to make sure she gets home safely, I don't reach my aunt's apartment until late. Feelings that haven't flared since before I lost my virginity return to me in a rush.

Why'd God invent women, anyway? Why give them so much control over a man's body and his mind? Not even a cold shower keeps unfulfilled dreams from punishing me through the night.

The next morning at school, people who've never spoken to me before make a point to cross my path when I walk through the halls. They all want to pat me on the back or shake my hand. I'll never let on that I'm only on the team due to blackmail by Kasili. And I've got to admit that I've missed the perks of being the team's high scorer. Girls stop and talk, even Nicole manages to brush her thigh against mine. Students applaud as I head into my classes and even the Lit teacher shakes my hand.

Then Yolanda stalks in and the class becomes a nightmare. She goes out of her way to get to her seat just to avoid passing in front of me. And every time I look around at her, she's staring right through me as if I'm not even here.

I can't remember anything about Hamlet, can't answer the teacher's questions and I don't even care. I'm way too focused on Yolanda and every time she moves. I bet if I turn around to look, she'll be licking those glistening lips. Although my eyes are staring straight ahead, the thought of those lips make me so hot for her, I'm left squirming in my seat and praying for the bell to ring so I can find some relief.

I don't have to worry about facing her—once that bell rings, she's flying out of her seat.

"Nice going last night," Neill says, as he gets between me and the door just as Yolanda rushes out. "Let me touch you, my man," he continues.

My lips tighten in frustration as I lose sight of Yolanda, who disappears into the crowded hall.

When I turn to him, Neill jumps. "Sorry. I wasn't trying anything funny with you."

"I know. I'm not mad at you," I tell him.

He glances at Yolanda's empty seat, then looks back at my face. As we walk down the hall, he says the one thing I'm most afraid of: "Some things just aren't meant to be."

Yolanda and me—never gonna happen. She'll patch things up with Malik—probably already has. Being the school queen is too important to her—she won't give it up that easily. I'll spend the rest of the year on the outside looking in, watching them showing off to the whole school. I'll always be shut out of what I want, and what I want is her.

Fourth period and she doesn't show in study hall. I'm not sure why I head to the cafeteria when the fifth-period bell rings, and I don't check out Malik's elite table until I'm settled beside Barney.

Yolanda's not there. But Malik is, with his arms around two new girls—who take turns feeding him his lunch.

Carl points to Malik with his chin. "Guess the rumor's true."

"Rumor?" Barney's lips twist as she says it and I'm grateful not to have to ask that question.

"The Golden Couple isn't, anymore."

Bad-to-the-bone Malik grins and his girls laugh like he's Ludacris or something.

"What's he see in those two?" Barney huffs as she shifts in her seat, looking like a snarling lioness.

"His latest worshipers," I reply. They were selected to make Yolanda jealous enough to come crawling back.

She was right to be mad at me for getting involved. I made her lose her spot as school queen. She could've handled Malik fine without me. They'd probably have made up by now. All I've done is damage her. Maybe I should apologize to Malik, help her get back to being queen.

I hate doing the right thing. Not that a girl like Yolanda won't pick up someone else right away. Maybe she's already found herself another top dog and maybe this one'll treat her right.

"By the way, we're back together again," Barney says, nudging me and leaning close.

I nearly choke on a bite from my dry sandwich and force it down with a gulp of milk. "We are?" I gasp when I can breathe again.

"Aren't you glad?" she teases.

"Fine. And okay, I'm glad."

"Wanna know why? 'Cause you're in charge now," she continues. "You're bigger than Malik."

Big whoop. I was born bigger than Malik.

Barney waves her fork in the air. "Bigger than—Oh my God."

Silence blankets the table, and everyone's staring at me. Or rather, at the space by my left shoulder.

"The world ended and they forgot to tell us," Neill says. There's awe in his face, but not worry.

Still, I'm unprepared when I turn around, because it's Yolanda Dare who's standing behind me.

There is a God.

"What the hell's The Dare doing here?" Renata asks in a phony whisper. Tyrone's looking at Barney like a guard dog waiting to be told to attack. But Barney just stares silently at Yolanda.

I jump to my feet. But only as I stare down at Yolanda do I realize my sudden move could scare her off. Her head's high and she's defiant, yet I can see she's trembling, as if she expects me to slap her—as if she's preparing to get hurt. Doesn't she see how she makes me feel?

"If you all don't mind…could I sit here?" She looks and sounds like my Linda pleading for some forbidden treat.

I don't know what to say, and as the silence lengthens, I glance at Malik's side of the room. He's standing next to the table, and the look on his face could separate the stink from a wino. His hands curl into fists, but he won't do anything. He's all bark and no bite, the loud and arrogant type with nothing to back it up. Malik says something that makes the other guys laugh before falling back into his chair.

Yolanda frowns and looks down at her tray. "Guess not, then. I'll sit somewhere else. Sorry I bothered you."

As she turns away, Neill gets up, too. "You can stay, I don't mind." Then he throws a glance at me.

I can't let Yolanda leave. I take her tray and set it on the table. As I pull back a chair for her, she sighs, as if she'd been too scared to breathe up until now.

"This is social suicide," I whisper in her ear as she sits down.

The half dozen bracelets on her right arm jingle as she moves, just like the beads tinkling at the ends of the micro-braids hanging down her back. She stares into my eyes and says, "This is where I want to be."

I so regret letting Barney reclaim me as her boyfriend.

The material of Yolanda's blouse is so light and thin, it flutters every time she breathes, teasing her breasts. Teasing me.

One by one, the others finish eating and drift away. Neither Yolanda nor I say anything else until the bell rings. Barney's the last to leave, and only goes after throwing a frown and a glare in my direction.

I stand and pick up Yolanda's tray, then say, "Tomorrow. Fourth period, the library."

She goes stiff and her eyes narrow and she's not understanding

"The report, remember?" I say.

PULL

Yoyo Dare, the girl I once called a puppet, stares at me for a long time. Then she nods and says, "Tomorrow." Then she walks away. The only string being pulled is mine.

CHAPTER 23

As the assistant coach lines up the team for drills, Kasili pulls me into his office. He takes his seat, strokes his chin and then sighs. I recognize the act designed to calm his patients. The man forgets he's not my therapist.

"Interesting game last night—one that'll figure in my memoirs." He drums his fingers on the desk.

I shrug. The team finally got a win, so why's he bitching?

"What do you want from me?" I ask. If he wants to talk strategy, I'm his man. If he wants inside my head, he can kiss my ass.

"What I want is for you to understand that you're not responsible for everything. I'm still not sure I did the right thing letting you foul Malik that way." He sighs again, the long suffering kind of sigh that parents use when they're upset with their kids.

"*You* weren't doing anything."

"I expected you to shake things up. Just something...smoother." He wants smooth? There's a 7-Eleven down the street. He can pick up any flavor smoothie he likes.

"You need sand."

He sits up in his chair and blinks. "Pardon me?"

"You need sand, not oil for this machine. I'm the sand that's messing up the works."

Kasili chuckles. "Maybe so. At least it worked. But, David, you and Malik need to settle things. Bury your differences."

Getting old must mean you forget what real life is like. 'Cause he might as well have said we should bury the hatchet. Nothing less will end what's between me and Malik. We're two dogs fighting over the same bone. The struggle won't end until one of us lets go. And it isn't going to be me.

◆

Yolanda meets me in the library the next day as planned. She puts her books on the table, says my name and I shiver.

"What's wrong?" she asks.

"I'm sorry you're not top of the school anymore. I shouldn't have interfered."

She closes her mouth and her eyes narrow into that look girls get when they want you to back the hell off.

I need to be smart now and keep quiet. But I've been pretty dumb lately.

"If you want, I'll talk to Malik. I could—apologize."

Her head jerks up. "You do and I'll smack you. Malik doesn't matter. I'll find a new man soon."

"Oh." A knot fills my throat. I sit and open a book, but

the words jumble on the page in an unreadable pile. "Who?"

Her head's bent over her papers. "I'll know him when I find him. He'll have everything, be the perfect man."

I think of things girls say they want from guys. "Someone understanding?" Another word for sissy.

She nods. The papers rustle in her hands.

"Caring?" Meaning he'll let a girl stomp up and down his back.

Another nod.

"Sensitive?" Cries at the chick flicks. Lies as necessary, so she can pretend he's not a playa.

They're all things I can never be.

Yolanda reaches for her pen. Instead, she sends it rolling across the table. I trap the pen and put it back beside her trembling hand.

"Add in smart and strong, and super good looking— and that's you," she says.

Her voice is so soft I can barely hear her and need a few seconds to realize she actually means me. Now my hand shakes, too.

"What do you want from me?" I ask.

"Nothing more than you want to give," she whispers.

Then she's in my arms. I don't know if I went to her or she came to me. Doesn't matter. We're together and I want her. I need to kiss her. With my fingers entangled among her velvet braids, I tilt her head up and our lips meet.

Mine.

She's soft. The promise of a new year and a future, and all this warmth floods through me. No other girl has ever made me feel like this. I'm ready to make a big-assed public display of my love right here in the library stacks.

Frantic hands push at my chest as she twists away from my arms. As I release her, she stumbles back against the desk and a boom sounds as one of the heavy books falls over the edge and hits the floor. Something squeezes my chest as she runs the back of her hand across her mouth as if erasing the feel of my lips. The electricity between us remains in the air.

"Yolanda."

"*Don't* you touch me. Don't ever do that again!" She's shaking with anger as she says, "I don't want you. God, I shouldn't have come here."

With trembling hands, she gathers her books and papers together.

I want to pull her back and kiss her again. That feeling wasn't something I imagined. But when I grab her arm, she just freezes.

"Don't, David—I didn't know you were like this."

I won't hold her against her will. "Don't you like me? Even a little?" I sound like a whiny girl, and if she turns and laughs at me, I don't think even the Grand Canyon's a big enough hole to crawl into.

"I *can't* like you."

Can't? My sin must be written on my face. I kneel to pick up the fallen book and she's crying when I hand it back to her.

"At first…I was going to get you," she says. "I knew I could so totally take you in. But she's so sweet and nice, and she wanted to be my friend. I mean a real friend—not just pretending and waiting for a chance to tear me down. She really likes you and she's always saying how wonderful you are. And I can't betray her, even though she hates me now."

"Who?"

Her brow furrows into such a confused expression it makes me want to kiss her again. "And here I thought Barney was lucky. Men! Maybe you *are* all the same."

When did my sister enter this conversation? "You're angry because I want you for my girl?"

An exasperated shriek fills my ears. "What about the girl you already *have*? Barney adores you!"

I laugh and pull Yolanda against my chest. This time when she tries to pull free, I tighten my arms even more.

"Didn't you hear me? I said I can't betray—"

"My sister."

She's speechless for a moment. Then says, "Your...sister?"

The second kiss beats hell out of the first.

"You're lying," she says when our lips separate. "How can she be your sister?"

"Usual way—same parents." I swear this is the last time I'll ever claim Antwon Murhaselt.

She sniffles as she stares into my eyes. "I suppose...you do kind of look alike."

I look like Antwon. Barney could be Mom's twin.

"You pretended to be your sister's boyfriend?"

I see I'll have to fill her in. "It's the guy code. If she's my sister, my friends can nail her even if I beat the shit outta them. As my girlfriend, she's untouchable—unless she comes on to them."

"And that worked?" Yolanda sounds more amused than angry.

"Well, for about a day," I admit. "Is this why you've been giving things to Barney? Because you thought she was my girlfriend?"

"She liked the scarf and the other things, and I just thought your girlfriend should dress better," Yolanda says. "I saw you with her, saw you so gentle and protective. You kissed her on the forehead, like she was the most precious thing in the world and I—I kinda hated her."

Yolanda was jealous? *Hot damn.*

"I mean, I knew I could so totally take you from her, and watching you be so nice made my insides melt. But I couldn't 'cause that would hurt Barney, and I knew she was number one in your heart, so—"

I have to do a public display of affection, just one more time.

I shouldn't feel guilty. I have every right to Yolanda. But that frown on Barney's face when she sees us walk into the lunchroom together tells me I'd better explain things to her—now.

After helping Yolanda to a seat, I lean over Barney's shoulder and whisper, "We have to talk."

She turns to Renata, acting like she didn't hear me.

"Barney," I say.

A heavy sigh and a long-suffering, "What?" is her reply.

"We need to talk."

"That's how it begins." Renata's whisper in Barney's ear is loud enough for me to hear, and probably the entire room, too. "Next he'll say it's him, not you."

My sister turns to me with narrowed eyes. "So talk, David."

"Can we just—go somewhere private?"

Another huge sigh, then she says, "Fine."

It's not fine, but it will be once I explain.

As she gets to her feet, Malik and one of his friends come towards us.

"Hey, teammate," Malik says. "Was that a great game or what?"

"Not now. I'm busy." Barney's gone stiff and there's a shine in her eyes I really don't like.

Malik leans on the table. He puts his elbow in Julian's face, as if Julian wasn't even there. "Me and the guys, we took a vote." His companion nods and grins.

When I say nothing, Barney asks, "A vote? About what?"

"You've been promoted, man. You get to come sit over at our table." Malik turns a toothy grin on Barney. "Bring along your girlfriend, too."

Barney's eyes widen and her smile fills her face. I don't dare look at Yolanda.

"I'm fine right here," I say. "You've got nothing I want."

Malik throws a glance at Barney. "You sure about that?"

"Positive."

His gaze moves over Yolanda. "Not everyone's happy with leftovers. But, it's your loss." His laugh echoes through the room as he and his friend head back to their seats.

Barney's hands shake. "Why, David? Don't you know what that would mean to me?"

I know how much she wants to be with the in-crowd. I also know it's not going to happen. "I'm not going over there."

"But I want to. You're my guy. You're supposed to think of me," she says as she moves around me to stand behind Yolanda's chair. "But then, I guess you're not still *my* guy, are you?"

"I said we have to talk." *Please, Barney, not here.*

"About you and The Dare? Oh my God, how could you?"

"He's a guy," Renata mutters.

"This doesn't concern you." I've had more than enough of her remarks about my girl.

"No, it affects me." Barney's neck's doing that snakey thing, like she really is my girlfriend. "You can't just dump me like this. Not here, in front of everyone. Don't you care about me at all?"

I can't say she's everything to me anymore. I can't, I won't give up Yolanda.

"Guess not," she says when I say nothing. "Just tell me one thing, David. Why her? Why Yolanda Dare?"

Because. She's beautiful. Smart. She likes me. And when I touch her, I want more. She makes me feel worthy. Her hands are soft, her eyes dark and...she listens to me.

"Because." I say. Barney turns and walks out of the lunchroom.

Stop her. Don't let her go, I tell myself. My body refuses to obey, and I drop back into my seat.

Barney's asleep when I get home. Or she's pretending—which is even worse.

CHAPTER 24

Sanderson sits at the worktable inside the construction trailer. He's pouring over a stack of papers as I clock in.

"Seems you and that punk team won a game," he says.

I wait to hear more.

Without raising his head he continues, "Get to work. I'm not paying you to play basketball."

Right.

"Eighteen points," he says as I turn to leave.

Eighteen points, eight rebounds and six blocks. But who's counting?

Apparently he is. "Plus eight rebounds and you blocked six shots." He still hasn't lifted his eyes from the papers, but I'll bet he's grinning. If I've pleased the man, I'm happy.

◆

We win our next two games. Even Malik's starting to relax.

Barney refuses to talk to me. The more I do, the less it

seems she understands, or cares. I've given up hoping for gratitude, or even respect.

"Hey, dawg, heard you're looking for work."

Malik laughs and moves closer to our table. "Dad says I can hire you. We need help back in the storeroom. You know, the kind of brainless shit any dodo with a strong back can handle. I'll be glad to show you the ropes."

"You told Malik I needed a job?" I say to my sister. Whatever's beginning between her and Malik has to be stopped, now, before she gets too far under his control. "Sharing my business with Malik Kaplan's no help," I tell her.

Barney won't meet my eyes. "You said you needed to find work. I'm trying to help. I know he likes me. He listens to me. Not like the shrinks who get paid so they *have* to listen. Not like you, too busy playing with The Dare to have any time for me anymore. You've been running around with that—"

"Don't say it."

"What I say or don't say doesn't change the facts. She pretended to be my friend, when all the time she was laughing at me, 'The Giant.' She was perfectly happy stealing the guy she thought was mine. What does that make her?"

"You're wrong. Yolanda wouldn't have anything to do with me until I told her you were my sister."

Barney's eyes widen. "You told her? So much for your identity being a secret. You let that witch worm herself under your skin."

"She's no witch. She likes you, Barney. She'd still like to be your friend."

My sister blinks and then draws in a deep breath. For a second I see my best buddy again. Then she laughs. But there's nothing funny in the sound. "She's got you fooled, David. You really think she's special? Just how often do you think about her?"

Every minute of every day. Every time my heart beats. Always.

◆

I don't want to enter the room, but the smell of gingerbread draws me to the kitchen where Mom's baking. Only, she's short and long, thin braids hang down her back. I touch her shoulder, and when she turns her head I see...Yolanda.

"David, David."

Yolanda's face hangs in the air before me, and I know I must still be dreaming. I take a deep breath of her perfume and close my eyes to try and return to the kitchen.

She shakes me again. "You have to wake up. The bell rang, lunch period's over."

"Lunch," I murmur. "Love gingerbread."

"Sixth period, David. You have to get up and get to class."

My eyes spring open. I've slept through study and lunch? I'd only planned to rest my eyes for a few minutes. "You shouldn't just let me sleep." She's already stacked our books. For the second time this week, I've slept instead of helping with our project.

"I know you needed the rest."

"I needed to work. The paper—"

"It's almost done." She sounds so reasonable. "Relax, we'll have it ready in a few days."

What am I contributing to this partnership? She even went out to take photographs of couples because I couldn't get away from the gym and work. "You're doing all the work—you're doing everything," I tell her.

"I'm fine with that," she says.

"But *I'm* not." Yes, I needed sleep. I don't get home until around midnight. Maybe the nap makes me feel better, but now I owe a huge debt to Yolanda.

As we join the people rushing through the halls during the all-too-short passing period I say, "I need to pay you back."

The eyebrow she lifts makes her even more appealing. "I'm pretty demanding," she says. "Sure you really want to do that?"

Oh hell. That look on her face spells danger. But I owe her. "Whatever you want."

"You make the presentation to the class." She turns and heads for the staircase.

That's no consequence. I've been trying to think of a way to get her to let me handle that for days. I run after her and grab her arm before she can start up the stairs.

"That's not payment. I wanted to make this presentation," I say.

"Then you're getting your wish. Now let me get to my class."

"But it isn't fair. That's not a consequence."

Her eyes narrow. "You think consequences have to hurt to be real?"

Well, duh. I nod.

She giggles. "Then I'll think of something painful. Now let me get to class before the teacher slaps *me* with a consequence." She pulls free, runs halfway up the stairs, then turns and winks.

During practice that evening Kasili calls me aside.

"It's come to my attention..." the man actually looks at a loss for words, "... that I'm working you too hard."

What's Malik been saying about me now? "I'm fine. I carry my weight."

"And then some. But classes, a job, practice and extra work with some of the team—don't think I haven't noticed."

I knew he did, but just didn't think he cared.

"That stops, now. You don't need the extra drills."

"The team's gonna resent me if I'm not drilling with them."

"I'll handle that," he says. "And one more thing. I've spoken to some of my contacts about you. We win a few more, I think they'll come take a good look at you. A scholarship's a possibility."

"Scholarship? You mean for college?" My heart pounds against my ribs. It's just what my mother wanted. Is it possible that even after everything I've done wrong, I can still live out her dream for me? But to me, the thought of college is like four more years of prison, just like high school has been.

"Absolutely. Especially if you keep your grades up, which won't happen without rest. This team's my responsibility, David. You don't have to take over for me. I'd sleep through classes myself if I had to carry your load."

"I don't sleep in class." *Thanks to Yolanda.*

"From now on, you leave immediately after practice ends. Use the time to rest. And spend some quality time with Barnetta."

Like she'll let me. My sister grows more sullen every day. In fact, I've barely seen her all week. "Why? What's wrong with her?"

The muscles on his face tighten. Yolanda would read his expression in a second. All I can tell is that whatever he's thinking, it isn't anything good.

"I can't talk about her," he says. "I have to keep confidentiality. Just keep a close eye on things at home. Your sister needs you."

CHAPTER 25

I'm still thinking about Kasili's words as my shift ends. The full moon, combined with the high-intensity security lights, leave the construction site almost as bright as noon when I finally clock out. The walls of the building I've spent hours working on loom over me as I stop in the doorway of the construction trailer. Like everything else here, that wall's almost done.

Sanderson looks me up and down and says, "Shift's over, David. Go home."

"Sometimes I feel like this *is* home."

He smiles and I know he accepts this as truth. "I know. Can't honestly say I'd be doing this job if they didn't pay me, but I'm damn glad they do. There's nothing else I'd rather do with my life."

"Me, too," I admit.

"Not everyone's cut out for this. The job's dirty, back-breaking and dangerous."

I know.

He's spent years mastering this trade through hard work and dedication. There's a lot of stereotypes about dumb tradesmen. A lot of people who don't know jack about men like Sanderson and the other people I've found here.

"Have you heard anything about other jobs?" I ask.

"Not much around here right now, David. I've asked around, but haven't yet found anyone looking for a part-timer."

That's no real surprise. This job was one in a million. Sanderson and I have a unique deal. Few jobs are big or urgent enough to need a second shift, and even fewer have bosses willing to bet on a kid. I'd lucked into heaven with this gig.

"Still, if you find out about anything..." I say.

"I'll let you know." He stubs out his cigar. "Oh, and I want to let you know, this is my last day."

A sinkhole opens under my feet. "I thought there was another month of nights."

"Yeah, and I'll be replaced here until things end. I found a spot leading a crew in Ohio. That job won't wait, so I have to jump now or lose it to the next guy. It's a long-term project—may last a year or so. And it's close enough so I can get back to my family on weekends."

Back to his family. That, I understand.

"I get to pick a team to come with me. There's even a spot for an apprentice. You got any interest in that?"

The opportunity to learn from the best and move down the road to mastery? *Oh, God, yes.* Escape Kaplan's Auto Body, and four years of college drudgery to work in the world I love? But reality forces me to say, "I can't. I have school." School, plus the guys on the basketball team who depend on me, my sisters who need me here with them, Yolanda. And not necessarily in that order. "I envy whoever you choose, and I wish I could go. But I can't."

Sanderson shrugs like he expected that answer, but hoped he'd be wrong. "Probably for the best. You go on the way you're going. Stay in school, get yourself that desk job. Soon you'll be on the top floor of some skyscraper, enjoying the good life."

A skyscraper built by someone else. At a desk in an office full of suits who laugh at men like Sanderson.

"I've let my replacement know the kind of work you do. And I'll keep looking around for something else you'd fit in with."

He doesn't say *don't hold your breath*. He doesn't need to. Then he shakes my hand.

"Good luck, David," he says. "It's been great having you on my team. No matter what, I still bet you'll be my boss someday."

Unfortunately, praise, no matter how warm it leaves my heart, won't buy food or pay the rent.

Or solve my problem with my sister.

I'm looking for a new job, working the old one, studying, and trying to figure out how to fit a real girlfriend into everything else. Not to mention keeping my sister as my friend.

Barney may need me, but she's less and less willing to talk to me. My full schedule means there aren't a lot of chances for us to be alone together. We don't walk home from school together anymore. She runs out of the apartment every morning while I'm still trying to get my tired body out of bed. She's asleep when I get back from work, and she's moved to sit closer to Renata and Francesca at lunch, which makes it even easier to ignore me.

But I'm not giving up. After setting my alarm early and forcing myself out of bed, I get ready and follow her when she walks out the door in the morning. I tell her, "We have to talk."

She just moves faster. And all she says is "No."

"Barney, you've got to understand—"

"No, I don't." Barney's really good at *no*.

She's no longer using her little girl backpack. I don't remember when that changed. I remind her: "You wanted us to stop pretending we were going together."

At least that makes her talk. She stops and plants her hands on her hips. "I never wanted to be humiliated. And Yolanda Dare! You know what she is."

"I want her."

"Well, you can't have us both."

"Barney, you'll always be my sister."

"Really? I'm still a Murhaselt. Do you even give a crap about me, now that you're so determined to be someone else?"

"Doesn't matter. Murhaselt or Albacore, I'm still your brother David."

Her nose goes up. "Just go, before someone sees us together. You don't want word getting back to The Dare that you're cheating on her."

She runs off for school, leaving me frozen in place. Mom once told me I'd make a great father. Then she added, "Sometimes what a girl needs most is her mother." Not sometimes. Barney and Linda need her all the time. And so do I.

Mom was wrong about me in another way, too. She thought I loved school, and that I was a good student. Math and I understand each other. Math's solid, tangible and predictable. And if you work hard enough, you can understand the rules. To me, every other subject is boring and confusing, if not downright impossible. Without my mom's constant push, I might have left school a lot sooner. I thought about leaving at seventeen, when I became old enough to opt out. And I could never confess to Mom how depressing I found the idea of struggling for four more years. Not when having me in college was so important to her.

She was always there to give me that extra push, just when I needed her. Right up to the end, she was thinking only about me. When I hurt my arm in that last game, she was right there at my side. She forced her way into the ambulance, held my hand and gave me that brave smile. At home, she sat beside the bed with me, not worrying about anything else. But I was thinking only about myself, focusing only on my pain. Mom ignored my irritable words. She stayed with me until the medicine took effect, until I fell asleep.

Until I left her defenseless, like the worthless fool that I am.

I'm not depressed or sleepy when Yolanda shows up in the library. Maybe my one-sided argument with my sister has revived my energy. Or maybe I just need to complain. Since I also feel the need to win at least one argument, I start off before she even takes a seat.

"Wanna tell me why you went bitching to Kasili about me?" I ask her.

Yolanda doesn't even blink. "Well, you weren't going to. Not even if you keeled over from exhaustion."

"That's my business."

"Even if you end up sick? Or failing? What happens then? Either take care of yourself or I will."

"You're not my mother," spills from my lips before I even think. "I don't want you interfering in my life. Get it?"

Her books hit the tabletop, sounding like a crane dropping a load. "I understand you perfectly."

This is all going wrong. I don't want to drive her away. "I'm sorry, Yo. I know you're trying to help me. I...I appreciate that."

"I don't want your *appreciation*."

"It's just right now, things are a God-awful mess. I don't know where to start solving the problem my life's become."

"David, life isn't a problem to be solved. It's not a class. There's no pass or fail. Life just *is*."

For me, life's a test I've already failed. "Says who?" I ask, sounding nastier than I intended.

She doesn't seem to notice. There's laughter in her eyes when she says, "Kierkegaard."

"Kirk who?"

"Gotcha." Her lips join her eyes and it's like a hundred tiny flares lighting up.

"You made that up."

"No. Kierkegaard was a Danish philosopher."

"Oh, no." I slap my forehead in mock disgust, just to

make sure she laughs again. "Not another wishy-washy Dane? I've had enough dealing with Hamlet. Back to reality, Yo."

"That's just what he says. His philosophy is that life's not a problem we're supposed to solve."

"What is it then, Miss Know-It-All?"

"Life's just reality." Her voice is soft and husky. "All we're supposed to do is experience it. There's no win or lose."

Maybe my life would be easier if I could believe Kirka-whoever he is, if I could believe I never failed the test. Believe that I really did care about school. Or that four years of college wouldn't be worse than trying to use a fork to dig a ditch through clay in a thunderstorm. When I found out Mom was dead, I actually thought I'd have an excuse to give up. But then I remembered what she wanted for me, and that I had to pay my debt for not protecting her. So the challenges and the tests and the struggles all had to go on.

Maybe I'm not actually being tested; maybe the real word is *trapped*.

Yolanda doesn't say *Tell me about your mother*, but I want to tell her. What if I just admit the truth out loud? That I'm the one who killed my mother. But I can't.

Because if this girl pulls out that old, tired 'not your fault, that it was God's will', yadda, yadda, crap-load of sympathy, I don't know what I'll do.

"Here's how it is," I say. "My mother had a lot of plans and dreams for all of us. I have to make sure those dreams come true. Call it life, or reality, or a test…call it whatever you want. I can't let myself fail. I just can't."

She's silent for a long time. Then she says, "I think
I've found your consequence. And it won't even hurt. Not
too much, anyway."

Another demand. Whatever. "Your wish is my command."

"Then I command you take me out on a date."

I need a few seconds to think. "You're asking me out?"

"No. You have to ask *me* out."

*This can't be the same girl who bowed her head and
acted terrified around Malik.*

"You wanna go out? With me?"

"Why thank you, Mr. Albacore. I'd love to go out with
you."

I feel myself snap to attention below the belt, while
every bone in my body turns to mush. Me and My Dare are
going out. On a date. Together! *Using what for cash?*

"I suppose...dinner?"

"McDonald's will do just fine."

She understands—I can swing that. "And then...maybe
a movie?"

"I'd love to go to a movie with you."

This isn't going to hurt after all. "Tomorrow, after the
game? Deal?"

She extends her hand. "Deal."

Yolanda's hand closes over mine. She smells so sweet.
I bend my head to her hair and breathe deep. My guts grow
tight as something comforting surges from her hand to my
skin. For a moment, I almost feel forgiven.

When I arrive at the jobsite that evening, I meet
Sanderson's replacement and fail the test again.

"I don't need you, kid." The stocky man who replaced Sanderson won't even let me through the gate.

"Talk to anyone," I say. "The guys'll tell you I'm a good worker. Sanderson said I was one of his best men."

"I heard what he had to say. Doesn't matter. You're not a man and I don't need a water boy or a gofer. I don't deal with kids. That's it. Not when there's men and women who need to feed their families and are willing to put in a full day's work to do it." He pauses. "Sanderson spoke highly of you. See me in a couple of years and I'll put you to work then."

A couple of years won't help me. I need a paycheck now. I need to feed my family, too. Even if that means talking with Kaplan senior. In the absence of winning the lotto, a game I have too much sense to play, I'm left with only that one miserable choice.

◆

This can't be happening. Malik grins when I enter his father's shop. Then he howls with laughter when I explain I'm after the job. He grabs my arm and yells across the room.

"Yo, Pop, this here's Davie."

Earth, please open up and swallow me.

The older version of Malik sitting behind the counter looks like he never smiled in his life. "Is this boy a friend of yours?" he asks.

"Absolutely. Davie and I share a lot, don't we? School, the b'ball team. Our taste in women."

The old man's lips pull together even tighter. "I was really looking for someone older. Someone with experience."

I tried. Thank God I failed. "Fine, I'll just go."

But Malik won't let go of my arm. "Davie's got loads of experience, don't you? He's real good with his hands. I need him in the back." His voice lowers. "Hire him," he demands.

Kaplan shrugs. It's easy to see who's the ruler in their house. "Fine. Welcome aboard, Davie."

"It's David."

Kaplan never stops talking. "Follow Malik's lead, and for God's sake, both of you, stay in the back. I don't want my customers seeing you." He surprises me by turning his lips into a plastic smile when a man walks through the entrance.

Malik pulls me through a door in the back of the office. *Barney. Linda. Aunt Edie.* I say the names to myself, to remind me why I'm here, why I have to put up with this. Malik leads me to a storeroom then flips on a light. I see piles of crates and lines of shelves stacked with car filters, accessories and assorted parts.

"We gotta get this crap organized, fish-face." Malik says.

Naturally, *we* means *me*. He points at a set of work gloves lying in a corner, sits himself in a chair and props his feet up on a box. I'm the one shelving crates full of parts and accessories for who knows what kinds of cars and motorbikes.

"Chop-chop, fish-face, we don't have all night."

Between one ridiculous order after another to move boxes around the shelves, he peels an orange and talks about his life. And he talks about Yolanda.

Barney. Linda. My Aunt.

"Sometimes that girl gets all pouty. Bet you've noticed that already. Then I gotta push so damned hard to make her come it ain't hardly worth the effort." He extends a slice of orange and grins. "Wanna share?"

Barney.

"Then again she'll make these little noises. Goes all fucking crazy, too. She do that for you, fish-face?"

Linda.

"Kinda like oh-uh-oooh baby. Oh yeah, Malik, oh, man, that's it." His voice lowers. "I hope she hasn't made a mistake and called you Malik."

My Aunt.

"No, no, no, fish-face, the edges have to be even. You're gonna have to restack every one of those. My dad wants things done right. Sure you don't want to share a piece?"

I don't want this job, and if I have to stay here any longer, I'll be sharing a cell with Antwon. There *has* to be something else. Anything else.

"So tell me, what's that big-assed amazon of yours like when she comes? She howl at the moon or—Fucking shit!"

I hurl the box I was holding and it smashes against the wall behind Malik's head. Glass shatters and metal pieces roll across the floor. Malik's not a complete fool—he's already running for the door.

As I strip off the work gloves, he stands in the doorway. Apparently he's regained a little courage. "You pick that crap up. Anything's broken, it comes out of your pay," he warns.

But they don't print enough money to pay me for this shit. After tossing the gloves back in the dust, I head for the door.

"Pick the junk up your own damn self. I quit," I say.

"You can't," Malik says as he backs out of my path. "I'm not cleaning that mess up. You can't leave."

My fingers curl into fists. "Be real sure you want me to stay. 'Cause if I do, you'll join the rest of the shit on the floor. Probably in just as many pieces."

The pissed-off look remains on his face, but he doesn't say anything more. Like I said, he may be an asshole, but he's not a complete fool.

But I, however, am jobless.

CHAPTER 26

Malik's still giving me that pissed-off look in the gym the next afternoon, as we get ready for the game. I'm just looking forward to getting the ball in my hands. At least when I'm on the court, everything goes my way. Every move feels right and my body knows the right thing to do, always.

"We won't be taking this team by surprise," Kasili says in the locker room. "Nobody expects to run over the no-name team anymore."

'Course not. We were featured as the October Surprise in the local sports section of the *Chicago Messenger*. They even spelled my name right. That wasn't always true when I was a Murhaselt.

Kasili continues, "So get out there and play with emotion. I want good, hard, aggressive basketball. Let them know you're for real, and you'll have no trouble."

Play with emotion. No problem there. Play with emotion and win with power. And afterwards—?

Malik's still staring at me as we line up for the opening tip. Maybe thinking about how well we worked together? Or is he just feeling his own loss? I feel Yolanda's eyes on me. That she used to be Malik's girl doesn't matter. What she will be tonight is *mine*.

It's obvious right from the beginning that Malik's out to stir up emotions, all right. One of our guys bobbles the ball and kicks it out of bounds. Malik yells at him, which just makes the guy hang his head lower. As we hustle back for our defensive positions, I whisper to him, "Relax."

The other team inbounds the ball. I rush forward and snag it before it reaches their player's hands. I see that Julian's clear. He grabs my pass and surges for the basket for an easy two. The rest of the half goes like clockwork.

In the second half, Malik goes for a shot and has the ball stripped from his hands. "I was fouled," he shouts. While he continues his tantrum, his man runs the length of the court and scores. In seconds I'm toe-to-toe with Malik and I just let him have it.

"Stop whining about the refs, Malik. Deal with the calls as they come."

"Fuck off, fish-face."

He's already lost the war between us. I turn away, saying, "You're gonna need to learn to do better than that. Guess you still don't know me." *Or the coach*.

"Kaplan, take a seat. Jeffries, go in." Kasili says.

Let the coach fight this. I'm just here to play. I'm here to win. *And then to score*.

◆

I won't think about my job problems tonight. Or about money, or my sister who acts like she hates me. *Not tonight*.

Used to be I wanted just any girl. In sixth grade, I just stared at them. Wished for some way I could charm, coax or even beg a girl to let me do that mysterious *it* with her. But I was too embarrassed to actually try anything. If ever a guy could be called innocent, that was me.

Then Marybeth Nagle came home from college for spring break. I was thrilled when she drew me down to her parents' basement for "a little fun." Thrilled, confused, shocked and so scared I couldn't stop shaking, I did what she told me to do. Tried to do everything right. That near non-event almost ended before it began, and Marybeth wasn't exactly pleased. "I didn't know you'd never done this before. God, that was nothing," was all she said.

But at least it happened early—I'd had that first lay over and done with, while most guys on the block were still scared they never would. By the time I reached high school I could do the job and performed exceptionally well. I was the man to have at Grogan Hills, and girls threw themselves at me.

But for months after that spring afternoon, I walked past Marybeth's parents' house with my eyes nearly glued shut.

Tonight things are gonna be different. Since I joined the team, a lot of the girls here at Farrington have let me know they'd like a piece of me, too. But only one has my nuts ready to pop. It's like I've been waiting for her forever. And tonight I'm taking my time—about everything. Tonight the only girl in my head is my Mighty Mite, and she's waiting for me outside the locker room. Before the night's over, she's gonna scream my name and be glad she's with me now.

Her hair is pulled into a ponytail that hangs down her back. I grab a handful of braids and free them so I can run my hands over those soft, ropy coils.

"What's this thing you have with my hair?" She grins up at me. "Don't tell me you only hang with me because of my hairdo."

"You said I could pull your string." I grab a braid and tug gently.

She laughs and I'm a bomb on the verge of detonating. I have a pocket full of condoms and my heart's beating faster than during the game. I feel something stirring below and I say, "Let's go."

The McDonald's across the street from the movie house is packed. Half the guys inside come over to congratulate me when we walk in. Girls hustle over, too, and claws flare as Mighty Mite sends them running.

I tell her to order whatever she wants. I want her to be happy. The happier the girl, the better things will go when I get her alone in the dark. That top row in the movies is make-out heaven, especially during monster flicks.

"Why 'Witch Doctor Zombies'? " she asks as we eat. She grimaces and my blood heats up, knowing what's in store when the monsters are up on the screen. "What about 'Holiday in Spring'? I heard the music's great and it's supposed to be really funny. I know you guys like those scream-fests, but I don't think I'll be able to watch."

And that's exactly the point. Movie Monster scares Girl. Then Girl crawls into your arms and puts her head in your lap. We both enjoy what comes next, and who cares what's on the screen? Didn't Malik ever take her to the movies?

"I'll be right there with you, babe," I say.

She pops a fry dripping ketchup into her mouth. Just watching her makes the room too damned hot. She licks her lips and the air's so heavy, it even hurts to breathe.

"I've never liked being scared," she says. "Watching people sliced and eaten by monsters and...uggh. I had nightmares when I was a kid. I thought monsters ate my parents and might come after me next."

"Nothing to fear, you'll have me right beside you." I'm the only thing eating her tonight. Soon she won't be thinking about the past. Or about any kind of zombies.

She laughs. "I'm older now. I know monsters aren't real. My folks just forgot about me."

"Forgot? How? I mean...how old were you?"

"Eight. It wasn't the first time I came home to an empty apartment. But this time they didn't come back. So DCFS came and took me." She swallows her last fry, takes a swallow of Coke and gestures at my tray. I nod, and she reaches for my fries.

"I know all about DCFS." The Department of Children and Family Services. The same "helpers" that descended on us and decided our future.

"I bet you do," Yolanda says as she munches. "I kept hoping my folks would come back any day. Any month. I decided they couldn't find me because of the homes I got stuck in, so I ran away a couple of times. They called me a habitual runaway—you never want that label slapped on you. It just gets you some hellish placements."

Hellish? "The people you're with now?"

"They're fine. This home's better than most. It's a big

house, I have my own room, they're really nice. It's just—
they feel guilty about having so much. So they asked for a
foster kid so they could 'give back.' They didn't particu-
larly want *me*. Any kid would do. They had someone else
before me. And there'll be someone else when I'm gone."

"When you're gone? You're leaving?" Something
catches in my throat.

"Relax. I have no plans. But…you always know you
might have to leave any day. Once—after Trey…" She
shakes her head as if trying to dislodge a bitter memory.
"Anyway, I've been here over two years, so maybe this is
the end."

"Who's Trey?" Why does the memory of leaving him
redden her cheeks? Not even the sight of Malik coming
through the door with his posse a few minutes ago had that
effect on her.

"No. I'd rather talk about the zombies." Her voice has
a toneless quality and she gets up. She talks as if her life's
a third-rate book she's had to do a report on for class. And
this Trey sounds like a chapter she'd rather skip.

I stand beside her, take her hand and put my arm
around her shoulder. One kiss and she'll stop with the past.
She'll know right away that I'm better—better than Malik.
And better than this Trey of hers, or anyone else she's ever
known.

"And the Yoyo swings on," says Malik, who's standing
by our table.

"Shut the fuck up," I say. If I didn't have my arms
around Yolanda, I'd deck the grinning bastard right here.
We're not on school grounds and I can't get expelled for

knocking him out here at Mickey D's. But my girl's shaking and some things are more important than fighting.

"I'm congratulatin' you, Davie. Hope you took your vitamins. Takes a lot to satisfy our little Yoyo. Ask the quarterback. And the halfback, and the center—hell, just about anybody'll tell you how she always rolls back for more."

Yolanda's hand on my arm is all that keeps me from swinging at his face.

"Don't," she says. "He doesn't matter."

Malik turns to her. "I'm the guy who always wanted you. I took care of you."

"Wanted me?" Her chin lifts. "Oh, please. Any body would do to meet your needs."

"And you think fish-face here's different? I thought you were at least smart enough to know the one thing you're good at. *He* certainly does."

She doesn't release me, or look or sound scared. She's wearing a warrior scowl and is breathing so hard and fast, I wonder whether she's holding me back, or using me to keep from punching him herself.

"Let's just get on to the movie," she says through clenched teeth.

"The movies?" Malik laughs as we start for the door. "That the best you can do, Davie? Hope you remembered protection, Yoyo, my love. He doesn't seem the type to think of the little extras."

She whirls. "For your information, Mister Kaplan, we're going to enjoy the show."

"He's out to enjoy *your* show. Take a good look at his tight-assed pants. Once the lights go down, so will you."

The cold outside bites. We run across the street, but one of Yolanda's heels catches on the curb at the other side and she stumbles. I grab her and pull her back against me until she gets her balance. I hold her so tight that, even through the coat, she's gonna feel what I've got waiting for her, know just how badly I want her. She's gonna forget Malik. Forget Trey and the football team, and everyone else. She'll be as eager for me as I am for her.

She stiffens. Beneath the brown, her skin goes from red to gray.

"What's wrong?" I ask.

"Nothing."

I have two sisters. A girl says that, and she really means A-helluva-lot-you-stupid-male.

"Yes, I want you. Why's that wrong? I'm not Malik, I'm not gonna hurt you. We won't do anything you don't like. It's gonna be good for both of us."

"That's what *he* said."

"Malik?"

Her head shakes. "Trey."

Him again? Her body's so tense, she could be posing for a straight-jacket ad. Whoever this joker was, she still feels something for him. "Is Trey someone you...lost?"

"Someone I found. We were placed in the same foster home and I thought it was like having a big brother or something. After three years, I'd begun to accept that my parents weren't coming back. So I thought, a big brother would be nice. And when he said I'd like it, I thought, *okay.*"

Like it? I want her to tell me more, and I'm afraid she'll tell me more.

"He said it only hurt because I was dumb and didn't do it right. That we'd have to practice a lot, because that's what guys wanted from me, so I better learn to be good."

Eight plus three is...*eleven?* God, Linda's *eleven. Yolanda was only eleven her first time—that's rape.*

The memory of my first time springs into my head again and I fight down a shudder. At thirteen, I'd been embarrassed. At eleven, I'd have shit my pants in sheer terror.

"Why didn't you tell someone?" I don't mean to sound accusing, but her head jerks as if I'd hit her.

"I finally did. And DCFS took me away."

Took *her* away?

Drops of sweat bead on her forehead. "They yanked me out so fast, I didn't even have time to pack. 'Course I didn't have much, so I didn't have much to lose."

I can barely breathe now, thinking about how much she *did* lose. And I want the son of a bitch who raped her. I want his mutilated body on the floor at my feet. I won't be quick about anything I do to that bastard.

"If you want, I'll take you home," I say. How had she held all this inside her for so long? I never knew how strong my Mighty Mite really was.

"Oh, no. It's okay. I'm not a kid anymore. I just thought—" She sighs. "Let's get inside and...and get busy."

Part of my anatomy agrees with her. But as we join the slow-moving ticket line, something's wrong. I want Yolanda. Want her happy to be with me. With *me*, not just with fucking me.

The guy in line in front of us is already halfway inside his date's pants. Their kiss is hot, noisy and wet. As he purchases two tickets for "Witch Doctor Zombies," his date giggles so goofily, I wonder how old she is. "I don't think I can watch this," she says.

He pinches her ass as they enter the theater. "I gotcha covered, baby," he says.

The picture on the wall shows blood dripping down from a maniac's fangs onto a bikini-clad girl screaming at his feet.

"Two," I tell the old woman behind the glass. "Holiday in Spring."

Yolanda looks surprised. "Are you sure? That's PG-13."

My groin's so tight I want to moan, but I say, "That's right where I want to be."

In a theater full of giggling middle-school girls.

Yolanda's head rests on my shoulder and I feel her laughing. She looks up, her eyes glistening in the darkness. That's worth the uncomfortable chair, my too-tight jeans and my body's disappointment. We kiss, and the stupid movie doesn't matter. I slide my arm around her shoulders, to hold her tight. To let her know I want her. And that she's safe.

She relaxes against my chest. It's all good.

CHAPTER 27

We hold hands all the way up the stairs to her house. When Jerry arrives with outstretched hand, I send him running back inside with an autograph.

"Advantage of being a ballplayer," I say when the door closes.

"That's the first autograph he's ever gotten. Now he'll be after me to take him to all your games."

"Malik never gave him one?" One second too late, I realize I've opened mouth and inserted a big foot.

But Yolanda doesn't look offended. "Malik didn't believe in real dates. Or in seeing me home." Then her lips grow tight. *"The football team thing."*

"Doesn't matter." I talk fast to keep from gagging.

"You didn't believe that story, did you?"

"'Course not." Hope I sound convincing. The knot in my chest melts. I take two steps down from the porch, then turn. We're almost eye to eye. I place my hands on the sides of her face and kiss her warm soft forehead. "I had the best time tonight."

"Note to self," she murmurs. "Never forget you are the luckiest girl in the world."

I need to get home and make a few notes of my own.

The minute I'm back in the apartment, I stop in my sisters' bedroom. I've got to see Linda and remind myself that she's safe. When I walk in to say goodnight, Linda's head rests on her pillow. But Barney's bed is empty.

Linda opens her eyes and she lifts her head. She stares at me through eyes that reflect the moonlight streaming in from the window.

"Where's Barney?" I ask.

"Out on a date."

Part of me relaxes, but the other part starts preparing for the talk I'll have to have with her. After saying goodnight to Linda, I pick up the phone in the living room and dial Barney's cell. Six rings later, I realize she's not going to answer the phone my money still pays for. It's off, or she recognized the number and doesn't want to talk to me tonight.

"She's with her friend," Aunt Edie tells me, but she can't say which friend, or if the friend is a male or female. "I can't keep track of her," she adds in a complaining tone, before her shoulders shake with a heavy cough. She sounds almost as if she cares, but I know the truth, so that must be anger I hear in her voice.

Barney must be with Tyrone, and they're both out after curfew. *Calm down*, I tell myself. I'm not her parent. Just the guy whose gonna scare the living shit out of little Mister Tyrone whenever he brings her home. 'Cause fourteen-year-old boys I get. Girls—of any age—are just mysterious. And I live with one of the biggest mysteries yet.

Music sounds from outside the front window, music so loud the window panes rattle. A car stops across the street—Malik's car. As I watch through the window, the passenger door opens and my sister climbs out. I'm struggling to breathe through the ridges in the steel rebar rod staking my throat as I race through the door, down the stairs and out to the street.

Malik and his car are gone before the cold outdoor air hits my face. I'm sweating and furious, and I can still smell exhaust fumes as the music grows faint. Barnetta's waving at Malik with a dopey smile on her face. But her smile disappears when she sees me heading towards her.

This was supposed to be Mom's job. She'd just give her that look, and Barney would snarl and mutter under her breath, but in the end, she'd obey.

I take a deep breath and push back what I want to say and settle for, "What do you think you're doing out this late?"

She shrugs and tries to walk around me.

"I expect an answer," I say.

"You think I'm scared of you?" she asks me.

"I think you should act like you have some sense."

Her eyes flicker for a second. Then she looks at me and says, "Malik invited me out for a bite to eat. He wanted to talk. We're both feeling a little dumped these days, so I said yes. It's not your business, anyway. Aunt Edie said I could go out."

I remember the tired look on our aunt's face.

"Did you tell her you'd be out past curfew? Do you want us thrown out of this place? It could happen if she decides she can't handle us. Or were you just planning on moving in with him?"

I don't know what I expect her to say, but it's definitely not what she tells me: "Maybe I am."

"Hell no!" Things were so much easier when Barney was a tomboy. Then her only use for guys was on the baseball field. She's a hell of a pitcher, and baseball's practically non-contact, and that's more to my liking than this. Unfortunately contact appears the only thing she's interested in right now. It's the reason Malik's chasing after her.

"Bastard couldn't be bothered seeing you safely inside?" I say.

Barney flushes and her hands curl into fists. "I told him to leave. I knew you'd cause us trouble."

"You don't know what trouble is."

"You're such a bully. You've got everyone scared of you."

"He's using you, don't you see that? He's out to make Yolanda jealous." *And to hurt me.* With my sister helping him succeed.

"You're saying no one could ever care about me, is that it?" She asks.

"Not what I said," I tell her.

"But it's what you *meant*. He likes me, David. Has from the first day, before he even knew you existed. I won't let you ruin this for me. He helps me forget everything."

"That's not good enough."

"He's good enough for *me*. He's alone now that you

stole his girl. And I'm alone because you deserted me. Maybe Malik and I—we're just meant to be."

"Did you let him...?" *God. I can't say this to my sister.*

"Malik respects me. He's a gentleman. We talked. Then he brought me home. That's all."

I want to believe her. I *have* to believe her.

I also believe Malik's only made his first move. He's taken the inbound pass, next he'll be driving in for the lay-up.

"This should make you happy," Barney says. "You're free to hang around with little Miss Dare now. You like her better than me, anyway."

"That's not true." *Or is it?* I'm not even sure anymore. "What about Tyrone? You and he look close. He's a great guy and—"

"Tyrone's a...a toad." She swallows and her eyes stare at the building behind me. "He's just another nobody. He can't do anything for me the way Malik can."

No way in hell I'll ever let Malik do you. "You can't see him again. I forbid it, you understand?"

"You *forbid* it? I hate you, David. You're worse than Dad."

She can't mean that.

It feels like somebody punched me in my throat. Malik Kaplan and my sister *cannot* happen. No matter what she thinks, he's using her. He may have lost the earlier battles, but if he takes Barney, he'll win the war.

◆

I remember the Murhaselt household in the old days. Smiles and laughter and weekends spent together. And I remember when the smiles turned to tight faces and then to loud, angry words, drinking and cursing and slammed doors. No one helped. No one thought there was a need. Mom went back to work. Antwon yelled and postured like a corner thug, the kind of guy who never takes a swing until his crew's around to step in and keep a real fight from starting. Mostly smack talk and no real action.

And I learned what outsourced meant when it happened in my own family. Antwon dropped from successful breadwinner to a janitor who had to depend on his wife to go back to work and help make ends meet. I get that he felt humiliated. But that doesn't explain what he turned into.

Or what I might become someday.

"Who do you blame for all this?" They train shrinks to ask these silly questions.

I know I'm supposed to say, *Me. Help me, doc. Make me all innocent again.* And then she'll say, *Here, take these pills. Don't worry, be happy.*

Barney gave me the silent treatment this morning. I follow her lead with this shrink and say nothing.

"After your father left—"

"Antwon," I correct her.

Another long silence.

"Have you spoken to your father since—"

"Antwon."

"How did you feel when…Antwon didn't ask for help after things went bad?"

"Men don't ask for help," I say. "We deal. I get that he

was pissed. High-paid factory worker one day, unemployed the next. He should have fucking dealt with it."

I want the memories to stop. Remembering brings nightmares of a gun held by a man I should have stopped.

"Besides, he did get help," I say.

I've surprised her. In spite of her training her jaw falls open. She takes a deep breath and tries hiding her reaction.

"Tell me more," she says.

I grin. "He got a gun, didn't he?"

She sighs. "There's no shame in asking for help."

Spoken like a female shrink. Maybe I'd have done better with Kasili after all. At least he's a guy. He'd get this. And we could get something accomplished, maybe diagram a few plays, or discuss the next opponent's weakness.

"Why should I need help?" I take care of business. I even hated having the teachers at Grogan Hills "help me." The makeup tests I took because practice and games kept me out of class were made idiot proof. The tutors they assigned even did my homework for me whenever necessary. They wanted a winner, so they did whatever they needed to keep me on the team. *I hate school.* History, English, Social Studies—it all swirls in my head and I just don't care. And I've never been able to tell anyone. Not when Mom was so proud of my grades.

"Are you angry at yourself?" she asks.

Who the hell does she think she is? "Don't you guys just hand out drugs and tell people to be happy?"

"David, do you think you need medication?"

No! Hell no. Never again.

"Stop with the questions, okay?"

My head aches. Where's that damned bell?

◆

"Statistics aren't getting us anywhere," I say as I close the laptop we've been using to search the Internet.

Yolanda nods. "Lies, damn lies, and statistics, remember?"

I know I'm right. Marriage is bad for women. But the numbers we're finding prove nothing. And I can't bring up the story of Wilhelmina and Antwon Murhaselt.

I know how buildings are put together. Piece by piece, with precise measurements, attention to detail and careful planning. I can make my case the same way.

After pulling a piece of paper from my notebook, I draw a line down the center, label the two columns and look at my partner across the library table.

"Skip numbers," I say. "Real people. Pro or con: Queen Latifah?"

As I expect, Yolanda laughs. "No fair, David. Unless you balance her with Perez Hilton."

"Okay then." I search my brain for the little I remember of history. "Queen Elizabeth I. She could have had anyone, but she knew better than to get married."

"Fine. How about Mary, Joseph's wife? She's the mother of God and still she decided to spend her life married to a man."

"You play dirty."

She points at the pro column. "Just write them down."

I obey and counter, "Ivana Trump."

"Don't pretend she didn't benefit from that marriage," Yolanda says. "Queen Victoria and Prince Albert."

"Oprah," I counter.

"I'll give you that one. But I'll raise you Melinda and Bill Gates."

My pen flies across the page. This is so much fun, I don't even care which column gets to be longer. "Bill and Hillary Clinton."

I stop writing. Then we both say, "Could go in either column," and we laugh.

"What about Mother Teresa?"

Yolanda frowns. "Uh, David, she was a nun."

"And too smart to get married. Gotcha!"

She laughs again and the happy sound pulls me deeper under her spell. *What about David and Yolanda Albacore* trembles on my lips. All the air in the room disappears with that explosive thought. This beautiful, strong, perfect girl and the son of a man who murdered the woman he claimed to have loved? *Never gonna happen.*

The bell rings. No class period has ever moved faster.

Between the shrink and Barney's you-don't-exist silence this morning, I'm ready for a calm, quiet lunch period. Since Barney no longer talks to me, that should be easy to accomplish.

Yolanda tries to protest when I tell the cashier I'm paying for her lunch. But this time I won't let her refuse. It feels good to do something for her and I need to feel good today.

Barney's not in her seat at the table yet. Neill won't

look at me when I sit down. Neither will Carl or Julian, or any of the guys. But the girls won't stop staring at me.

"What's up?" I ask.

Neill sighs. "Your girl's gone."

"What'd you expect?" Julian says. "We get dropped when a better invite comes along."

"What better invite? Where's Barney?"

Yolanda grabs my arm. "David." She's looking over at Malik's table.

As I turn to look, Renata says, "Did you think she'd just hang around here crying, when you moved on?"

I don't need to ask who she's talking about. My sister's sitting at Yolanda's old table. In Yolanda's old seat. Next to Yolanda's ex.

CHAPTER 28

I'm standing behind my sister's chair gritting my teeth, my hands in fists, and I'm ready to rip into everyone seated at Malik's table. "Get up!" I say.

When Barney refuses to even turn her head and look at me, I say it a little bit louder. "GET. UP."

Every face at the table turns toward me—every face but one—Barney's.

"You can't make me do anything," she says. Her back's stiff and her voice all scratchy. "We're nothing to each other now."

Malik laughs. "Have to love a lady who speaks her mind."

Once I wanted to throw my sister away. Now I'm aching to throw her over my shoulder and carry her off to safety.

"Let's go, Barney," I say.

Malik leans close to her. "You want to leave me, Boo?"

Boo? I wait for Barney to punch him for that knobby name.

Instead she bats her eyes and giggles. "No, Malik. I want to stay."

Triumph jets from the narrow eyes Malik turns on me. "The lady's free to eat wherever she wants. So back off."

I take my sister's arm. "Let's go, Barney."

She cries out and my hand slips away.

One of the lunchroom monitors moves in. "Get back to your table," she warns.

"I need to talk—"

"Back to your table or go to the principal's office. Now move."

Barney still hasn't looked at me.

Malik chuckles. "Guess *you're* the one who doesn't know, fish-face."

"Face it, you've been dumped," Julian says when I return to our table alone.

"Didn't you tell her you needed her back to complete your harem?" Renata's voice drips sarcasm like a sausage drips grease. "You can't blame her for going after something better. Or maybe *you* can."

"Shut up." Neill's command earns him a frown he ignores. Then he turns to me. "Malik didn't make her go. She just walked over there and sat down all on her own. Give it up, it happens."

Give up my sister? Never.

I should have watched her more closely. Should have been here to stop this.

I turn to see Barney looking at Malik and laughing the way she used to, *before*. Maybe it won't be as bad as I'm afraid of. Maybe Malik really likes her after all.

Then he looks across the room. He points one finger at me and pretends like he's shooting a pistol. Then he wraps his arm around the back of Barney's chair.

What am I going to do?

"You don't lecture her," Yolanda says as we leave the lunchroom. "Maybe you should tell Malik she's your sister."

"That'll just up the ante." The prick would know he had more ammunition. "He's turned on the damned charm, and I'm just her brother."

"Malik's not so bad as long as he's gets what he wants. But when he doesn't…" She sighs. "You've got to get Barney away from him."

Agreed, but how?

"He has a thing for new girls. Girls who don't understand him, or what he's after until they're sucked in and he's got them. He starts slow and takes his time moving in. You don't realize what you're into until…"

"Is that what happened to you?"

"I've always known about guys like Malik. I knew exactly what he wanted from day one." She shakes her head. "I was thinking, maybe if I talk to him…"

"No." I don't want her having to get close to Malik. Her eyes flash and I'm left wondering if I really am too forceful sometimes.

Yolanda says, "Then I'll talk to Barney."

"What'll you say?"

"A private message. The kind of thing a boy, especially a brother, probably wouldn't understand. So don't ask me because I'm not going to tell you."

"She may not listen. She thinks you're her rival for Malik."

Yolanda shakes her head. "You're wrong. I'm her rival for you. She's afraid she's losing her brother."

"That'll never happen."

"I know," she says as she walks away.

Now what? Have I upset Yolanda? Opened mouth and inserted my big foot all over again? What I feel for each of them is totally different. I want them both. Why can't they understand that?

◆

Sanderson said I understood planning and risk management. On the way to practice after my last class I decide to use that. If I organize the problems and risks, maybe I can come up with a plan.

Number one, my sister's running with a guy who wants to use her to diss me.

Number two, I have no job and I wouldn't go back to Kaplan if he begged. That won't happen anyway.

Number three, my girl's mad because I don't know how to tell her she's number one, and that she's not in a race with my sisters.

Number four, Kasili's after me about college. At least that's never gonna happen, so I cross that off the list right away.

Anything else? Oh yeah. Number five, Malik's tailing me.

Just as I reach the door of the gym, I whirl and face him. "What do you want?" I say.

"Whoa, big fish, peace. We're both just going the same way. And I wanted to give you an invitation. I'm having a party for the team after Friday's game. My place. It'll be fun. You can even bring your little friend."

"No thanks."

"I'm having the best—of everything."

No chance in hell either Yolanda or I will show up at his place Friday night.

The rest of the team sounds excited when he tells them about his plans. Only Julian throws a worried glance in my direction before accepting the invitation.

While everyone talks with Malik after practice, I finish dressing and leave. Outside the locker room door there's a first—Barney's waiting for me.

Before I have a chance to hope she jumps at me. "Did you send The Dare after me?"

"She knows some things about Malik. So, yeah, I wanted her to talk to you."

"Don't you ever sic your little slut on me again."

I raise my hand to slap that word from her lips. She flinches and I realize what I'm about to do, and I end up frozen in place.

Yolanda's my lady. No one should ever talk about her that way. But Barney's my buddy—my sister. I can't believe what I almost did. As I'm lowering my hand, she turns and runs down the corridor.

A laugh sounds behind me. When I turn, I see Malik standing in the doorway.

"That's the trouble with women," he says. "Hard to just let go."

Maybe Kasili's right and names don't matter. Maybe DNA trumps everything. Because deep down, I'm too much a Murhaselt. I won't go to that party. And no matter *what* I have to do, my sister will *not* be going, either.

CHAPTER 29

I'm staring at Yolanda in Lit class the next morning when an office flunky brings the teacher a note. She frowns as she walks toward Yolanda's desk. "The principal wants to see you in her office, now."

Funny thing, Yolanda doesn't look surprised. She's got her books and papers already stacked and she gets up like a gazelle. When she passes, she pauses for a second and looks down at me. Her lips part, but then she heads to the door without saying anything.

She hasn't come back to class by the time the bell rings, and I hear the first rumors when classes change.

"A bunch of them were picked up last night, and I hear they're still in jail."

"Who was picked up?" I ask. "For what?"

"Cops arrested girls stealing at Ford City Mall last night," one girl says with a snicker.

"I hear a bunch of those skanky ho's escaped, and the cops are down at the principal's office picking them up now."

"Who?" Don't say Yolanda. Please don't say—

"Nicole."

"Joelle."

Don't say,

"Yolanda?"

The girl beside me shrugs. "Probably. They all hang together."

Shit.

There's status in being picked up by the cops. No status in being an expert with a sewing machine. The cops can't have any proof Yolanda was involved because she wasn't. But if she is accused, she wouldn't admit the truth.

By fourth period, I'm getting frantic. Yolanda isn't in the library so I head for the office in time to see two big, burly, uniformed Chicago cops leaving, armed with their billy clubs, handcuffs and guns. But there's still no sign of Yolanda.

Kasili's nowhere to be found. My shrink's door is locked and the secretary won't talk or let me go in to see the principal. And Devontae just shrugs.

Which all leaves me wandering through the halls, trying to figure out what to do. Head for the police station and say…what? She'd rather be in a cell than tell people she's a phony. She wouldn't want me to betray her, but I can't just stand here and let her get punished for something she didn't do.

I hear Renata's voice as I pass by the girl's washroom. "You may be The Dare, but you can't just go waltzing around like some kind of goddess. You don't even have the grace to look ashamed."

"I have nothing to be ashamed of," Yolanda says.

Basic kindergarten rule—never go inside the girl's bathroom. Never. Not for any reason.

Basic grade school rule—never get in the middle of cat fights. Never. Not for any reason.

"What did you do?" Renata continues. "Hand the other girls your orders? You get to keep your hands clean while your friends get screwed? Maybe that fooled the dumbass cops but we're not stupid, are we, girls?"

"We think it's time you paid." That was Barney's voice.

Fuck basic rules. The sound of the door crashing against the wall echoes through the bathroom when I storm inside.

Five female faces turn to stare at the male invader.

Renata, Barney and two others I don't know are circled around Yolanda. The four look like dogs ready to pounce on fresh meat. But the Mighty Mite's shoulders are squared and there's something in her five-foot body that's kept them from moving in.

She's safe. The police let her go. Nobody, not even Barney, gets to hurt her now.

My sister doesn't wait for me to speak. "So now you see, now you know the truth about The Dare."

I do know the truth, but can't share it. I promised to keep my mouth shut. "You don't even know she's involved." I move to stand at Yolanda's side. "She wasn't arrested."

Renata raises her eyebrows as if she's just heard the most foolish thing ever. "Of course not. Ringleaders never get caught."

"What makes you think she's a ringleader?"

I should have kept my big mouth shut. All four girls laugh, although Barney ducks her head.

"You having the hots for her doesn't change the truth," Renata says.

"Back off," I say. "Yolanda never stole anything. I know. I bought those things for her." I don't mind lying if it forces them to leave my girl alone.

Barney looks at me like I'm some evil monster. "David, how could you?"

Renata turns to Yolanda. "So those knee burns pay off? Is he easier to swallow than Malik?"

Before I can yell at that little witch, Yolanda takes a deep breath and smiles up at me. "It's okay, David. You don't have to lie or cover for me anymore."

"I knew it," Renata says.

Yolanda steps forward. "No one bought these things for me. And I've never stolen anything."

"You're out casing the mall all the time," Renata insists.

"Looking for ideas. Those are the only things I ever take." Yolanda plucks at her blouse. "I made this myself. I make all my things. Everything I wear is a genuine Yolanda Original."

Four faces stare at her in silence.

"It gets better. I'm a foster child. My parents abandoned me. I've seen my mother only once in the last eight years. I was thirteen and she had a new husband and a new family. She barely remembered me and had no interest in a souvenir of the past."

"My God. Talk about freaky." Renata laughs. Like stealing or using Daddy's money or getting on your knees to get a guy to open his wallet would be better.

The door opens and another girl steps in. She stops, looks at us and then backs out. Then two more girls follow, leaving me, Yolanda, Barney and Renata. Barney stares at Yolanda and shakes her head before running out. Yolanda takes my hand and we leave the bathroom together as the bell rings.

◆

At lunch I see there's trouble between Barney and Malik, so not everything's going wrong. Something's got them arguing. Maybe seeing Yolanda in a different light is helping her see through Malik's disguise. My sister's smart, and a little Malik goes a very long way. She won't need more than a few clues and she'll figure him out sooner or later.

She's shaking her head and she looks as crushed as if her puppy dog died. She's sitting beside Malik and saying something that makes him lean back in his chair and snort. The sound of her chair hitting the floor when she jumps up echoes around the lunchroom. She says something and his grin vanishes, then he looks in my direction and that ugly smile returns. This time whatever he says sends my sister running from the room.

That's when Yolanda takes my hand and says, "Go ahead, David. Go get her."

I don't like leaving Yolanda alone with the haters at our table, but I know she's right. I have to go to my sister.

When I find Barney she's at her locker, pulling and ripping at her things like a dog searching for a lost bone.

Kneeling beside her, I take her chin and lift her face. "What's wrong? What did Malik say to you?"

She shakes her head and says, "Nothing."

The word comes out too quickly. She's having trouble meeting my eyes. I insist. "Whatever it is, let me help."

She's always been a lot like me. That's why we made such good buddies. She never asked for help, never asked me to slow down and wait for her, or tackle her problems. She's always been fearless, like a lioness Now her jaw sets and I see the return of my stubborn, determined sister.

Maybe that's what she needs to be right now. It's okay with me. Better that then have her falling apart.

After taking a deep breath, I force myself to say, "If you want, we'll go back and I'll tell everyone I'm really your brother. We'll say it was all a joke and that I forced you to pretend. Then they'll laugh at me, not you."

She shakes her head. "No. That's not what I want. I just…I lost something, that's all. I bet I left it at home."

We work together to pick up her scattered books and papers and little girl trinkets, and stuff them back in her locker.

"Come back to our table," I say as she locks the door.

"I can't. The bell's going to ring in a minute anyway."

"Tomorrow, then."

She hesitates. "No. I have to be with Malik. Don't worry about me."

That's easy to say. But impossible to do.

At least my sister's not as distant with me the next

morning and even waits to walk to school with me. Not even Yolanda walking up to the school doors makes her frown. Maybe I can relax. Maybe she's coming back to me. I even see her talking to Yolanda in the hall just before fourth period. Her head's bent over my Mighty Mite. Neither of them are smiling, but they aren't yelling at each other, either.

As I approach, Yolanda pats Barney's arm and says, "The bell's about to ring, so you better run."

Barney looks at me, nods then goes tearing down the hall.

"What's up?" I ask my girl.

"Private girl talk."

"Meaning I should keep out of this?" I'm too happy to see the two of them talking again to push things. With the back of my hand I rub Yolanda's cheek. "Staying out of girl stuff works for me."

Her lips grow tight. "Would you mind if I don't study with you today? There's something I need to do."

She's the best tutor I ever had, and I'll miss this hour together. But there'll be plenty of others. "Okay," I say. "See you at lunch."

The bell rings. A few last pairs of feet go rushing down the hall. But Yolanda doesn't move. Instead she takes a major deep breath. "I need to ask you something," she says.

She's suddenly so serious, I'm worried. "Um...ask me anything you want."

"Do you love me?"

An easy one. "Yes. Absolutely."

"More than anything?"

"Yeah."

"More than...Barney?"

She can't still be jealous of my sister? I don't know how to answer her.

As I hesitate, Yolanda laughs. "You don't need to say anything."

I'm relieved, but still wary. "I love you both. Just in different ways."

"Relax, David. It's not a test. Besides," her voice softens, "I love Barney, too."

Great. "So, see you at lunch?"

She hesitates before nodding. "Yeah. See ya later."

Which is why I'm almost knocked on my butt when I get to the lunchroom and see Barney sitting on Malik's left side. And to top it all off, Yolanda in the chair on his right.

"You've been dumped again, man," Neill says.

CHAPTER 30

Yolanda escapes me after lunch, but she's not getting away again. The minute Mr. Martin stops talking, I'm going after her. And so help me, she's going to explain. Because there has to be an explanation. This has to be a mistake.

"You guys keep wanting to grow up too soon. Slow down, be glad you live in a time and place where you're allowed to still be young. Adulthood will catch up to you soon enough," Mr. Martin says.

I'll be adult about this. She'll explain and—I'll be able to breathe again.

She'll explain and we'll laugh. I hope.

"Remember, full-fledged, productive, responsible adulthood takes more than just brains and brawn. Life experience provides the final ingredient. It's hard to get the right mixture packed into only eighteen years. Frankly, I know more than a few thirty-somethings I'd consider adults in name only."

One guy raises his hand. "What do you mean, life experience?"

"Things like travel."

A groan goes through the room.

"Like where we gonna go?"

"Yeah, like when I spent that year in Paris."

"Go ahead and laugh, guys," Martin says. "But everything, even a weekend at the Dells, or a day trip to visit relatives, or even just visiting a different neighborhood around here opens the mind and pushes you towards maturity. So does dealing with problems."

Yolanda lifts her head. She turns to stare at me.

Kids call out comments such as, "I don't like problems." And "Growing up is hard." And "What about happy times?"

"We all want happy times," Martin says. "But facing our problems and responsibilities provides us with opportunities for growth."

"What about when you care about someone," I say. I'm still staring into Yolanda eyes. "Care so much that you want them close, no matter what? You'd give anything and everything to keep them with you."

"What if they don't deserve everything?" Yolanda says.

I know she means me. Her eyes narrow, her lips get tight and I don't know what I did to make her so angry.

"Then I guess you have to let them go," I say and pray she'll tell me I'm wrong.

From the corner of my eye I see a puzzled look on the teacher's face. All I care about is Yolanda's answer. I know I don't deserve everything. But all I want is *her*.

"I guess you're right, Mr. Albacore," she says before turning her back on me.

♦

I'm watching the seconds count down. Class ends and I'm up before Yolanda can collect her books and escape.

"What's wrong?" I ask.

She refuses to look at me and pushes her way into the hall. "Why does something have to be wrong?" she replies.

"This isn't real, this can't be real, you can't mean this. What's happened to you? To us?"

"It's over, David. You and me, we're done."

"You're over and out, fish-face."

Over her shoulder I see Malik pushing through the crowded hallway. Yolanda stands motionless as he places his arm on her shoulder.

It hurts to breathe. I can't think. This cannot be real. She can't be saying, "You were fun at first, David, but frankly you've gotten a little boring."

Boring? "What? What do you want from me?"

"Nothing. You played your part." She looks up at Malik and smiles. "Thanks to you, Malik's learned his lesson. I'm grateful for your help in making my man jealous."

"Grateful." *Oh, God. I'm a parrot. I'm a fool.*

Malik dips his head and catches Yolanda in a big, noisy lip-lock. Then he lifts his head and winks at me. "Yeah, fish-face. Thanks for helping me see the error of my ways. Oh, and you can take your giant back."

He prefers his tiny bitch?

Yolanda licks her lips and again I feel the urge to finish the job for her. Except that's Malik's job now.

"Go away, David. I don't need you anymore."

I obey her and walk through the locker room doors. Like a robot, like a tool she's been using in a sick game to make Malik come crawling back to her.

Like a man with a claw hammer ripping his heart from his chest.

◆

My practice shot hits the backboard and falls to the floor as the stands fill just minutes before the game begins. Barney comes in and sits a few rows above the team's bench. If she were one of those super-powered comic book mutants, the stare she turns on Malik would leave him as a puddle of goop on the floor. She obviously knows he just used her to get Yolanda back. Just the way Yolanda used me.

I'm grateful for your help.

Kasili snaps his fingers in my face. "What's up, David? Look alive."

"Sorry."

"Come here, there's someone I want you to meet."

He leads me to a man standing near our bench. In spite of the suit and tie, I can tell he's at home on a basketball court. Six-six, just over two hundred pounds, obviously a former player, and probably a good one. "David Albacore, meet Peter Ellingswood, assistant coach at DePaul University and my roommate at college."

"Hakeem won't stop talking about you," Ellingswood says as we shake hands.

Kasili nods. "Peter's doing some recruiting, and since

he was in the neighborhood, I asked him to come take a look."

"Asked? Your wife refused to hand over a piece of that apple pie until I promised I'd come."

"He's here to see if I really know how to coach."

Ellingswood turns back to me. "And get a good look at you. My old roomie's been singing your praises so now I want a look-see for myself."

Over his shoulder I see Yolanda walk into the gym. She climbs the bleachers, pausing for a second when she reaches the row where Barney's sitting, then continues to the top and sits by herself.

"David, did you hear me?" Kasili sounds annoyed.

"Sorry. I—I'm just anxious for the game to begin."

"Can't fault the boy for being eager," Ellingswood says. He takes my hand again before turning to Kasili. "We'll talk again after the game."

As he goes to sit in the stands, Kasili says, "You can do yourself a lot of good tonight, David. He's still got slots to fill."

And I care because?

The home crowd groans when the other center takes the tip, leaving me to hustle back on defense. My man scores twice before Kasili calls a time out. "What's going on with you?" he asks me as we all huddle around him.

"Davie looks tired. Think he could use a little bench time." Malik's trying to make his face look like he's concerned. I can't even make myself feel angry.

Kasili substitutes for me and holds me at his side while play resumes. "Want to tell me what's wrong?"

Yeah, let's discuss my love life. Former love life.

"Malik said it, I'm tired."

"Whatever's between you and Malik—"

"I'm over it. I never wanted to play again, anyway."

"Not want to use a talent God gave you? Never settle for mediocrity. You have a major opportunity tonight. This is a chance for a full scholarship."

"Oh." DePaul's located right in the city. If Ellingswood recruits me, my life can continue exactly the way it is. Nothing changes but the name of the school holding me prisoner.

"That's what you want, isn't it?"

It's certainly one item on that long list of things I'm supposed to want. Things I have no choice about. Like getting over that beautiful bitch. I nod.

"Then get back in there and focus. Show Peter the real David Albacore."

Focus. *Yeah, Right.*

Boring? I'll show her boring.

"I'm over it, Coach. Put me back in."

Yolanda is just another girl. If I just say that often enough, I'll begin believing it.

Just another girl. Just another....Just.

The ball squirts free as Julian uses a move I taught him and strips his man. I dive for the loose ball, scoop it up, pivot and shoot. My game's back. More, I feel the zone settle over me. Every muscle tingles as I step into the shooting trance where I don't have to think or feel. Where not even a lid over the basket could make me miss. I'm back where no female can make me care.

When we come out of the locker room as half-time ends, I'm surprised to see Yolanda and Barney together in the stands. They look like they're arguing about something, so the subject has to be Malik. Yolanda looks up and our eyes meet. My throat tightens. Then she turns away and goes back to her seat in the top row.

I don't know a lot about marriage, but I finally see the purpose of a boyfriend. It gives girls at least one guy to make a damn fool of. I can turn my back on her, I can score a hundred points—a thousand. Nothing really changes. She may be just another girl, but I'm still caught on a leash. Me. Stupid Number One.

'Cause if Yolanda crooked her finger right now, I'd fall over myself running up those steps to get back to her side.

In spite of the bad beginning, I end with a triple double, seventeen points, ten blocks and eleven rebounds. We win by thirteen.

Kasili's happy.

Which makes one of us.

◆

My sister's waiting for me when I leave the gym. Malik and most of the others are still inside. I hurried to dress and escape, unwilling to stay near him any longer than I had to. And I didn't want to chance Kasili dragging me back to talk to Ellingswood.

And maybe I hoped I'd see Yolanda out here, even if she was just waiting for Malik.

Barney and I join the stream of triumphant students singing a victory song on the grounds in front of the school.

"Maybe you should go to Malik's party," she says.

"No. And neither are you." I wait for a protest that never happens.

"I'm not going with him anymore." She won't even look at my face. Malik's defection must have hurt her more than I realized.

"You shouldn't be angry at Yolanda," Barney says.

"I'm not gonna talk about her." Hard to believe the two girls have made up. Maybe this is just more of what girls do. Stick up for each other and screw guys. Someday my sister will make some poor guy beg while she laughs at him. Make him believe she cares until she's had her fill, then leave him feeling like a fool.

Meanwhile, I have to forget Yolanda. Forget I was just a choke chain she used to jerk Malik around until he returned to heel.

Other teammates pour out of the gym. Malik's standing in the doorway, waving at the celebrating students who cheer and call his name before he sets off to the parking lot.

Julian comes up behind me and slaps my shoulder. I almost fall. "We're off to Frank's for pizza."

Yolanda stands beside Malik's car. She sweeps the hair back from her shoulders as he approaches and I almost feel the vibrations from her beads move across my skin.

"What happened to the party?" Barney asks.

"Last-minute change." Julian looks at me. "You left the locker room too quick to hear the party's off."

Barney looks like she's just awakened from some nightmare. "Guess his parents came home."

Malik still hasn't learned to be a gentleman. He climbs

behind the wheel then sits waiting. Yolanda walks around the car, opens her door and settles into the passenger seat.

"Nope," one of the guards says. "But he's decided to have some kind of private party, so we've been un-invited."

Of course. He wants to celebrate their reunion in private.

"I'd rather have pizza anyway," Julian says.

"Count me out," I say as Malik's car rolls into the street. Which makes absolutely no sense. Once I get home, all I'll do is lie in bed and think about her—with him.

My teammates gather around me. "You gotta come, man."

"You're the hero."

"Seventeen points."

Seventeen meaningless points. "You guys get moving. I need to rest. It's too cold to just stand here." With my hands thrust deep in my pockets, I start the long walk home.

Barney comes running after me.

"Get back to your friends," I tell her. "All the pizza you can eat." She can have my share. I need to be alone. "Tyrone's gonna be happy to have you around."

Instead of smiling, she grabs my arm and forces me to stop. "You have to go to Malik's party."

"Canceled, remember?" Her grip tightens and she frowns like she's worried about me. "I'm fine, promise," I tell her.

"You look like you're in a bad way," says Barney.

That forces a laugh out of me. "This is my normal state, Barney. Relax, I'm tough."

She continues following me. "I have to make a confession."

"About Malik?"

When she nods, I stop and put my hands on her shoulders. "Forget him. He's not the only guy in the world."

"But he knows about you. About David Murhaselt, I mean."

"What can he know?"

She takes a big breath and squares her shoulders. "We were talking and...I guess I said something. Then I guess he went looking and found my diary. Everything's in there. He said he was going to tell the coach, the whole school."

I'm glad I can kill this worry. "Relax, Barney girl. Malik can tell Kasili whatever he wants. The man will laugh and Malik'll look like the dickhead he is."

"You won't get kicked off the team?"

"Kasili knew all about me before I even joined the team. Nothing in your diary can hurt me."

Instead of looking relieved she grabs my arm. "I thought I'd ruined you. Malik was so nice at first. I didn't know he just wanted to...I didn't listen to you. And then he said he'd tell everyone unless I agreed. He wanted me to go out with him. *Be* with him. You know."

Yeah, I know. Somehow I control myself, take a deep breath and give her shoulders an extra tight squeeze.

"At least now you know the truth," I say. "Tell you what, I'll take you to Frank's, and we'll both have a slice and forget. Tomorrow you'll make up with your friends, and the last few days'll be forgotten. Now let's haul ass before we freeze to death."

But Barney still doesn't move. "He wanted me to go with him to his party tonight. Upstairs. I didn't want to, but he said I had to or he'd go straight to Kasili. I know how important basketball is to you, and school and your name and—and everything. I was scared, but it was my fault he'd found out, and I couldn't let him hurt you. So I knew I had to go."

I can't believe what she almost sacrificed for me. Guess maybe I have a reason to thank Yolanda after all.

"Don't apologize. He can't hurt me, and even if he could, you don't owe me anything." This time when I laugh, it almost sounds real. "You never were a good liar. I shouldn't have expected you to pretend for me. You don't have to any more."

"But he's got Yolanda now."

Why'd she make me see that painful vision? "They deserve each other. We both learned important lessons today. Neither of them is worth our trouble."

I turn to keep walking but she grabs my arm. "But Yolanda."

"What about her?" Had she been part of the scheme to use my sister? Yesterday I would have said *impossible*. Today I see that I never knew her. "May they both be happy together."

"She's all alone with him."

I shrug and thrust my fists into the jacket pockets, careful to keep her from seeing how that thought rips me apart.

"Neither of us needs to worry about her. She got what she wanted." The crown will rest securely on her head again before the night ends.

"No," Barney says. Her voice is so soft, the chilly breeze almost carries her words away before I hear them. "David, she *hates* Malik."

Riiiight. That's a hell of a lip-lock for hatred.

"David, I know you think I hate Yolanda because of what she said to me."

"No."

"Don't lie, David." Her lips twist. "Maybe I did—a little. Mostly I hated her because I knew I was going to lose my brother. She was taking you away from me."

"It really doesn't matter anymore."

Barney's crying now. "But David, it does. I told her what happened, what Malik wanted from me. She got him to take her instead. I thought you'd go to the party and save her. I didn't know he'd have her alone. David, he hates her so much!"

CHAPTER 31

Three miles to Malik's house and my legs won't move fast enough. I can barely draw breath past the fire in my lungs, but I'd have to be dead to stop running.

There's no sound inside the house when my fist pounds his front door. No screams, no laughter, no music, but I know they're in there. His car sits in the driveway and light streams from the front window, but there's no light in the second-floor bedroom windows. "Malik! Open the God damn door!"

I'm searching for a rock to throw at the window when the door opens a crack. Malik has the gall to yell, "What the fuck's going on?" as I push past him into the house.

"Where is she?" I can't wait for an answer. I'm halfway up the staircase when I hear the rattle of beads behind me.

Turning, I see her on the sofa.

There's an overturned beer bottle on the coffee table. Moisture stains her torn blouse. She's shaking and one shoe is in the middle of the rug. Yolanda won't look up at me when she says, "You have to go, David. You can't be here."

"You heard the...lady." Malik moves to stand by the sofa near her head. His hands are on his hips. like he's some kind of overlord. He has no idea how close he is to a violent uprising.

But only Yolanda matters now. Our eyes lock as I cross the room, pick up her shoe, then kneel at her feet. The room's hot, but when I take her foot her skin's icy. A red scratch on the flesh above her right breast leaves me biting back a growl as I take her hand and help her to her feet. "Come on. We're leaving."

"I can't. I have to be here."

She's shaking even harder now, and I can't let myself look at the scratch or her torn blouse or I'll lose it. Instead my hands cradle her face and I tell her, "You're coming with me."

"Now you're boring both of us, fish-face," Malik says. "Or should I call you by your real name?"

"Call me whatever you want." *Let the whole world hear.*

Yolanda takes a deep breath. "It's okay. I made a deal."

"There's no deal with the fucker who threatened my sister." How could I have believed for one second that Yolanda didn't care about me?

"So you admit the truth, Murhaselt." Malik says the word like the insult it is. "Barney baby was quite taken with me and told me everything. Now you better pray this bitch keeps her end of the deal."

I'm going to have to hurt him. My heart races, and my fists argue over which one gets to go first. Yolanda takes my arm when I lunge toward him. "No, David, don't," she begs.

She might have stopped me if the hand on my arm weren't still icy cold. If her movement didn't make fresh blood seep from that scratch. *If* Malik had enough sense to stop laughing.

My right fist wins and an uppercut to his jaw sends him falling back against an end table. The lamp from the table crashes to the floor as my left gets its turn. The jab takes him in the stomach and he goes down hard.

Broken glass crunches under my shoe when I step beside his head. And now it's my turn to laugh when he whimpers. "Did Barney tell you everything about the Murhaselt family?" I ask. "What happens when we get really mad?"

The blood dripping from his whining mouth and his bug-eyed stare leave Malik ready to star as victim number one in the next zombie movie. Fat tears stream down his cheeks and mix with the blood and snot dribbling out of his nose.

"I didn't touch your precious sister. And that ho's not worth—"

Some people just don't understand self-preservation.

Yolanda grabs my arm. "No. He's not important, David. *You* are."

"You don't have to sacrifice yourself for me. Got it?" I speak softly. Partly so she'll know I'm not mad at her. Partly so my voice won't cover up the soundtrack of Malik's sobs.

She nods and buries her head in my chest. "He's going to tell the school. He said one of us had to...I couldn't let him hurt your sister. It's okay for me."

"No, Yolanda. It's not."

Malik scrambles to his feet and backs toward the door. He looks like he expects me to pound him again. Guess he's not a complete jackass.

"I'll tell everyone," he says. "The Principal. Coach. Everyone."

Yolanda stiffens.

I tighten my grip so she can't move away from me. "Go ahead."

His jaw drops. "You're a fucking pretender. Everyone will know about you and your old man. Don't you know what'll happen? What people will say? Be careful of that Murhaselt. He's a liar and a fraud. And his father's a murderer. You won't be able to play, either."

"You should read the papers, Kaplan. My name change notice was printed a while back."

"What the hell?"

Yeah, keep that expression on your ratty face. "You're too little, too damned late. Be concerned about yourself when you walk into the office with this story. Kasili has strong feelings about blackmail. The guys on the team aren't too fond of it either."

One arm's around Yolanda. The other pulls Barney's camera phone from my pocket and snaps a picture.

Malik lunges. I'm forced to release Yolanda to push him down again.

"Bastard." He straightens and wipes the back of his hand over his face, which only smears the glistening snot ball hanging from his nose. I have to get another shot of this.

"I'm so glad I got the best phone for my sister. Sound

and video. I can send copies to anyone I want, mister can't-get-any-on-my-own-so-I-have-to-blackmail-girls-for-sex."

He tries clearing his face again. "What do you want to make that go away?"

"Tempting—" I say. And just as he begins to look smug I add, "—but too late. There's a party at Frank's place, with entertainment by Malik. Right about now, you're a hot topic at the pizzeria." I lift the phone to my ear. "You guys get all this, Julian?"

As Malik gapes, I turn to him. "Say hello to your fans."

Now he tries to hide his face and I laugh. "You know what they say about nothing ever disappearing from the Internet?"

Mom once told me about an old TV show called *Candid Camera* that caught people acting like fools. YouTube is much, much better. I wonder which of the guys will post Malik's fall from grace first.

After tucking Yolanda's coat around her shoulders, we brave the wind chill outside. There's no hurry now.

"David, really, what about school? What about your name?"

"My name really *is* Albacore. Judge signed the papers and everything. It's done."

"Malik really can't hurt you?"

When I shake my head she sighs. "I feel like such a fool."

"And I feel so loved."

The phone rings before I can kiss her. Our home number flashes on the screen. It's Barney, checking up.

"Relax, Barney girl," I say. "Everything's fine, I'm taking Yolanda home now."

But my sister's sobbing. "Come home. Come now, David. It's Aunt Edie...I think she's dying."

CHAPTER 32

The doctors call it a stroke. "And now, ladies and gentlemen, on tonight's fight card, we bring you the fifty-eight-year-old lady fighting for every breath." That's right up there with domestic abuse.

"You can talk to David," my aunt says. Her face looks crooked. She can't move the muscles on her right side, and even her right eyelid and the side of her lips droop. Her words are slurred and her voice is breathless in spite of the oxygen tube at her nose.

Today's Sunday, the first day they let us in to see her. I hate hospitals. They smell like crap and feel like death. The woman in the other bed even *looks* like death. She's loaded down with machines, bags and tubes, and something that never stops hissing. Only she never moves or makes any sound.

The doc doesn't want to talk to kids about the medical issues, but I'm all she has.

"Mrs. Crenshaw, I really don't think it's appropriate—"

"Tell him."

Yeah, there's Murhaselt blood in her, too.

The doctor shrugs. "If you insist. There's damage to the motor section in your left hemisphere. That means—"

"She's paralyzed." I already know that. "Is it permanent?"

He seems relieved not to have to go into details. "We won't know everything until we do further testing. And of course there will be physical and occupational therapy."

"Is the paralysis permanent?"

"Things are still uncertain."

"So you mean yes. I'm *young*, not stupid."

He frowns. "I mean things are still up in the air. She has her age on her side, but, frankly, she's very run down. She'll need extensive therapy."

She'll need someone to care for her. And everything will fall on me. "I'll handle things," I tell her after the doctor leaves. A man takes care of his family. Linda, Barnetta—even Aunt Edie. They all belong to me.

Barney and Linda come in after the doctor leaves. They needed to come see our aunt and be sure she'll be okay. I can't make myself tell them she won't. Barney stands by Aunt Edie's head and Linda stands at the foot of the bed. I take the hand plucking at the blanket covering her chest. The narrow, blue veins jut through the thin layer of mocha skin. Her eyes are wide, and the bags underneath suddenly seem much darker and deeper. I know my aunt didn't get sick just to hurt me.

But now I have to force down regret and abandon my future, the plans Mom made, the plans Kasili's trying to make. None of them can be allowed to matter. Not with all this going on.

"Don't worry," Barney tells our aunt. "I'll take care of you."

I know she means it, and I know she'll try.

We all try keeping our eyes away from the woman on the other bed.

My aunt tries to tighten her fingers around mine. She's even weaker than she looks. "You kids. I love you all so much."

"You love us?" There's something cold and tight inside my chest, something I never knew was there until now, as I feel it fall apart. It *hadn't* been just about the money.

"Did I ever thank you? For taking the three of us in?" I ask her, even though it's kind of late.

She laughs and pats my arm. "I should thank *you*. I'd been so worried about the three of you. I wanted to do something to get you out of that stupid system, but I had no idea how I'd handle things."

"I know we put you out when I forced you to take us."

"Don't overestimate your own power, young man. I know how to say no. You three…you're my family. And it hurt to think what was about to happen to you." She pauses and her eyes darken. Talking is obviously still hard for her. "You're *all* my family. When your mother died…when my brother killed your mother, I was so angry at him. And so worried about you kids. And then you called, David." Her hand squeezes mine. "I couldn't have done this without you."

She wanted us? All of us?

Even me?

And here I'd resented having to beg her to take us.

Been certain she resented me for insisting. Instead she was hurting because she cared. Why hadn't I been able to see that?

◆

When I enter Kasili's office, he looks up and grins. "Just the man I wanted to see. Peter's eager to talk to you. Bet on it, there's going to be an offer. I've spoken with your teachers. Some of your grades are a little iffy. Guess that's to be expected. You've been carrying a hell of a load. I'm sure I can get you a little assistance to pull things up—"

"It won't help." It's just another offer that won't pay the rent. At least turning this one down won't be difficult. It won't hurt me a bit.

He's not listening. "You've been through a lot of stress, and the school will make allowances."

"Won't help."

He finally stops talking.

"I'm just here to tell you I'm leaving school."

He doesn't jump out of his chair and yell, but he does take a deep breath. Then he picks up the phone and calls his assistant to get practice going. His eyes never leave my face.

"It's okay," I say when he hangs up. "You should go, the team needs you."

"So do you. I was afraid you'd want to make some heroic gesture when I heard about your aunt's stroke. How bad are things?"

"Didn't Barney tell you?"

"I want to hear it from you." He waves me to the seat facing his desk.

"She's never gonna fully recover. The doctor says— she's been under too much stress these last months."

"I see."

Does he? Really? "I have two sisters who need me, a sick aunt and no income. I have no choice. I have to leave school and get a real job."

"There's always choices. Maybe some of your other relatives can help."

"Been there, done that. And no, I'm it. Next month, either I have a full-time job or we don't make the rent. My sisters are gone and I'm out on the street. And I'm not leaving my aunt helpless." Maybe if I can work full time, Sanderson's replacement will give me a chance. Even flagger or water boy will pay better than selling burgers at Mickey D's. "I have no other options. School's gotta go."

His fingers beat a march on the oak desktop. "In other words, you waste your life. Is your aunt asking you to sacrifice yourself?"

"My mother."

He frowns. "Your mother's dead."

I know. "I have to take care of her children."

"*You're* one of her children. You've been on some kind of mission. I noticed that from the beginning. What's eating you, son?"

"Don't call me that."

Kasili sighs. I can't tell if that's a coach's sigh or a shrink's. "That's what I thought. You're sacrificing yourself."

Lifting the picture of his family from his desk I ask, "What would you sacrifice for them?"

"Not the same thing." He laughs as he takes the photo from my hands. "No one expects a seventeen-year-old to assume full responsibility for a family, David."

I suppose his laugh is his attempt to be kind. "I expect it of me. I'm old enough to make this decision. I can't be selfish."

"So you throw away everything you could become?" He leans back in his chair and fiddles with a pen while his eyes glaze over and he stares at the wall over my head. "What about your future? Graduation. College. What do you want to do with your life? Have you given any thought to five, maybe ten years from now? Where you want to be?"

My future? Who cares? Right now, today, all I can think of is my family. "Do you know what happens if the state puts my sisters back into the system?"

"I know they'll be taken care of. Homes will be found for them where they'll grow into healthy, happy, productive adults. You're not living in Oliver Twist's time; they won't end up on the streets or dumped in a workhouse. They'll get placed. Maybe not exactly what you want, but things will work out for them. You're the one I'm worried about. What happens to you if DCFS steps in?"

"The joy of being an adult." I force a laugh from my tight throat. "I'll be eighteen before they could finish processing the paperwork. They probably won't even bother doing anything, except tell me to take good care of myself and get lost. It's not me I'm worried about."

"You leave school now and you'll always regret giving

up." He heaves that sigh again. "I can't bring your mother back, but I know she'd never expect you to toss away your future. Let me help you do what she'd really want." His voice trails off. For a second I think he's unable to find words.

Then he says, "What if I put you up?"

My chest grows tight. "What did you say?"

"You could stay with me and my family. I'm not saying this because of the team. Yes, you are a great player with tons of potential, and looking at a college scholarship that will secure your future. But the way to give back is to live your own life and become the best man you can be. Take care of your own future. And your own future family."

A vision of Yolanda and me, together with our future children, flashes in my brain. Then a hot knife twists in my guts.

"Just tell my aunt and sisters to go to hell?" How can I think about winning when they end up losing everything?

"When we do things out of guilt, it turns to resentment. And sometimes even hatred. What happens when the day comes and you look back and think of what you could have had? When you're just another statistic, and resent your family because of that?"

"I'll never resent my sisters. Never."

But the truth is, I already do.

◆

"What are we going to do?" Linda asks.

"I'll be getting a new job."

"You found someplace?"

"Frank's needs a busboy, and the garage is looking for a cashier." The mechanic at the corner gas station needs help during the day. Doesn't pay much, but I need every penny now. Frank's needs someone for the evenings. A look at what stores and gas stations pay, and I see I'll need two jobs. After a few minutes calculating what I'll make if I take both jobs and I know. Even at twelve-hour days, I'll barely make my old part-timer's wage.

"What about school?" Barney's face changes as she begins to understand. "You're leaving school? Because of us?"

"Things have to change," I tell my sisters. "When our aunt comes home—"

"I'll take care of her."

"She needs everything, Barney. She can't even use the bathroom by herself, or get in and out of bed."

My sister gulps, but nods. "I can handle that."

Day and night? I'm still thinking about that when the doctors let my aunt come home. Aunt Edie is still weak. She can't navigate stairs. I have to carry her up to the apartment. Now she's trapped up here, same as me.

She has a wheelchair with a bag of medications, follow-up appointments with specialists. And she's lost her job.

I love my sisters. But when do I get my turn? Everyone's got a piece of my life. Mom. Barnetta. Linda. Kasili. Aunt Edie. Everyone but me.

CHAPTER 33

Sanderson's replacement still refuses to take me.

At first all's quiet when I return home after that disappointment. I feel like such a failure. I desperately want to go find a hole where I can hide. Get far away from here and leave all the problems behind, give up on everyone's dreams.

Linda's fingers move like lightning bugs in the early dusk, flicking over the controls of her video game. Her little devil races across the screen in the pointless quest to build and destroy.

"Time for bed," I say.

Her fingers never pause and her head never turns.

In the kitchen, my aunt's calling for help. Her voice is a deep croak. I look inside. She's alone, sitting in her wheelchair staring at her hands. She's spilled her dinner. Food is all over the table, the floor and her. Barney was supposed to be helping her. Where is that girl?

My aunt's weak voice follows me into my sister's bedroom. Barney's there, just sitting on the bed with her arms wrapped around herself as she ignores Aunt Edie's calls.

"What's with you? Don't you hear our aunt crying for help? You need to get over there and do something for her."

"I can't, David."

"Can't? You mean you won't."

Everything's left to me. Everything's falling apart.

I turn back to the living room and Linda's still bent over that game.

My aunt ceases her cries as I get her cleaned up. Her head's hanging. She's old and tired, and I can't let this happen to her again. When I wheel her into the front room, Barney's standing there.

Barney steps forward, looking like she's been ordered to crawl backwards over a cliff. "I'll take her now," she says and grabs the handles of the wheelchair.

"What, now that there's nothing more to do? What if she'd been sick again? You have to be dependable. I am not the designated slave so you get to have fun."

She doesn't protest, but her eyes fall to the floor as Aunt Edie protests for her, "David, please, she's young."

"And undependable. But then, everyone knows they can always leave everything for old David to come and do it for them. Just dump everything on David." I turn to Linda, who's still playing with the devil dice.

"Didn't I tell you to stop?" I ask her.

She ignores me.

Before I can think about it, I've grabbed the controller from her hands. "I said stop." Tossing the controller to the rug, I stomp on it. A loud crack and the plastic crunches under my heel. "Maybe now I'll get some respect. And look at me when I'm talking to you."

When Linda lifts her head, her eyes are wet and her hands shake. She flinches when I try to take her arm and a firecracker explodes inside my stomach. My Linda's looking like a puppy backed into a dark alley by a pack of snarling strays.

And I sounded just like Antwon.

Maybe Kasili's version of the future will be better for all of us. Maybe Linda will come out of that dark place she's tucked herself into once she's in a new home. Maybe Barney can learn to be—not just a girl, but a woman like Mom. Maybe I just want them with me to quash my guilt, and anyone else, anywhere else, will be better for them than me.

I haven't done any better for my sisters or my aunt than I had for Mom. My mother's dead because of me. Aunt Edie's ill because I talked her into taking us in. Linda's addicted to that game and stares at it or the walls for hours. Barney—I remind myself that all I've done for her these last few months is make one mistake after another. I have no choice. No matter the cost to me, I have to pay my debt to all of them.

And Yolanda. I still have nothing for her—not even a future.

◆

The social worker arrives two days later, wearing that false smile on her face, the I'm-so-tired-of-this-shit depression darkening her over-painted eyes. She sits in the kitchen with her papers spread over the table and all of us staring, trying to pretend we don't know the message she's brought. Barney made coffee only to find that the woman wanted tea, and now has the kettle on.

Dirty dishes fill the sink. Barney'd promised to get them done but forgot. I know she's embarrassed now, but I also know it doesn't matter. The decision about their future was made before this woman left her office.

"This means—what?"

I'm glad Barney saved me from having to ask that question. Especially since I can guess the answer.

"None of you need worry." The woman looks at the contents of the folder spread on the kitchen table. "David, you're almost eighteen, correct?"

"I know. I'm on my own."

A shrill whistle makes her jump. Linda stares at her hands while Barney shoots from her chair to the stove. As a cloud of steam rises from the tea kettle she fills a china cup, dumps in a tea bag and rushes back to place the drink in front of the social worker. Only a few drops spill over onto the lace tablecloth.

The woman frowns. "Is there any honey?"

Barney looks at me with a frantic expression on her face.

"We don't waste money on extras." Maybe I'd jump to do the woman's bidding, too, if I thought it would make a difference.

"What are the plans for taking care of your aunt's needs?" the woman asks.

"I'll take care of her," Barney says.

"My aunt's moving in with her sister-in-law," I say.

The look Barney shoots at me would shut up Benedict Arnold, and I can only hope that someday she'll understand this is reality, not betrayal. I'm tired of this farce. The woman already knows the answer to all her questions. The papers hold the plans she's already made for us.

"I'll be moving in with Mary...my husband's sister," Aunt Edie says. "I have to give up this apartment." Two old ladies with a pitiful income, stuck in a place that's a tighter fit than this hovel—and with no room for anyone extra.

The woman turns back to me, sighs and shuffles some papers. "What about you? There are services I can direct you to."

"I don't need them, I have a place." When she raises her eyebrows I add, "Coach Kasili's able to put me up. I'll be staying with his family." I can't look at Barney.

"I really should talk with them," the woman says.

"I'll be eighteen in a few weeks," I remind her.

Her lips purse, but she backs down and returns to perusing her papers, too tired to show how thrilled she is to have one of us off her plate, I guess. She turns to look at Linda. "My dear, your aunt and uncle in Jamaica still want you with them."

Linda never even looks up.

Aunt Edie smothers a sharp cry. "So far away?"

"Jamaica's a lovely place. I truly envy her," the social worker says.

Maybe she does, but she wasn't the one being sent far from everything she knows and everyone she loves.

"We'll never see her again." The anguish in Barney's voice pummels my heart. She's too scared to ask about herself. We both know she's going to be warehoused to an overcrowded group home, because no one wants a six-foot tall fourteen-year-old still trying to recover from stepping in her mother's blood to grab the phone to call for help.

The woman's eyes narrow into an impatient frown. Like so many others, she looks at Barney's size and doesn't see that she's still a little girl. One who's almost as young and scared as Linda. "You should be happy for your sister. And, of course, we'll find you a home. I'm still looking into a few possibilities. I'll have a placement for you by this weekend."

She closes her folder, glances at her watch, frowns and gets to her feet. "Well, that's it. Everything's all taken care of. I understand you're leaving this weekend, Mrs. Crenshaw, so I'll be back on Friday. Be ready, girls."

She nods at Aunt Edie and ignores me as she leaves.

"All taken care of?" Barney says as the door closes behind the woman. "That's it? Be ready, and we'll all be somewhere else next Friday night?"

In a halting voice, Aunt Edie says, "Well, maybe there's a reason for all this. Maybe it's the Lord's will and all for the best, in time. Meantime we need to get packing."

Barney throws a spoon across the kitchen. "I don't like that stupid school anyway. I don't like living here, and I don't like you, any of you."

Aunt Edie reaches for Barney's hand. She jerks free and runs to her room.

How can I blame her? She's being tossed again, like so much dirty laundry. She's losing everything, and for Barney, life's just not fair.

But I'll still have Yolanda.

"I feel so guilty," Aunt Edie says. "I'd have done anything to keep her, and all of you."

◆

The twin beds fill my sisters' room. Even though it cost more, Aunt Edie insisted on buying two beds so they each could have their own space. Easy to see the signs of how much she cared, now that it's too late.

Linda's asleep, but her lips still frown. I'm scared—I frightened her so badly. When she's a thousand miles away, how will she remember me? The way I used to hold her and play with her? Or the way I've acted today?

Barney's hair spills over onto her pillow. She'd been a bald baby. Mom taped one of those dumb pink baby ribbons to her wrinkled brown little scalp. I don't know what'll happen to us now. How long will it take for us to become total strangers?

Kasili said, "Survivor guilt is a common human failing. It's also pointless and harmful. You have a right to save yourself. That's not being selfish. It's doing the right thing."

So why does doing what's right make me feel so hollow inside?

CHAPTER 34

The next day after practice ends, Yolanda's waiting for me at the gym. I've invited her over to our place for dinner so we can all be together, even if it's just this once. It's gonna be cramped in the tiny apartment. Things are already tight with just the four of us eating at the kitchen table. But I just want everybody I care about together—just one, last stinking time. Sure, we'll have phone calls and letters, and I'll still have Yolanda. But we won't be together again, at least not like this.

Before we leave school, I take a ball and shoot hoops on the deserted court. Yo sits on the team bench while I play around and she applauds every time I fly up for a dunk.

"Your turn," I say and hand her the ball.

"You're crazy." There's a gleam in her eye as she steps out of her heels. "I don't really know how to do this."

I guide her across the floor to the free-throw line with my hands on her arms. "You just have to concentrate on what you want. Stare at the basket. Will the ball to go through the hoop."

"Just mind over matter? It never worked when I tried making myself taller."

She's the only person who always makes me laugh. "You're the perfect size," I tell her. "Now raise your arms and let it fly."

The ball sails a few feet into the air, then falls far short of the net. She laughs as it bounces weakly across the floor.

I shake my head. "Pit-i-ful."

She shrugs and puts up her hands. "I'm a girl, what do you expect?"

"But you're so strong willed. And lots of girls play basketball."

She puts her hands on her hips. "David, I'm five feet tall!"

I run across the court, snag the ball and take it back to her. Then I take her hand and move her closer to the basket before handing her the ball again. We stand directly in front of the basket, and I look up at the net, and then down at her.

"This will not help." She sounds like a patient mother, trying to soothe her sick baby. "It's just not gonna happen, David."

I reach down, grasp her waist and settle her on my shoulder. Then I tell her, "Now shoot."

She giggles and drops the ball easily through the hoop.

"And the Mighty Mite scores two points!" I say as I lower her back to the floor.

"What did you call me?"

Oh hell. "Uh—"

Her hands go back to her hips. "Did you call me a mite?"

"Uh…yeah." Now I wait for the huff. The pout. The explosion. She scowls and I shrivel like a slug on salt.

"Mighty Mite." She repeats. She's thinking, then nodding. "I like that."

Man, am I lucky or what?

◆

"Maybe someday I'll look back on this and we'll all laugh, and maybe talk about how well things turned out," I say as we head for the apartment. "I mean, I know this is the right thing to do. The only thing I can do. But I *hate* it."

"You think people blame you, don't you?"

"*I* blame me. I tried blaming basketball, the cheerleader, the doctor, the medicine. Everything except the one person responsible."

"Your father."

That shocks me. Of course I know who pulled the trigger. Antwon never even pretended he was sorry. I went to the trial. Saw him when he insisted on taking the stand, where he claimed it was my mother's own fault, that she somehow made him shoot her. But if I'd been there, been awake, he'd never have gotten close to her. She'd never have been shot.

"Not him—*me*. I let a game be more important than my family," I tell Yolanda.

"But your father pulled the trigger."

"And he's in prison for that." There was no prison for me. I looked at my arm and remembered how crooked it was after I hit the gym floor. It didn't even hurt—not at first—and the fracture didn't seem real. "At the hospital I wanted painkillers. I had an excuse to get high and I took it."

Now Yolanda does give me a huff. "You and Barney are way too alike."

We're walking into the apartment just as she says that, so I don't have a chance to ask what she means.

Things start out fine when Yolanda hands over the present she brought for my aunt, a shawl that has Aunt Edie gushing.

"It's just lovely, Yolanda. And you're so different from most girls these days. I'm glad David will be seeing someone like you—when I'm gone."

"I love making things," Yolanda says. "I see material and it speaks to me. When David invited me over to dinner, that piece just begged to come along."

For this one day, I have a real family. Barney and Yolanda work together to set the table. They've been chattering like the kids in the church nursery these last few days. I'm glad, because my sister needs friends. Even one she's about to lose.

I know who did the cooking, and it's not either of my sisters. Aunt Edie planned it well, and the smell of fish and greens fill my nose. And there's spaghetti, a mountain of pasta with ping-pong ball–sized meatballs, dripping with sauce. It's more than enough for five hungry mouths. Even in a wheelchair, Aunt Edie fixes a good meal. But no one matches Mom's cooking.

I had something special with Mom. We always understood each other well. Barney claims she was Mom's favorite, and probably Linda feels the same. That was Mom's gift—she made all of us feel special and loved. I always felt lucky to have her, but I never got around to telling her. And now it's too late. I never even got to say goodbye.

With that thought, grief kicks in. My heart sinks like a thousand-pound anchor's dragging it down.

After dinner I leave the others in the kitchen and walk into the front room. Outside the window I see the snowfall beginning. Yolanda's right behind me when I turn and she touches my arm. Suddenly everything pours out and I can't stop it.

"Mom meant everything to me. She loved me no matter what I did. Like in first grade—I flunked this spelling test. I didn't study, and didn't care, until I saw that almost every word was wrong. The teacher said I couldn't come back until that F paper was signed by one of my parents. I seriously decided the world would come to an end if Antwon ever found out. And I was ready to run away forever.

"The next morning I was at the door shaking, 'cause I couldn't go to school, and I couldn't say anything to anyone. Antwon had already left for work, and I stood in the doorway, frozen. Then I just pushed the paper toward Mom."

"And?"

"She signed it, patted me on the shoulder and said don't worry. She never mentioned it again, never said a thing to Antwon. I was only six years old, and I was so glad she was my mother. Now she's dead and it's all my fault."

"She blames herself, too."

Yolanda's words confuse me. "What are you talking about?" I ask.

"She means me," Barney says from the doorway. "*I'm* the reason Mom's dead."

My sister's shaking and crying big, wet tears. Her sobs make her hiccup, and I've never seen her cry like that. Not even at the funeral.

I cross the room and pull her against my shoulder. "Don't cry, Barney. Please." I feel helpless, and don't know what else to do or say.

But Yolanda certainly does. She gets a glass of water and makes Barney drink it. "Go on," she says. "Every drop."

"I woke up and heard them arguing," Barney says between sips. "But I was too scared to go out there. If I hadn't been such a coward, I could have stopped him from shooting her."

"But he had a gun," I tell my sister.

"Daddy loved me! I could have talked to him, could have made him go away."

"But Barney, he came to the house to kill her. You wouldn't have stopped him. If you'd gone in the kitchen, there would have been two dead bodies on the floor."

Barney tries to cover her ears, but I grab her hands and stare into her guilt-filled eyes. "He'd already stopped caring about any of us, Barney. He'd stopped loving all of us."

No man who loved his children could ever walk into a house where they lived with a loaded gun in his hand, out to destroy their mother. Barney's pleas could not have stopped him because he was there to kill. My sister couldn't have stopped that bullet.

And neither could I.

In my dreams the sling falls from my arm and I race into the kitchen, where I wrench the gun away from his hand. Antwon cowers, backs away and cries. Swears that he still loves us.

But my dreams aren't reality. If I'd gone into the kitchen and confronted Antwon and his gun, I'd be dead along with Mom. Even without a broken arm, my blood would have mingled with Mom's on that kitchen floor. That would have left Barney and Linda to bury both of us, and they'd have been even more alone.

I loved my mother, I didn't kill her. I am not my father and I won't ever be him. I wasn't the one who pulled the trigger, and I wasn't responsible for what Antwon did. And I couldn't have stopped him anyway, even if I'd been awake.

So I don't owe Mom my life, or the future I want to plan for myself.

◆

The next day after school, Yolanda and I take a bus to the construction site. I take her hand and lead her to the fence, where we stare at the building I helped create. The ground's ugly with mud, gravel and debris, the rut tracks made by the bucket loaders and the heavy wheels of wire and other equipment. I know she won't see what I do, but I want to make her understand.

"This is what you want?" she asks.

"Will you help me get it?" I hold my breath, afraid of her answer.

But it comes with a smile. "Of course, David," she says.

"You don't even know what I'm going to ask yet."

"You're going to have to leave and chase your dream, aren't you?"

I touch her cheek. "You're my dream."

"No, I'm the reality. And yes, David. I'll help you get there. What do we have to do first?"

CHAPTER 35

Sanderson confirmed that the job in Ohio was still mine and said I could room with him during my apprenticeship. Aunt Edie and her sister-in-law will be the girls' official guardians, and two adults were enough to convince DCFS. Maybe the social worker wasn't completely happy with the plan, but I already had the rest of my argument ready. "Just think—you can call us a success story," I told her. DCFS seems to like that kind of thing.

I'll make sure they always have money. And Barney's agreed to take the job at Frank's. Not big bucks, but she understands now how every penny counts. I'm still amazed how quickly she stepped up—once I stepped back and let her. With that and my pay as a full-time apprentice, we've even upgraded our home. We signed a lease on that house near my aunt's church, the one I always pictured us living in. We move in over the weekend. It was a stitch watching Barney and Linda pull together to take down that FOR RENT sign. They'll each have their own rooms now, and Martha and Edie will share the first-floor master bedroom. And I get my place on top, my own little spot in the sky.

Both old ladies are excited about the move, and they feel like they'll have a decent future, with family around them as they age. And my sisters are pumped about it, too. We spent a day packing, and then they move into their new home. And I get ready for the move to Ohio.

I confront Kasili last, now that I have everything figured out.

He's achieved his goal. The team won't have a goose egg in the win column. Julian's grown sharp, and I'll take my share of the credit for that.

"I'm not suiting up for tonight's game," I tell the coach on Thursday. "Tomorrow's my last day at Farrington. I'm withdrawing from school and leaving for Ohio next week."

"You still intend to drop out? I thought we agreed you'd do the right thing and stay in school."

"We agreed I shouldn't feel *guilty*. And I don't."

"Then why are we back to this?"

"I'm not back to anything. I'm moving ahead, going after my future."

"And your diploma? The scholarship?"

Those were other people's dreams. I look down at hands that ache to create things.

I try to paint him a picture so he'll understand: "Have you ever stood on a scaffold, a hundred feet off the ground, just you and the air and freedom? When I'm up there, even birds have to envy me. It's just me and my dreams."

I can tell he still thinks I'm crazy. But that's not important to me. I'm doing what *feels* right—what *is* right. For me, for my family.

Like Sanderson said, a man takes care of the things he loves.

"But college—you could have a free ride," Kasili says.

"I'm not college material."

"Not true."

Very true. "I'm not knocking college, Coach. Or myself for that matter. I know you think I'm making a mistake. But I think I've finally stopped making them. This isn't a mistake, I'm sure of it."

I'll be fine. This decision finally feels right. It's my choice, the right thing for me. And this time there's no pain involved—for anyone.

I'm looking at Kasili, who's skin has gone so gray, I'm wondering if he'll be needing an ambulance soon. "You're throwing your life away, David. Just stay in school until June. It's only seven more months. Then you graduate. Once you have that diploma, the world opens for you. Drop out now, and you'll just end up another statistic."

But June will be too late. My family will all be scattered, and my apprenticeship filled by someone else. And I'd find myself still stuck scrambling to fulfill someone else's dream.

"I'm way too big to fall between the cracks." I laugh at the man who talks like every adult who believes in the Big Secret of Success. But I'm happy with my own little ones. He means well, he just doesn't understand how selfish I'm finally letting myself be. I don't need basketball or a scholarship for the future I want to build. I'll get what I want so I can live the life I'm supposed to.

But I'll never convince Kasili, and it doesn't really matter to me. *I'm* convinced that I'm making the right choice—*and* for all the right reasons.

"David, for God's sake, think of yourself. Don't let guilt rule your life."

I smile at his mistake. He's a good man. But, like the social worker, he sees me as a child, something I had to stop being the day my mother died.

"You asked me what I wanted for my future. I want the wind. And mortar and bricks, too. I want hours working at a job I know so well, I'll have time to think of—well, just about anything. I want to look over the plans for something that never existed before. I want to dream up those plans and make them real. I know I can learn some of this in school. But I'll learn it faster doing it instead of reading about it. And I'll be taught by a master. In the meantime, I'm keeping my family together. Not because I feel guilty, and not because I have to. I'm doing it because I want to. Don't worry, Coach. I won't become another dropout statistic. After all, there's always the G.E.D."

I stand and shake his hand.

"I won't give up," Kasili says.

"Just don't give up on Barney. That's all I ask. She's feeling that survivor guilt thing, too. She told me that she thought she killed Mom because she was smart enough not to confront a madman with a gun. She ever tell you that?"

He frowns. "No. Barney's only been talking about finding the body. What that meant to her."

"That's why girls need Moms." And best friends. "When you see Barney next time, talk to her about guilt."

◆

Yolanda's the only thing that might make me crumble. Other guys may come into her life. They'll be here, and I won't. Sanderson and I, we'll live for the weekends. But it won't be enough. Not with Yolanda Dare, the one and only Mighty Mite, whose confidence and beauty fill a room. I'll become something someday, no doubt about that. But it may take me years, and it's not fair to expect her to wait.

Yolanda's going to make someone a dream wife and partner in life. But whoever he is, there's one thing he'd better understand—be good to her or find himself fish bait.

◆

Yolanda waits for me when I arrive at school the next day. She smiles as I go to her, bats her eyes, moves in for the kiss and I'm ready to give up everything for her.

"Kasili asked me to talk to you," she says. "I'm supposed to remind you that you and I can be together forever, live happily ever after and all that crap—if you stay here in school like he wants you to. But he picked the wrong girl for this mission. You go for it, David. I know you'll keep your promise."

I try laughing and hope it sounds better to her than it does to me. "I don't recall making any promises."

She smiles. "I distinctly heard you say you love me."

"I—I did. I do. I mean—" I don't even know what I mean.

"I do have one condition for you."

It figures. Just when I started to relax.

"Not sure I can go along with any conditions."

"You are so lucky I was born, David Albacore."

More than luck. A real miracle from God.

"No one else would put up with you," she says and hands me a box.

Inside I find dark blue fabric. "Blue?"

"Royal blue, Mr. Albacore." She lifts the material. It's a shirt. Inside, she's sewn a handmade label informing the world that this is *A Yolanda Original.*

"How'd you know my size?" I ask. The fit's damn near perfect when I try it on. "You never took my measurements."

She stands on tiptoe to reach my shoulders as she runs her fingers over my chest. Sparks trail those hands in every place they touch. "I don't need a tape measure to know my man. I'll expect you back here every chance you get, and you'd better be wearing this shirt."

"And I'll expect you to be waiting for me."

She nods, and I swear she'll have everything. Beautiful house, car, and a house full of kids.

And she'll also have me.

◆

It's my last day at school. At least Barney's life is back to normal. I listen to her and Yolanda talking as they carry their lunches to our table.

"None of the guys likes me," Barney complains.

"That Tyrone still has his eyes on you," Yolanda says.

"He's always belching and making stupid noises when we're together."

"That means he likes you."

Barney frowns. "And he always groans when he sees me."

"Wow—he really likes you."

She perks up. "Are you sure?"

I can't keep from laughing when she sits down at the table. Sure enough, Tyrone groans, and Barney tilts her head and smiles at him.

"You still want to marry me?" she asks.

Tyrone freezes except for his eyes, which sneak a glance my way.

I still don't get girls, but I can tell that my sister's gonna be all right.

◆

It's the last class of my last day. Yolanda and I stand on either side of the poster she's put together.

"Life can be hell," I say.

The class laughs and Martin frowns. Yolanda nods. She understands.

"The pros of marriage." I pause and look at her. "First of all, regular sex."

Even Mr. Martin cracks a smile as he holds up both hands to silence the laughter circling the room. Yolanda's cheeks darken as she blushes, but she returns my smile.

"The pros of marriage?" I ask. "Ask a ship the pros of an anchor. Or a building the pros of a solid foundation. When you're putting up a building, something big and solid that's intended to last a long time, you begin with the foundation. The bigger you want that building to become, the more important that base. You want it to be strong, so you start deep with thick concrete and reinforce it with steel bars."

"That's what a marriage should be. Two tough materials coming together to make something even stronger when they're joined." *Which is the concrete, which is the rebar— it doesn't even matter when they're one.*

"The pros are simple: shelter from loneliness. A cheering section when everyone else thinks you're wrong." I point to a picture Yolanda took of an old couple holding hands on a park bench. "When it's right, it's awesome."

"And the cons, Miss Dare," Mr. Martin says.

The voice of the true Yolanda Original is strong when she begins, "Unless people come together for the right reasons, the foundation will crack. You have to be caring and complete by yourself, and strong enough to stand alone before you try to stand together. Don't get married because society or family and friends say you should. Or because you're looking for someone else to make you happy, or you're scared to be alone. Making a marriage work is hard. So you better be ready to keep working at it.

"If things go wrong—" she shrugs, "—remember, marriage involves people, and it has to be a true partnership. Both people have to be unselfish and willing to accept each other's faults. No man—or woman—should try to make their partner change. And don't expect them to stay the same, either. They'll change in ways you never dreamed. If you can't accept that, then stay single. Life is better as a happy single person than as part of an unhappy married couple."

I look at her face and smile before ending our talk. "People can learn if they're willing. Learn to live their own lives, and overcome their own faults. They can decide not to let things crash and burn, and not to be ruled by other people's dreams. Until you do all that, don't let money or worries or anything like that be the reason you tie the knot. But once you do—grab onto your spouse and your life, and then hold on tight."

◆

Kasili lets me into the locker room to say goodbye to the team before the game. No chance they'll let Booger Kaplan—his new nickname—take over again. He can barely raise his head, and people still snicker when he does, even Joelle.

Julian looks eager to take over as center. He's learned a lot and doesn't take himself too seriously. "Just watch," he tells me. "We're gonna crush these guys." You gotta have confidence to make it. He's gonna have a great time, no matter what happens in this game.

Yolanda stands beside me at the entrance to the gym as the game begins. Barney's hanging around the side where the band sits. Poor Tyrone may not have much choice but to date her, now that she's following Yolanda's advice on how to deal with guys.

The whistle blows and I feel my fingers twitch. Part of me still wants that ball.

Julian takes the tip for Farrington. They're playing well. A forward takes a shot from beyond the three-point line. Daring, but the ball slips through the hoop. Then Julian steals the inbound pass for another two.

"Does it hurt not to play?" Yolanda asks me.

I laugh. "Nah. It doesn't hurt at all. That's just a game. I've got my life ahead of me." I love that feeling of flying, both in the game and when I'm working. That's why I can't wait to get back up on a scaffold or walk on a beam. My childhood dream has been put aside now, right next to everyone else's dreams for me.

I've got my own damn life to live.

I take my girl's hand and leave the game behind.

Acknowledgments

First of all, a huge thank you to Andrea Somberg. Your enthusiasm and love for *Pull* swept it from an impossible dream into reality. I will never forget that feeling when you said you loved my words and wanted to work with me to get them published.

Thanks also go to Evelyn Fazio and WestSide for taking a chance with me. You loved my David and found him a real boy, and spent hours working with a newbie to help me shed my amateurish ways.

Big thanks to the members of Illinois Society of Children's Book Writers and Illustrators for their continued encouragement; and to the members of both the Chicago North and Wisconsin chapters of Romance Writers of America for critiques and encouragement, and the examples their members provided.

To my teachers:

Jacki Bogolia, my very first fiction editor, who not only used my "Charlie the Church Cat" children's story to inspire Sunday School classes, but also taught me that no matter how well I think I write, there is always more I can do to make the writing better.

My first fiction writing teachers, Steve Alcorn and Lori Wilde. I got so much more from your on-line classes than from many traditional classrooms, and you were very patient with a slow learner. Your classes taught me about the importance of Theme, and Scene and Sequel, and the all-important Black Moment. I thought I knew how to write, but you taught me how much I didn't know. Thank you both for letting me in on the Big Secrets of writing.

Natalie Tilghman and Harper College in Palatine, Illinois, for the fiction writing workshops that helped me see my work the way a reader would, and taught me to give, and gracefully accept, critiques.

To Shelley Coriell, *Pull*'s beta reader, you let me know that sometimes a basketball is really something more.

To Mary Jo Lepo, Dave Gran, members of The Writing Place, and all the other usual suspects inhabiting the Arlington Heights Library who cheered me on over the years.

And to Jim Elgas, who invited me to submit to *The Arlington Almanac* and published my very first short story in 2008.

Last, but not least, special thanks to the young construction worker who shared pizza with me one cold night at a construction site and shared his story. He'll never know how much he inspired the creation of young David Albacore.